ABOUT THE AUTHOR

James Warden was a teacher for forty years and retired in 2006. He now enjoys his retirement as much as he enjoyed his time in the education service and is catching up on those things which he left undone and ought to have done – in particular, his writing. He writes every morning between nine o'clock and noon, for thirty-six weeks of the year.

He is fortunate enough to be able to act in several Norwich theatres – the Maddermarket, the Sewell Barn and, with the Great Hall Players, at the Assembly House – and this experience informs his writing. His stage adaptation of Laurie Lee's *As I Walked Out One Midsummer Morning* was performed at the Sewell Barn Theatre in November 2009. His original play, *Letters from a Boy in the Trenches*, which was based on the letters of a WW1 soldier, was performed in Marchington, Staffordshire in 2015.

James is married – for the second time – and lives in Norfolk. He and his wife travel as much as possible. They have visited Italy (where they were married in 2002) several times, Canada, Bermuda, Egypt, India, the Czech Republic, New England, Poland, Slovenia, Antarctica, the Falkland Islands, Alaska, the Galapagos Islands, Australia and Switzerland. In 2018, they travelled across the USA on Route 66. They have also taken several holidays in various Mediterranean resorts – the basis for his first novel, *Three Women of a Certain Age*, which was published in July 2010.

During his years in education, he wrote about twenty play scripts for children. These included the one that formed the basis for his children's story, *The Great Gobbler and his Home Baking Factory at the North Pole*, which he wrote in 1982 and published in December 2010.

He has three sons by his first marriage, and they inspired three of his novels – *The Vampire's Homecoming*, published in 2011, *The One-eyed Dwarf*, published in 2012 and *The Haunting of Thornham Staithe*, published in 2022. With them and his first wife, he also travelled to the southern states of North America, France, Germany (West and East), Estonia and what was Czechoslovakia.

WRITING BY JAMES WARDEN

<u>Stories of Our Time</u>
Three Women of a Certain Age (2010)
The Age of Wisdom (2015))
Swinging in the Sixties (2016)
Benjamin Rudge: A Tale of the London Riots of '11 (2024)

<u>'Tales of Mystery and Imagination'</u>
The Vampire's Homecoming (2011)
The First Rendlesham Incident (2017)
The Search for Edwin Drood (2020)
The Haunting of Thornham Staithe (2022)

<u>Stories for Children</u>
The Great Gobbler and his Home-Baking Factory
at the North Pole (2010)
The One-eyed Dwarf (2012)

<u>Biography</u>
The Boy in the Photograph: Bill Pieri's
autobiography (2014)
A Child of the Fifties: autobiography of
my childhood (2017)

<u>Plays</u>
As I Walked Out One Midsummer Morning
*(Adapted with the permission of Laurie Lee's estate
and performed at the Sewell Barn Theatre in Norwich
in November 2009.)*

Letters from a Boy in the Trenches
*(Adapted from the letters home of Sydney Harrison
and performed by the Marchington Amateur Dramatic
Society in November 2015.)*

BENJAMIN RUDGE
A TALE OF THE
LONDON RIOTS
OF '11

BY

JAMES WARDEN

Grosvenor House
Publishing Limited

This book is published by
Grosvenor House Publishing Ltd
Link House
140 The Broadway, Tolworth, Surrey, KT6 7HT.
www.grosvenorhousepublishing.co.uk

This book is a work of fiction. Any resemblance to
people or events, past or present, is purely coincidental.

A CIP record for this book
is available from the British Library

ISBN 978-1-80381-043-0

To my sister,
Linda Edwards,

who raised three children,
one a son with autism,
more or less alone,
all of whom knew right from wrong,

with thanks for her advice on autism.

INTRODUCTION AND ACKNOWLEDGEMENTS

This story is a work of fiction, but the events and incidents are based upon those experienced by people at the time of the London riots in 2011.

In particular, the confrontations between the police and the rioters are taken from two main sources, *The Riots* by Michael Matthews and *Reading the Riots* by The Guardian newspaper; **without these two sources of information, writing the novel would not have been possible, and to them I am indebted deeply.** The thoughts, words and actions of the police and the rioters are taken directly from these sources; nothing has been exaggerated for the sake of achieving an effect.

Similarly, the thoughts, words and actions of members of the public and of public figures are taken from newspaper accounts of the time.

Newspaper accounts have also been used, particularly in *Benjamin's Notebooks*, but these have been adapted to suit the fictitious characters. I did this to ensure that the outcomes of the violence, such as the sentences given, were correct for the crimes committed.

The books and newspapers used as reference for this novel are as follows:

The Riots by Michael Matthews: Silvertail Books 2016
Reading the Riots: Guardian Short Books 2011
Out of the Ashes by David Lammy: Guardian Books 2012
The English Riots of 2011 edited by Daniel Briggs: Waterside Press 2012
Riot City by Clive Bloom: Palgrave Macmillan 2012
The Guardian: August 2011

Daily Mail: August 2011
Evening Standard: August 2011

I also ought to acknowledge *Barnaby Rudge: A Tale of the Riots of 'Eighty* by Charles Dickens, since it was re-reading this novel that gave me the idea for the story. A few years before, I heard part of a Radio 4 interview when the interviewee was asked 'You never married did you - why?' and he answered: 'I didn't think I'd be very good at it.' I do not know who these people were, but the answer stuck in my mind: I thought society might be better off if we all gave the matter some consideration before we had children. When the idea of setting a novel during the London riots came to me, I read David Lammy's book, and the idea and the thought came together.

BENJAMIN RUDGE:
A TALE OF THE LONDON RIOTS OF 2011

Main Fictitious Characters

<u>Police Officers:</u>
PC Alex Willet
PC John Chase
PC Emma Hare
PC Edward Andrews
PC Geoffrey Dale
PC Wendy Rackham
PS Andy Warner
PS Doreen Manners

<u>Members of the Public:</u>
Keith Willet, Landlord of The Blacksmith's Arms, Alex's father
Mabel Willet, his wife
Gabriel Pilgrim, owner of Pilgrim's General Store
Martha, his wife
Dolly, his daughter

Daniel Solomon, father of Charlie Solomon
Vanda, his partner
Tom Drane, father of Lewis Drane
Jenny, his ex-girlfriend
Phil Meadows, father of Carl Meadows.
Lynn, mother of Carl

Mary Rudge
Benjamin Rudge, her son
Mike Rudge, her ex-husband

Katy, Alex's partner
Louise, her daughter

Named Rioters:
Simon Tippet, leader of The Blades
Meghan Marks (Miggs), his girlfriend
Hugo Battersby
Neil Stagg
Dennis

All other main characters are actual people: public figures or members of the public.

SATURDAY, AUGUST 6TH

Chapter 1
A KNOTTY PROBLEM

Alex Willet always called in on his father before going home from his occupation as a police officer. It was the habit of years. He had, after all, worked in the Tottenham pub, The Blacksmith's Arms, as a teenager, helping out behind the bar and getting to know the locals, which proved to be a bonus when he joined the force at eighteen. Not that this decision had been welcomed wholeheartedly either by his parents or the locals: it wasn't so much that any of them were against the police, more a kind of natural reserve. But he'd won them over with a blend of charm, humour and discretion; policing by discretion sat comfortably alongside policing by consent.

Apart from seeing the daily ritual as a duty to visit his parents as often as possible, Alex also liked the pub. It had been his home – he'd known no other from the day he was born – and he liked what it represented in the community he policed. The Blacksmith's Arms, as the name suggested, had started life as a Victorian staging post: coaches stopped here, horses were changed as well as shod, strangers arrived to find rooms for the night. None of this history was now apparent – the archway under which stagecoaches once clattered over the cobbles and the forge itself with its fiery heat and ringing of hammer on anvil gone forever – but the bustling nature of the pub's past was reflected in its present role as the staging post for Tottenham Hotspur Football Club.

A sign over a set of swing doors indicated the way to **White Hart Lane Stadium** with an arrow pointing to the right, photographs of players past and present graced the walls, scarves secured at away games brought colour (**ODDA FK, Mansfield Town FC, Fredrickstad FK, Taunton Town FC, Newry City FC**), trophies stood secure on shelves specially designed for the purpose, thanks was given in a framed testimonial by a writer who felt the pub had saved him from watching Arsenal, flags waved **Spurs on Tour**, signs indicated SPURS MEMBERS CLUB ONLY.

A full-size snooker table dominated one side of the room, one-armed bandits were placed against some walls, high stools ran along the bar but mostly chairs were placed at small tables comfortably seating four drinkers. The pub was blessed by its wide-open space, the central bar area rising by a short flight of steps to an upper level, beside the snooker table a door led out to the pub garden.

It was a pleasant pub, lit well by windows opening onto the street, with its original floorboards and bar of English oak. The bar always looked warmly and invitingly lit; it boasted a selection of fifteen keg beers as well as a plentiful supply of spirits from around the world.

It was home to Alex, a place where he and his mates sprawled contentedly as teenagers, a place tidy enough but not so tidy as to make the locals feel uncomfortable. Three of them sat now, at their usual hour, five o'clock, on this particular evening of Saturday, August 6th, each of them known to Alex, each of them in work, work that ensured they'd be at the pub by the same time most nights; and they greeted him with their usual chorus:

"Think you're good enough yet" followed by the expected burst of beery laughter.

The joke – because that's what it was: there was no malice intended – had come from a comment Alex made a few years previously. Once he was established as a copper, "in a good job" as his mother, Mabel, said, relief in her voice, she wondered why he hadn't got a steady girlfriend and whether he thought it was time to look around seriously and get married. He'd replied that he didn't think he'd be very good at it and the remark was overheard by one of the three men sitting around the table. Much to Alex's mother's annoyance and his dad's concern – at the time – the comment began a running vein of humour at The Blacksmith's Arms.

"Why don't you get married?"

"I don't think I'd be very good at it."

It said much for his sense of humour and the certainty he felt about himself, that Alex took no offence. Only his mother was annoyed; his father, Keith Willet, shrugged his shoulders and shook his head, giving the humourists a scant glance from the bar as he pulled their pints.

It was true that he'd had no girlfriend, let alone a steady one, but he'd already seen enough in the neighbourhood and from behind the bar to know what made a good marriage and, more particularly, a good parent; and it wasn't what the humourists were thinking about with their laughter: some seemed to think being good at marriage went no further than their dicks, and the three sitting round the table were prime examples.

It was Daniel Solomon who'd earwigged Mabel Willet's comment to her son. Daniel had a child, Charlie, by a woman he claimed to love "more than the stars above" but "we couldn't live together, we'd get on each other's nerves". "But my boy will lack for nothing in this world" was always Daniel's claim. Nothing material that is, Alex thought, but the boy – now in his early teens – could only be sure of seeing his father on match days. Daniel's work for the council seemed to keep him busy during the rest of the week.

Phil Meadows, who was shuffling the dominoes when Alex walked in, also had a son, Carl, but saw nothing of him. Once, on the boy's ninth birthday, he'd felt moved to send him thirty pounds, a generous enough offer but one that failed to cover the cost to the boy's mother of bringing Carl up for that number of years. Phil always claimed, when pushed, that Carl had been the result of a "one-night stand" and he didn't see why he should be tied down by the circumstance; besides, he wondered whether it was a deliberate ploy on the part of the woman to nab him as a husband. Phil worked at a local fun fair "where there was plenty of totty about" and so felt quite content with his lot in life.

The third member of the regular trio, Tom Drane, was placed in his position in life by neither choice nor circumstances: his girlfriend ditched him. Tom was a worrier, forever concerned with his health and what might go wrong for him, and his girlfriend felt she couldn't cope with him and his problems while, at the same time, carrying the responsibility for their home, their child, Lewis, and her job. All her friends agreed with her and that was a relief but Lewis missed his dad and, as he grew up, missed him more. Tom did see him when he could; there was no greater pleasure than kicking a ball around with his son at the local park but it wasn't easy and became less so when another man appeared across the horizon. Tom's girlfriend liked having a boyfriend around.

"Evening all," said Alex in his traditional *Dixon of Dock Green* take-off, as he walked to the bar to speak with his dad.

"What'll you have, son?"

"Nothing tonight, thanks, Dad. I want to get back to Katy and the girl."

Alex hadn't married but fell in with a single parent, Katy Simmons, who had one child, a girl named Louise, and her own house not far from the pub. Alex asked no questions about how she came to own a house in an area where the cost was prohibitive, and Katy offered no explanation. They got on well – well enough, Mabel Willet hoped, to bring about the sound of wedding bells – and the arrangement suited them both. Alex, though feeling no commitment to marriage, looked out for mother and child as if he did.

"What's this about this Mark Duggan?" asked Keith Willet.

"Nothing to do with us, Dad."

"It's on the news."

"The police shot him, didn't they?" chipped in Daniel Solomon, "A couple of days ago."

Daniel was a tall man with a long, hooked nose, so tall and conscious of it that he walked with a permanent stoop, his shoulders rounded, peering at the ground; but he missed nothing. The six o'clock news, which would soon be rolling across one of the large screens in the pub always caught his eye. His work with the council obliged him to keep up to date: the latest news was the usual topic of conversation when he and his colleagues arrived at work in the morning, heading for the coffee machine.

"They said he was wanted by the police and they fired his gun at them first," continued Daniel, "but then the story changed and they said Duggan was unarmed."

"There was a picture on Facebook of a copper – sorry Alex: police officer – standing over Duggan's body minutes after he was shot," said Tom Drane, who – when he was free of his work as a painter and decorator – spent many hours on various forms of social media. There wasn't much Tom didn't know about everything.

"What's that got to do with anything?" questioned Keith Willet, seeing his son was being placed in a difficult position, "Of course they were standing over his body. He'd been shot."

"Just saying."

"Well don't, Tom Drane. Gossip's dangerous."

"It was nothing to do with us, the local police" said Alex, quietly, "As far as I know, and the truth will come out, Mark Duggan was being followed by officers from Operation Trident. It's the Met's Specialist Crime Unit. They concentrate on gang and gun crime. And that's all I know, but the officer wouldn't have fired unless he thought the suspect was armed and a threat to him and his colleagues."

"He was a gangster, wasn't he?" cut in Phil Meadows, "The family's well known for it. We get them hanging round the fun fair looking for kids to sell drugs to. If the police were following him, they must have known he had a gun."

Alex Willet didn't want to get involved in any of this talk: discussion would have been too good a word to describe what these men were saying, he thought.

"I'm off, Dad," he said, "Katy will have a meal waiting unless I'm very much mistaken and it's rude to keep her waiting and let it spoil."

He gave the three men still sharing the local gossip a wave and was about to leave the pub when Gabriel Pilgrim walked in from the street. Gabriel ran a grocery store on Tottenham High Road. He was a well-liked local man, married with one daughter, who he worshipped along with his wife, a fact not always to their benefit, since the term 'spoiled' could be fairly applied to both Dolly Pilgrim and her mother, Martha.

Gabriel was a short man and stout with a wide girth. Keith Willet, who was a great reader and fan of Dickens's novel, always thought of him as Mr Pickwick, although he never said as much to Gabriel's face. Like his fictitious look-alike, Gabriel always had a ready smile for all his customers, rich or poor, and many of the latter group were thankful for his readiness to wait for his money until their payday arrived. Alone for most of the day with two women, he needed to get out occasionally and was a regular at The Blacksmith's Arms, where he'd drop in for a "swift half" when the chatter at home became too much for him.

"Evening, Alex, off for your tea?"

"Evening Gabriel – family OK?"

It was their usual greeting and meant nothing more than it implied: two neighbours passing the time of day on their way about their business. The older man held the doors for the younger and they went their separate ways.

"Just a half, Keith, to tide me over," said the grocer, "and then I'll get back."

"We were just talking about the Mark Duggan shooting," said Daniel Solomon.

"Least said, soonest mended, as my old mother used to say," replied Gabriel, sipping his beer and leaning back on the bar.

"You've not heard anything in the shop, then?" persisted Daniel.

Gabriel and Keith exchanged glances. They'd both lived in Tottenham all their lives and, as businessmen, were careful not to take sides in ongoing disputes: and there were always disputes ongoing about something or other.

"It's all over Facebook," chipped in Tom Drane, persisting in his account now that Alex had gone, "Haven't you heard anything in the shop?"

"Nothing worth repeating. It's one of those knotty problems we'll have to wait for an answer for," replied Gabriel, downing his half quickly and leaving with a cheery wave.

He had, though: he'd heard a great deal, which is why he'd left the shop for a break, so intense was the gossip between his wife and daughter. A regular had worked them up by claiming that Mark Duggan hadn't fired his gun and that not only had he been shot unnecessarily but that the police had shot one of their own. He'd also heard a lot of wild talk about protests. Gabriel wanted to be well out of it all.

It was as he was turning into his store that he saw a man he thought he recognised, a face, a demeanour he recollected from long back. It was a tall man, big and lumbering with a bald head and a black moustache. He had a wild look in his eyes, the look of a man who might be hunting for someone but wasn't sure who he sought. He was dressed scruffily; his clothes looking as though they hadn't been washed or even hung carefully for months. The man passed him with a sideways glance, quickly averted, and disappeared into the pub.

Alex Willet turned off the High Road on to one of the many smaller side ones and arrived at the house of his lady friend, Katy Simmons. Their meeting had been an accident: she'd come to the station to report an incident at a neighbours' house – an elderly woman scared by a few local louts in her garden – and they'd liked each other immediately. Alex moved into the little house within the week.

It was one of a row of terraced houses built in the 1930s with a high-pitched roof and a bay window that looked out on a very small, neat garden, shielded from the road by a privet hedge. A small, wrought-iron gate opened on to the pavement. At the back, Katy had a small garden, mainly grassed, beyond which a long stretch of old trees provided shelter and shade.

"Alex," said Katy, when he let himself in through the front door, "Your tea's ready but I don't know if you'll have time to eat it. There's trouble at your station. A mob has gathered shouting they want justice for Mark Duggan. There are about three hundred of them and it looks very ugly. It's on the news. They look very agitated."

Alex looked at the meal Katy had prepared, steaming hot on the neatly laid table, a pork roast with Yorkshire's, crisp roasted potatoes, carrots, greens and thick onion gravy. He'd just come off duty and Katy's little girl, Louise, knife and fork in hand, was waiting to start.

"Let's enjoy this lovely meal," he said, "There'll be time enough for the trouble ahead."

Chapter 2
THE HONEST SHOPKEEPER

"Justice – that's what we want. You've seen it on Facebook. Mark on the ground; the police standing over him. What were they doing? Trying to get their story straight?"

The youth, Shane, a friend of the dead man, had the crowd's attention. He rocked back on his heels, ready to deliver another blow when one of those listening, another youth, Brad, cut in.

"It was in the *Evening Standard*. They said the police shot him while he was on the ground."

"The police didn't tell his mum," said a girl, Michelle. "She had to hear it on the evening news."

The group of youngsters, all residents of Broadwater Farm, a 1960s' housing estate, the home for nearly four thousand people, gathered together in unity on a street corner, began to mutter and curse among themselves.

"Yeah, Answers are what we want!" yelled one girl.

"Answers and Justice," cried Brad.

"Yeah, Answers and Justice," echoed Shane, keen to regain the high ground of the conversation, "The family are marching now. They're going down to the police station to get answers."

"The police are trying to confuse things. They're saying they both fired but people know Mark Duggan didn't fire his gun ...," said a girl called Nicola.

"Duggan knew he was being followed. He put out a Blackberry message ...," yelled another girl, in support.

"How do you know that?"

"Because me and my partner have been invited to go with the family. We were on our way when we bumped into you lot," replied Nicola, her voice getting louder as she spoke.

"So, who shot the copper?" asked a youth, more cautious than the rest.

"The police!" screamed the crowd

"One of their own?"

"It was an accident!" Natalie howled

"Yeah, a ricochet!" bawled Shane, "Are you lot coming or not."

It wasn't a question: anger was in the air and the crowd of youngsters was fired up. All it needed was a spark and Shane saw himself as the incendiary.

"ANSWERS! JUSTICE!"

"JUSTICE! ANSWERS!"

The chant took shape and the crowd grew as it marched towards the police station on Tottenham High Road.

By the time – 5.30 on that hot, August evening – the marchers reached their target, Mark Duggan's family had joined them, although his mother remained at home. A crowd of over a hundred pushed and jostled each other, soon reaching three hundred in number as their righteous indignation flared.

"The police killed him for no reason."

"Yeah, you don't have to get shot for nothing!"

"It's a piss take! How can police get away with shooting someone with no gun and get away with it and not go to prison?"

"It's the police, init!"

A line of police officers stood outside the station, deployed to protect the building, aiming for calm. An older officer, Andy Warner, with vivid memories of another riot, twenty-six years before – when PC Keith Blakelock was hacked to death by a mob of rioters in a stairwell on Broadwater Farm Estate while trying to protect fire fighters who were under attack – looked on with particular dread in his heart. He remembered hearing the news of PC Blakelock's murder on his car radio while driving home after his shift; he had pulled over and wept.

Watching the crowd, who'd arrived for a peaceful protest, he realised how quickly the mood can change; the crowd becomes a mob and a police officer's job becomes dangerous, life-threatening.

The situation was calm. A senior officer spoke with the crowd: after all, they knew little more than the public. Operation Trident hadn't been their concern. They were as confused as those watching by senior officers having to correct stories appearing in newspapers and then having to correct their own press releases. Confusion didn't help any situation, but especially one as volatile as the one they now faced.

What happened next no one in the crowd or in the line of officers was sure. A bottle was thrown; a sixteen-year-old girl was pushed down to the pavement. She appeared to have cuts and bruises to her face. Someone in the crowd dragged her away. And then more bottles, followed by bricks and pieces of scaffolding, were hurled at the line of public order officers.

*

Alex Willet had finished his meal and was sitting on their settee with Louise cuddled onto his lap. He was reading one of her favourite books to the youngster, while Katy cleared the dishes and saw to the washing up – at her insistence, not his. Alex didn't think the book, *The Story of Tracy Beaker by Jacqueline Wilson*, was suitable for a seven-year-old – the central character was an angry, impulsive and violent child – but all her friends were reading it or had seen it on television and Louise didn't want to be the odd one out.

Alex preferred *Treasure Island*: he remembered reading that when he was young. His own parents hadn't read to him much because they were always busy in the pub at bedtime but he'd had the local library.

They'd just reached the part where Tracy is planning the types of revenge she would like to take upon her enemies, with Alex thinking that there was enough of that kind of thing in real life, when the phone rang.

"It's for you, Alex," called Katy, "It's the station. There's a riot going on."

*

Gabriel Pilgrim, puzzling over the stranger he'd seen and thought he knew enter The Blacksmith's Arms, recalled with pleasure the times he'd spent in the pub. He wasn't a great drinker – customers wouldn't appreciate him smelling of beer when he served them – but he enjoyed the company, the break from his wife and daughter (both spoiled by him, he acknowledged and, therefore, maybe it was his fault) and the ambience. It was true the pub had a friendly, comfortable ambience.

On match days it was the busiest place on Earth but such a great atmosphere: the bar staff were top notch people – always friendly with nothing too much trouble – and there was a real, London feel about the place. Even when it was full and you had to drink outside on the street, it didn't take away the atmosphere and the pleasure.

And the prices were decent; price was a key consideration in business, the prices and having the reputation of being an honest shopkeeper. Get the price right and you keep your customers. Gabriel made a good living for his family at his grocery store – and it was his, although part of a small chain, which made wholesale prices competitive.

He hoped that one day his daughter would take the shop on but she didn't seem inclined at the moment: too dizzy, too concerned about boys and what her friends thought of her. There'd be time enough for that when she got older, he thought. And his wife, Martha, encouraged her, while going on about how worried she was when Dolly was out.

His wife met him at the shop door, anxious, in full flight, her dander up, waving her arms, seeming to expect him to solve the problems of the world.

"Have you seen this?" she screamed, "It's just up the road. They're attacking the police station!"

*

Edward Andrews, known to all as Ed, was having a good time, a weekend away with his wife at a friend's wedding anniversary near Stoke-on-Trent. He and his wife, Joan, hadn't left the dance floor all evening, although by the time the last waltz arrived he wasn't sure what his dance steps resembled: it may well have been a quickstep. He wasn't a dancer but his wife watched *Strictly* and felt they should have a go, as a result of which they'd attended a few classes and picked up the rudiments of the four key ballroom dances: not that this mattered in the early hours.

The six – or was it seven – pints of Guinness hadn't helped, naturally, any more than they would help when it came to his later performance in bed; but the main thing was that they were happy, glad to be in each other's company among friends. Ed was glad they were staying after the reception: it was always exciting being away for the night in an hotel and it meant he could drink because he wouldn't need to drive home.

He didn't have to go to work in the morning, either; much as Ed loved his job as a policeman (he was a Level 2 public order trained officer), a day off, away from the demands of modern policing, was always welcome.

He was unaware that his phone, left in the bedroom, had been buzzing with messages all night.

It was the next morning when he woke late, shaken by Joan because his phone was "purring away" on the bedside table, that he realized he'd missed dozens of text messages and calls. He felt like a bag of rabbit droppings, as the phrase goes: splitting headache, rough throat, blurred vision, eyes sore. He knew what the purring meant and groaned.

He had a distant memory, one fogged by alcohol, of someone at the party talking about trouble in London but it hadn't meant much at the time on the dance floor. It did now. Ed called his borough headquarters.

"I had a few missed calls" he said, apologetically.

"We need you in work this afternoon," was the answer, adding, "or yesterday – whichever is the sooner."

Chapter 3
AN ILL-OMENED MAN

Alex Willet, wearing his usual uniform, the one he wore patrolling the streets of Tottenham, ran swiftly towards the police station, still buttoning his tunic. He'd realised the Mark Duggan shooting would bring about protests – genuine protests but protests that might be seized upon by the usual troublemakers, those citizens out to cause disorder whenever and wherever they could. Nipping trouble in the bud was always the answer.

What he didn't realise was just how quickly law and order would break down, how nipping was no longer a possibility. As he neared the station, hearing the din, Alex decided to make for the back door. Ahead, on the High Road he walked every day of his life, the crowd, now a mob, was jostling and shoving, shafts of wood were flying through the air alongside bricks, bottles and what looked to Alex like scaffolding poles. Groups of youths were pushing police cars over, rocking and propelling them across the road.

*

Mary Rudge, a small, attractive woman, her hair still keeping the blackness of its youth, a fact she refused to believe, began settling down to a night in front of the television, a glass of vodka handy on the small table by the side of her chair. Saturday was never a good night on the box in August but she looked forward to watching a film, *South Pacific*, a favourite of her father, who would often sing *Some Enchanted Evening* when taking a bath, if not tunefully then with vigour, a film she'd seen as a girl, one she talked about with her children and one her eldest son eventually bought for her birthday in June.

Mary had turned sixty in June, not an encouraging age for a woman but Mary bore it gracefully. She'd worked hard all her life, first in a local bank and then as a school secretary, later becoming the school bursar when the Conservative government, under Margaret Thatcher, decided to allow schools to manage their entire budget and not just the small equipment allowance. A trying time for headteachers, one they could have done without; Mary's, seeing her aptitude for handling money, promoted her immediately, thankfully and with great success.

Mary's professional competence with money was reflected in her private life, Despite two divorces, one when her first child was still a baby and the other, later in life, when Mary was in her fifties, she had retained the family home and was hell-bent on paying off the mortgage. Her house was only a few streets away from Katy's and similar in style: three up, three down with a bay window looking out onto a small garden and with an outhouse at the back.

She'd raised her family in that house and was proud of the fact. Her eldest son, now a graphic designer living in Manchester, rang home at least once a week. Her other child, still living with her and likely to remain doing so, was Benjamin.

Benjamin was a son with autism and his upbring had been a challenge, not helped by her second husband clearing off when the boy was still very young. Mary, in her mid-forties when the boy was born, reared him alone, a single parent in defiance of the world.

Benjamin was sixteen, a vulnerable age for anyone, particularly so for one who was seen and saw himself, as an oddball. He was happy enough in his own way and never happier than when in his room playing on his computer. Benjamin's fixation at the moment was on super-heroes,

Batman and Spiderman especially, and hours were spent indulging in their adventures.

Benjamin usually felt he was better off alone because he found people confusing; people didn't always mean what they said or said what they meant, and one single gesture could mean several different things. Raising an eyebrow, for example could mean that someone was angry with you or liked you: it depended on how it was done. He'd got into trouble once when he was out with some friends from school: he'd not understood what one of the girls meant when she looked at him with raised eyebrows and a smile. But his mum had gone to the school and sorted out that problem.

Benjamin's other fixation was storing facts and designing quizzes for his family to answer. He always found meeting up with his family and friends to be very exciting and he knew the birthdays and death-days of every one of them.

Once at a party, he'd approached a friend of his brothers to ask about the man's family: how many children he had, what their names were and, especially, when they were born. This had not gone down well with his older brother who told him to let his friends enjoy the barbecue before he started "firing questions at them", adding "if you need to fire questions at them at all".

Benjamin had gone off to find a quiet place. He was quiet now, alone and able to think and understand. It always took him a long time to understand. He could hear his mum's film: someone was singing.

Mary had reached her father's favourite song. It was certainly romantic, more so than life proved to be for her. Love was sitting on a beach having Rossano Brazzi, or someone like him, singing to you. Why had she grown up believing that nonsense?

*

Selim Akbas stood in the doorway of his 24/7 general store on Tottenham High Road watching the mob and fearing for his livelihood. He felt he needed to shut up the shop but there was little he could do. The shop had no doors, only shutters. He would need a van to move everything before the mob, which seemed to be moving his way, reached him and there was no time. He had come to England from Turkey and built a business. His family's maxim had always been, 'if you don't work, you don't eat'. Now, what was to happen? The mob looked ugly. All he could do was stand by his shop and try to protect it himself.

His neighbour, Janusz Wojcik, joined him to watch what was going on. Janusz, who ran a barber's shop and at 87 still worked mornings, stayed in Britain after coming as a fighter pilot during the Second World War. His wife, an English girl he'd met during those days, had died the previous year.

"I just want enough for today, Selim," he said, "Tomorrow never comes."

In the flats above the shops along the road, the people who lived there were hanging out of the windows, also watching in a mixture of fascination and horror at what was happening at the police station, where rocks and bottles rained down on the police officers. The mob, restless and angry, was moving towards their homes.

"Look at them," said one woman, her child held close, "they only want to run amok, with no responsibility."

In the doorway of his grocery shop, Gabriel Pilgrim, listened in horror. Only an hour or so ago, he'd enjoyed a pint at The Blacksmith's Arms, and now what was going on? From where his shop stood, he could hear rather than see the rabble, but hearing was frightening enough. What was he to do, if they came his way, with a wife and daughter to protect? And a shop! He had shutters: perhaps he should close now?

His wife, Martha, had no such doubts. Batten down the hatches, whatever that might mean, was her attitude, and Martha certainly had attitude.

In her bedroom, Dolly Pilgrim, his daughter, was rivetted to her television screen watching the news rolling on.

Her friends were out there somewhere. She must speak to them. Dolly went to the window from where she could see what was going on. She reached for her Blackberry.

Keith Willet, unaware that his son was fending off the attackers at the station, continued to serve pint after pint as always. Daniel, Phil and Tom were still drinking and their dominoes were still being shuffled. It wasn't until the pub began to fill with excited locals that Keith realized he might have a problem.

*

Mary Rudge sat upright in her chair. It was that noise again: the sound of stumbling feet and shuffling cardboard boxes: dull, heavy sounds. She paused the film. Benjamin was upstairs; she was sure her son was safe. This wasn't the first time it had happened; someone was in the passage that ran alongside her house. She had an uneasy feeling she knew the intruder.

Going quietly to the back door, Mary slipped the bolts and turned the key. The light was fading outside but it wasn't dark, and if she caught the man this time it was going to be a phone call to the police. A narrow terrace led to the side of the house and Mary crept carefully along, determined to challenge the man; and she was sure it was a man.

She peered round the corner, crouching low so that if he looked her way it would be at head height and he wouldn't see her. He was tall, big and moved among the boxes in a lumbering gait. Mary couldn't see his face but the man was bald. He was scruffily dressed; his jacket and trousers were rumpled as though he'd just woken after a night in a doorway.

Mary stood and stepped into the side passage determined to have the matter out once and for all,

The man saw her, his eyes wild, and turned and ran.

"Come back!" Mary called.

But he was gone, out across the small front garden, into the street and away.

Mary sighed with relief: she hadn't really wanted to confront, just frighten him off. He'd come last Christmas, poking around among the empty present boxes she'd left for the refuse men. But he mustn't come again. Benjamin wouldn't want him to, any more than she did; furthermore, Benjamin would be frightened, upset and when he was upset Benjamin would begin to shake and possibly scream; and then he would retreat to his quiet place and wait, wait for her to come and listen.

*

Alan Willet was exhausted and saw no end to the night. On arrival at his station, two orders had gone out: officers were to get fully kitted up in their riot gear – overalls, helmets and shields – when they had the chance, and the other had been broadcast from the station on the police radio, 'URGENT ASSISTANCE! URGENT ASSISTANCE! WE ARE UNDER ATTACK!'

He knew what that call meant, although he'd never before had the misfortune to hear it: the lives of officers or the lives of members of the public were in danger.

Alan kitted up at once and went out front to relieve one of his comrades: only in this way could each officer stand back long enough to don their kit. At once, a brick hit his shield, splitting it down the middle; and Alan saw that his comrades had taken such blows on their standard issue helmets and tunics. Someone was bound to be seriously hurt or killed.

Bottles, bricks and rocks continued to crash down on the line of police officers as they sought to defend their station. Along the road, two police cars had now been turned on their sides and set alight.

It was essential they held the line and protected their headquarters but the mob, its confidence growing, was laughing and jeering. Now several hundred strong it saw no challenge facing it in the thin line of police officers. It began to push forward. The only way was for the officers to go on the offensive, under-manned and under-equipped.

Chapter 4
A SWAGGERING BLADE

Dolly Pilgrim left the house quietly by the back door: she knew her parents would try to stop her and that wasn't on the cards. She wanted to be with her friends.

Dolly was an attractive girl, on the plump side but sexily so; she always knew she wouldn't be short of a boyfriend. Sixteen now and clearly, in her own eyes at least, a woman. Ever since birth she'd been the apple of her parents' eyes; her mum could be a bit starchy at times, but Dolly put that down to jealousy; her dad adored her. When she'd wanted to sleepover with friends and knew her mum would be funny about it, Dolly always had the sense to go to her dad first. It wasn't that her dad ruled the roost – far from it – but Dolly knew her mum wouldn't want to be the one to look mean.

The passageway behind the shop led to the River Heights Apartments, which were above the Carpetright store; her friend, Cathy, whose dad was a teacher, lived there. It was nearly a mile away from where the police station was being attacked and so they'd be safe enough and could watch what was going on. Dolly also had her BlackBerry smartphone to text other friends; with any luck there'd be a gang of them. It'd be fun.

"Oh my God, I just wanted to see what's happening," cried Cathy, hugging Dolly vigorously.

"Do your parents know you're out?"

"I said I was going to see you. They thought I'd be safe at your dad's shop."

"My dad'd go mad if he knew I was here," replied Dolly, excitement welling up in her eyes, "I wonder if the others'll come?"

"I've texted everyone I know," replied Cathy, "They'll come."

And they did, few by few at a time, some alone, some in pairs, some in groups; the youngsters, some schoolfriends of Dolly and Cathy, others who'd picked up the BlackBerry messages, drifted to join them.

"My little brother, he's always in trouble with the police," exclaimed a youth who joined Dolly and her friends. They didn't know him but he looked animated; they were thrilled to be in his company

*

Alex Willet could see that the mob attacking Tottenham police station was becoming increasingly audacious; confidence shone in its eyes, shamelessness in the swing of its arms as it rained down anything it could lay hands on at the line of police officers. The rioters surged forward against the line, which was in danger of being overwhelmed. It couldn't be long, Alex thought, before the order came to go on the offensive.

Further up the High Road, he could see more of the rioters, a dense horde of several hundred, scarves pulled up over their faces, hoods on their heads. Beyond them, through the darkness, from a Territorial Support Group carrier, its grills down to protect the windscreen, fellow officers, all in riot gear, spilled out to form a cordon across the road; three lines of officers against a crowd of, perhaps, six hundred. Simultaneously, as the order was given, the police began to move in on the crowd, forcing it away from the area.

The crowd fell back but only slightly. Alex realised it was essential that he and his fellow officers held the line; if it was broken the rioters would get behind them and they would be cut off. He looked across at Andy Warner, an older, experienced policeman for whom he held huge respect. Andy, who had been holding the end of the line was no longer in place.

*

"They have no respect, especially for my mum. She's always polite and stuff, and they're always rude to her. No respect for any of us. You get to the police station, and they think they can sit there and take the piss out of you. So, obviously, in my eyes, I don't see them as good people," continued the youth to Dolly and her friends who were full of anticipation and excitement, even admiration for the speaker.

He was a thin youth, the type a gust of wind might blow over, the leanness of his legs emphasised further by the tightness of his jeans,. His legs he held apart as though securing himself more firmly to the ground. His nose and chin were thrust forward and together resembled the beak of a predatory bird. As he spoke he rocked back and forth so that his sharp features appeared to stab his listeners. Every word he uttered was tantamount to an attack.

"Police don't think we're rioting for a reason. They believe we're rioting because Mark Duggan died and we have no other reason. Like we're rioting cos they're not giving us nothing other to do. They're taking away the education maintenance allowance, they're taking away free travel and other allowances teenagers have and they're not replacing it with anything good."

He moved off into the crowd.

*

Andy Warner had been cut off. Seeing a fellow officer separated from the line, he'd edged forward to bring him back, allowing some of the mob to get behind him. The horde pressing against the police was dense: a slight gap in the line was enough.

Andy cursed himself: with all his years of experience he should have known better. It was just that another officer was isolated, and he reacted instinctively to protect his comrade. Now he was cut off. He turned. Three men faced him, all dressed in black with balaclavas hiding their face, nervous and dangerous. They exchanged glances and stepped towards Andy, and he noticed the machetes in their hands. It wasn't just the weapons that horrified him; it was the clear intent of the men. They had come to kill.

One of the men lunged and Andy parried with his shield. Emboldened, another stepped forward and hacked downwards at Andy's riot shield. It wouldn't take many blows of that kind and he faced three such weapons.

What might have happened next became the stuff of nightmares for months. Andy would wake from a terrible dream in which his body was hacked to death while he watched from somewhere in the room, unable to wake, unable to save himself. Only when his wife shook him could he escape the horror.

On that night, it wasn't his wife who came to his rescue but another policeman who rushed forward with his personal issue fire extinguisher and discharged it into the faces of the prospective killers. They stumbled back, blinded momentarily. Andy and his fellow officer charged, shields raised, batons high. The machete men turned and ran.

*

The thin youth who had so impressed Dolly and her friends was now in the thick of the mob. Simon Tippet was a gang member and he and his mates had waited for this night for a long time. They'd expected trouble when Mark Duggan was shot but never in their wildest dreams imagined it would erupt so quickly; and they had their Blackberry smartphones to thank.

He'd brought some lumps of hardcore with him, stuff his dad was using to lay their new path but that was nothing to what the others were chucking at the cops. Some of them had got hold of scaffolding from somewhere – not just the hinge bits but whole bloody poles – and they were chucking them over the heads of the crowd. Simon almost wet himself with excitement. He pressed forward, trying to get near the front but it was impossible. He took the rocks from his pockets and chucked them. They hit something; he hoped it was a copper.

'If only the rest of the gang was here, we could get it together; if only we'd known it was going to be like this, we could have put down all the beef for one day. All the gangs together – Pembury, Red Bandannas, Ware Street, Well Street, Mother's Square – the whole of them, Holly Street, everyone getting on and on the same level against the cops,' he thought.

His own gang, the Blades – his idea for their name – met regularly in an old, abandoned storage place. It was dirty – grubby walls, old boxes and pallets spread around, dust and grit on the floor – but it suited them well; they'd put the boxes in a horseshoe with him at the top end. There was no electric but they brought their own torches and nobody bothered them: nobody would dare – not even the cops, if they knew what was good for them. And they swore their oaths there. He always took charge. He knew what's what: build up their anger, build up their resentment. They despised authority of any kind – coppers, mayors, politicians especially, the law, teachers who'd had it in for any one of them, do-gooders, bosses, shopkeepers who got funny with them, other gangs especially any who came on their turf .... The list of grievances was endless and Simon enjoyed working himself up remembering them as he swaggered forward.

*

For Andy Warner, the ferocity of the attack was like nothing he'd ever witnessed. His line, defending the police station, was in danger of being overwhelmed. The station wasn't just a building: there were civilian staff, prisoners and equipment.

If this mob broke through, the thought of what would happen if they fired the place was not to be borne.

He was beginning to wonder if baton rounds should be used; plastic bullets, as they were called, had never been used in Britain – at least on the mainland – and using them would change, maybe forever, the nature of policing: the level of violence would rise creating more violence in reply.

He looked across at Alex Willet, a young officer who must be shocked by what he faced. For now, they must carry on fighting with what they had, a riot shield and a baton, against a violent mob hurling everything they could lay hands on. If they failed to hold the line, no one was coming to save them.

Chapter 5

IMMENSELY FLATTERED

Meghan Marks, known as Miggs to her friends, was immensely flattered: she'd received a text on her Blackberry from Simon Tippet. Simon was respected in their neighbourhood. He was leader of a gang. Miggs wasn't in the gang – no girls were – but it was really something to be seen out with a gang leader. His text said:

'Everyone everywhere link up at Tottenham Hale station. Bring balaclavas, hammers. Police can't stop it!!!!

Miggs was at Spitalfields with some friends when she got the message. It couldn't have been easier on the Underground: Liverpool Street to Oxford Circus on the Central Line, Oxford Circus to Tottenham on the Victoria. Nice of London Transport to lay on such a service!

Laugh? Laughing fit to bust, as her dad used to say. They'd all got out their Oyster cards and were on the way. Miggs's dad paid for her card. He was usually tight with money but not when it came to getting her home; he didn't like the idea she might be stranded somewhere. The Underground was full of excited kids. She and her friends had thought about going to the cinema but this was going to be more exciting; this was going to be real.

They dashed like mad from the Underground station to the High Road. They couldn't believe the sight that met their eyes. It was like mayhem!

"Look at the police running down, Miggs!" cried one of her friends, "I've never seen police so scared before."

Bottles were flying everywhere.

"And the police cars," yelped Miggs, "They're just throwing rocks at them."

"Where's Simon?"

"I don't know," replied Miggs, "He must be in there somewhere."

*

Keith Willet watched "the proceedings", as he expressed the rioting to his regulars, in a less than sanguine tone. He thought the police would get a grip on the situation: they always did. But! Yes, there was always the 'but'! At the moment, everything was happening a safe distance from his pub but that wasn't to say it would stay like that if things got out of control.

His son hadn't been in touch, and with the wife, Mabel, in a bit of a tizzy, Keith felt it might be a good idea to give Katy a ring. If Alex was there at the station, he'd feel a bit better about what was happening. His son wasn't one to get into a flap.

Taking a break from the bar, standing in the street, Keith realized just how hot was the night. Never a good sign – a hot summer: confrontation never seemed far away. He'd read somewhere that the murder rate increased by thirty percent during hot weather. Mind you, that was in America and what you might expect with so many guns around.

He'd wander round to Katy's. The pub could look after itself for a bit. With Mabel concerned, he could do with the break and Katy was always so calm. That was what probably attracted his son to her in the first place.

*

John Chase watched the events unfolding on his television screen with a mixture of relief and anxiety. His station was

Ealing and these disturbances were happening elsewhere. When he arrived at work tomorrow, there was still normal policing to be done. He'd been in the force thirty years and had once been a riot officer but his days of running around with a plastic shield and having petrol bombs thrown at him were in the past – well and truly in the past. The constant cancellation of his rest days to work at football matches convinced him that enough was enough.

He could have retired on a decent pension years ago but he still loved being a copper, doing proper police work, looking after the community. He loved Ealing; it was where he was born and bred and he still lived there. He knew the local youths and they knew him. Ealing was a calm, pleasant place; he saw part of his job as keeping it that way.

It was a mixed community but vibrant: at one end the million-pound homes, trendy restaurants and pubs: at the other, Asian jewellers and restaurants. A bit rough at the edges in places, maybe, but busy and full of energy. It was an exciting place to work and a nice place to live. Whatever was happening elsewhere, life in Ealing would jog along as usual when he got to work tomorrow, August 7th at sixteen hundred hours.

*

Geoffrey Dale, known to all and sundry as 'Jeff' – everyone even spelt it with the 'J' – took a different view.

He sat watching what was going on in Tottenham, wondering why he, a Level 2 Riot Officer, wasn't being called in. Nip it in the bud! Get in early!

He phoned his local station, offering to come into work, but his offer was declined. Stay at home seemed to be the policy; but Geoffrey knew that if the situation got out of hand it would be a hundred times more difficult to contain it.

*

Benjamin Rudge heard the disturbance and, when his mother came back in, he went downstairs to ask her what it was. Benjamin didn't like disturbances of any kind; Benjamin liked order in his life. He could cope with things being the same. He needed to know where he was and where everyone else was, also.

"Who was that, Mum?"

"No one, Ben. It's all right."

She'd spent most of his sixteen years reassuring her son; it was second nature by now, and her 'no one' not a lie – just habit.

"I thought there was someone in the side passage."

Mary was about to say 'it was just a cat' but restrained herself. Later, when the truth came out – and it would have to come out one day – Ben would remember she'd lied to him; and he wouldn't understand.

But how could she tell him the truth tonight? It was so complicated. When Ben was a baby and a toddler, his father had doted on him, loved him, cuddled him, carried him everywhere; and then he'd buggered off – just like that, without a word. The boy had never forgotten the loss but refused to remember his father as anything but a figment of his imagination: someone who had existed once but existed no more. He couldn't cope with the memory and his strategy was to deny it.

Mike Rudge – and Mary was sure it had been him in the passageway – had come back before. She'd found him poking among the discarded present boxes at Christmas, trying to discover what his child had received or hadn't, perhaps. This time it was Ben's birthday. He'd celebrated his sixteenth only a week ago on July 28th and Mike returned like a bad penny.

Mary remembered the day she'd found him in the house, soon after he'd left her. He'd had a key at that time and let himself in; she'd found him with Ben, talking to the boy, staining his mind, turning her son against her. A friend had helped her then, a neighbour, the shopkeeper, Gabriel Pilgrim, who'd phoned the police when she didn't like to do so; and Gabriel had spoken to that young policeman, Alex Willet, who'd 'had a word', as Gabriel put it.

She was grateful for their concern, but that hadn't helped her with Ben, who had been distraught for months afterwards. 'What did Daddy mean when he said you were a bad mother?' How could she answer such a question? How could she explain that what Mike had said wasn't true, that it was something he'd said to turn Ben against her? Ben took everything literally; there wasn't room in his way of thinking for half-truths or half-lies.

"Can we talk about this another time, Ben?"

"What time?"

"Another day."

"You said 'time'."

"Yes, I meant another occasion."

"Is it going to be another time, another day or another occasion?"

Mary knew she should have got used to this by now, but she really meant 'never', not if she could help it.

Chapter 6

SURPRISE AND DISAPPOINTMENT

Charlie Solomon, Daniel Solomon's son, watched the car he'd set fire to smoulder. He waited for the windows to crack and the petrol tank to explode. He'd known nothing about the protest until he received the BlackBerry text and then he'd gone straight to Tottenham. When people in the crowd told him why they were there, he decided to join in. It was only 8.30: there'd be a long night ahead. He thought he might as well get started with the police car.

"I know what they stand for. I hate the fucking police," he told the crowd, "Let's cause fucking chaos. Let's cause a riot."

The image of the burning police car was circulating on thousands of mobile phones within minutes.

*

Keith Willet, returning to his pub, saw the rising smoke. His conversation with his son's partner was less than reassuring: Katy had heard nothing from Alex since he was called into work two hours before. That was unusual if a serious situation was in hand: in those circumstances, Alex always gave her a quick call, urging her to keep Louise inside. To Keith's mind the lack of a call didn't mean things were hunky-dory: it meant he'd had no time to call, and so the situation was deadly serious. Now, seeing the smoke rang the landlord's alarm bells. He'd been around in '85 when the mobs ran wild, looting and killing, and he didn't fancy another dose.

Inside The Bricklayer's Arms, most eyes were focussed on the television screen: not all – the dominoes players seemed oblivious to anything but their game. Mabel Willet looked at her husband as he walked towards the bar. He shook his head: it meant not yet, give me a minute. But Mabel wasn't to be ignored: she nodded again, this time at the screen.

The television cameras, quick off the mark, had caught the youth and the burning car, caught him as he watched and then sloped off as though nothing much was going on. He joined a group of mates waiting on a corner and then disappeared.

Mabel gazed towards Daniel Solomon; Keith shook his head. The pictures weren't clear; it was just one face among many. But Mabel wasn't having it.

"Where's your boy tonight, Daniel?" she asked, avoiding her husband's warning look.

"With his mother," replied the dominoes player without looking up, "She's a good girl, my Vanda. She'll have him off to his football practice. We've got a star in the making with Charlie. Be playing for Spurs, one day, Mrs Willet."

"You're sure about that?" insisted Mabel.

Daniel looked up, unconcerned but curious.

"Why wouldn't he be? His mum looks after him during the week."

"When did you last see him?"

"We had a kick-around on Saturday."

"This morning?"

"No, last week. I couldn't make it this morning. Had a heavy week. Needed a lie in."

Daniel's cronies round their table laughed, laughter joined by other locals in the pub.

"I'll be round to see my little girl later tonight. Big night Saturday."

More laughter and several comments Mabel stifled with a look.

"You might see him sooner than later," snapped Mabel, "He's just been on telly. He's at the police station."

Daniel stopped playing. He wasn't a man easily perturbed. He had his life nicely spaced out, everything in order, everything in its place: free during the week, see the boy at weekends along with his little darling. They had tried, him and Vanda, but it just didn't work when they lived together: always on each other's nerves and it wasn't good for the boy hearing them argue. But he saw the boy was all right, wanted for nothing and it meant he was free to please himself what he did during the week, which usually meant drinking with the lads and getting together with his rock combo. It was a nice life if you could get it and you could get it if you tried. It worked well because he was always fresh at the weekends and looking forward to it.

"You putting me on, Mrs Willet?"

It was funny but the men always referred to Mabel by her title: no one had ever thought of using her first name. It was respect, pure and simple.

"Why would I do that, Daniel? I think you'd better get onto Vanda and see what's going on."

"I don't think my boy would get caught up in anything with that lot at the police station, Mrs Willet."

"Well, perhaps you'd better go and find out," Mabel snapped for the second time that evening, "because it's my boy who they're attacking with bottles and their fires."

She stormed off, leaving the bar quiet and her husband embarrassed. Keith didn't like scenes but knew what his wife said was true. If she was right and it was Charlie Solomon on the television, the likes of Daniel Solomon – who saw his son at his convenience, usually once a week but not always – had something to answer for: another mother's son.

Other eyes on them, the three men at the dominoes table exchanged glances before Daniel rose and left: he wasn't sure for where.

Phil Meadows hadn't seen his son since the boy was born, and he'd be about the same age as Daniel's. He wasn't even sure what he looked like. But surely, one shag after a Christmas party didn't tie you down for life, did it? He and his bit of stuff had knocked around for a while, it's true, and yes they had sort of talked about children and that sort of thing, but nothing serious. He hadn't committed himself to anything. He wasn't having her putting one over on him. Too many women were like that: get a good bloke, present him with a kid and tie him down for life. She'd tried to get maintenance from him in the beginning but he wasn't having any of that nonsense: that would be admitting he was the father and he wasn't sure. Well, not for certain. Anyway, he'd no reason to suppose his son, whatever his name was – Carl wasn't it? – would be caught up in anything like a riot. He'd be surprised if he was.

Tom Drane looked across the table at Phil as Daniel left. He could see the other man was having similar thoughts to himself. He knew about Phil's son: gossip mainly, but it rang true. His own situation was different: after his son was born, his girlfriend, Jenny, threw him out. She said she couldn't put up with his constant worrying about himself. "You only ever think about yourself, Tom," she'd said, "and I can't cope with it." It was true up to a point: he did worry a lot about his health and spent time at the gym when he might have been lending a hand. But he had a good job – he worked for the parks department – and he did get on with his boy and they enjoyed each other's company. He knew Lewis missed him because the boy said so; he'd never understood why his dad and mum split up. They'd spent weekends together at first and then the next boyfriend came along. Nice enough chap but it made Tom uncomfortable being in his company and Lewis didn't get on with him. "I call him dad," he said, "but he's not and it's not like being with you." Tom had gone home and wept that time. But he knew his son. He'd be OK: it was in the genes. Lewis wouldn't be up to anything stupid. If he was, Tom would be disappointed. Nevertheless.

Tom stood up.

"I'd best be off," he said, "I'm going to see my boy."

*

Alex Willet could see that the mob was now beyond control: newcomers had donned masks and were jumping up and down with excitement, an excitement bordering on hysteria. Two police cars were now wrecks, scraps of twisted metal spouting flames.

He and his colleagues were exhausted. They'd been fighting the mob continually for more than two hours on a hot summer's night: beyond exhaustion, they were drained of energy and seriously dehydrated. No one was bringing either reinforcements or water, while the mob was growing in numbers as fresh rioters arrived by bus and tube.

Alex yelled as much to Andy Warner, who nodded resignedly and backed into the station. He came out a few minutes later, his arms laden with a varied collection of drinks, fizzy, still and bottles of water, all cold to the touch. Andy grinned as he passed them round, grinned with anger in his eyes.

And then the order came to move forward. In a way, it was a relief to push against the swelling crowd even though the number of missiles crashing down on them increased as the mob saw the advancing plastic shields.

Alex lifted his round shield over his head to protect himself and stepped forward, holding the line with his comrades. Bottles, rocks and cans smashed down against the shields. The line of officers increased their pace.

And then a fully laden bottle broke the shield roof and struck a female officer on the head. She fell unconscious. The crowd roared its approval and rushed at the stricken woman, as she was pulled back from the front line.

"Hold the line!"

It was Andy Warner's voice; the line of shields dropped as batons were raised, blocking the path of the rioters, forcing them back. They moved against the frenzied mob over piles of broken glass and bricks. The eyes of the mob and its intentions – for now it was behaving as a single animal – were clearly on the stricken officer; they were panting for the kill.

Unknown to Alex and his fellow officers, a small degree of help had been on its way. On a side street, just off the Tottenham High Road, a carrier with eight officers from Hounslow (an inspector, a sergeant and six constables) waited for the arrival of further reinforcements before moving in on the crowd. A few rioters spotted their vehicle and began taking pot shots at it; anything that could be found and thrown was lobbed at the carrier: bottles, bricks, lumps of wood. For a time, this continued unabated and then, suddenly, stopped.

A strange silence followed, strange and uneasy. The police officers looked at each other and realised what was about to happen; other rioters had joined the few and were about to charge the vehicle. The driver started the engine, revved hard and drove slowly but straight into the crowd, moving them aside.

The carrier was immediately caught up in heavy traffic: cars and buses carrying people about their normal, daily business, home from work or out for the night, oblivious to the chaos and danger surrounding them.

*

Alex and his comrades continued to move forward against the crush of the mob, forcing them further back. As they advanced, officers took up their positions in the side streets they passed: there was no desire in the minds of the police for any rioters to move in behind them, no wish that their frontline should be cut off.

As they progressed forward pushing the mob away, it became clear that the rioters' intentions were roused beyond merely attacking the police: ahead, the officers could see flames leaping. The mob had fired some of the shops along with the flats above them. People who only a few hours earlier had opened their windows to gaze at what was going on around Tottenham police station with little more than curiosity were now involved themselves. Fearful for their lives they called from the upstairs windows, screaming, begging to be rescued. Smoke as well as fire now took hold.

Alex looked about him. Surely there would be fire engines. And there were but beyond the mob. Unless he and his colleagues could clear the area by pushing the mob clear, the fire offices had no chance of getting through.

"Steady! Steady as she goes!"

Andy Warner's voice again, rallying them for what must be done. They charged the mob, shields down, batons high in an attempt to gain enough ground to give passage to the fire engines.

A rock – or perhaps it was a brick or a piece of slab some rioter had broken from the pavement – struck Alex's shield. He raised it higher and felt something else, something hard and solid, slam into his legs. He gasped and bore the pain: this was no time to pause, pain or not. And then there was another and another and another, slam after slam. Alex looked up. The sky was filled with smoke, cutting off any light from the stars, and through the dimness the missiles of the enemy – for that is how he saw the rioters at that time – streamed down upon them. Shoulders, arms, hands and legs all took the blows; but they took the next road junction.

The crowd retreated before the police officers who dropped back just slightly. The mob moved against them, and they charged, again and again, taking road after road. Around and above them the residents of the flats cried for help, fearful of the fires that threatened them and their families.

Eventually, the mob was forced to retreat far enough for the fire officers to move in, quench the flames and rescue those who were trapped. Even so, the barrage of missiles continued.

Behind the front line, the mob attempted to take the side streets and roads but the officers who had stationed themselves there held their ground keeping the High Road clear.

Ahead, Alex could see that looting had begun and he knew the shop. It was that of Selim Akbas, the Turk who kept the general store. He was a neighbour of Alex's! Katy shopped there! What the ... yes, what the ... Alex never swore but he felt like doing so at that moment.

Their line moved forward. The mob retreated further and as the officers paused Alex took the opportunity to speak to the man with whom he always passed the time of day.

"We're going to move, Selim," he said, "against these rioters and looters. You need to close your shop. We'll not be here to protect your business."

Selim repeated what he had said to his neighbour, Janusz Wojcik, only a few hours before, adding:

"I will try to move what is left of my fruit and vegetable stalls inside but ..."

He shrugged and smiled. He was resigned. Selim gestured that the officers should wait, before going into his shop and returning with an armful of chocolates and bottles of water. He thanked them all and wished them luck before turning to protect his livelihood.

*

Tom Drane's son, Lewis, was in Wood Green when the rioting started. His dad had been right when he said the boy didn't feel comfortable at home anymore, not with his mum being with the new boyfriend, and Lewis took to wandering off with his mates. Somehow they'd ended up in Wood Green. It was always a bit of a laugh. They never knew where they'd end up next. Someone would have an idea and they'd just go for it.

They were together and had been all day when the Blackberry texts and pictures came in. No one could believe what was going on in Tottenham just two miles away. Lewis wasn't sure how it started. They were excited and daring each other and then suddenly one of them dashed into a shop and came out with a handful of stuff.

Stuff – yeah, that was the trigger, really. Stuff pushed in your face on the television every day, stuff you can never have because you don't have the money: phones, jewellery and especially clothes – the Ralph, the Gucci, the Nike, the trainers. It's all the style. Everyone wants it and if you haven't got it you look like an idiot.

And in a way, it seemed these things were his just rewards. We live in a consumerist society fuelled by greed and the people to blame are the big businesses and the advertisers shoving stuff in your face all the time, making you feel inadequate.

It was exciting, yes, but it was all about money. It started like that with a load of shouting and anger: cigarettes, alcohol, One of the gang actually nicked a suitcase and they began to fill it up: laptops, i-phones, trainers.

All they knew that night were the streets and the running in and out of shops taking what they could grab. And him, Lewis, who'd talked about, one day, being a probation officer.

Chapter 7
BUOYANT AND HOPEFUL

Hugo Battersby felt buoyant and hopeful. He'd got a small group of his mates on the take, including the potential probation officer, Lewis Drane, but that was only the start. He'd waited years for this moment and while the others were looting in and out of the smaller shops, Hugo slid into a side alley and sent a few texts on his BlackBerry. He was going to shaft the big boys and shaft them good.

His aim was clear: he and his mates would take only from the major consumer brands – the ones shafting the kids. Industries and businesses, especially big businesses, international businesses, were raping the world, taking advantage of our labour and the labour of people worldwide. They'd talked about it over and over again: JD Sports making £50 on a shoe, using child labour! They were organised and ready. His BlackBerry text read simply:

The time's come. We rape them! Foot Locker, PC World, JD Sports, Carphone. You know the ones! Target goods with maximum resale potential. We've got the storage.

Hugo lit a cigarette and looked back along the Wood Green High Road. He'd leave the others to it now. They were enjoying themselves in and out of the shops, laughing, giggling, they couldn't believe their luck. Lewis Drane would make a good probation officer: he'd see it from the inside.

*

Keith Willet was determined that whatever happened his pub would stay open. Looking round the bar he took note of those locals he knew to be of a similar mind. All older men, men with families, men in work. The three dominoes players would be back once they'd sorted out their children and he'd get the others to round up some mates. It was going to be a long night but his son was out there fighting those bastards and he wasn't going to be doing it for nothing

"All right, listen up," he called, turning off the television screen for the moment, "We need to show these kids that they're not going to win and that we're all sticking together. If they come this way and start looting I want to be here. We can't let these bastards grind us down, come what may. The Blacksmith's Arms will stay open and I'm expecting you as locals and regulars to be with me. We'll stand a vigil 'til dawn."

While he spoke, Martha had come from the kitchen to listen. She looked around the bar, stepped from behind it and walked among the tables and chairs. She passed by the one-armed bandits – a definite target, she thought, for the mob – and ran her hand along the baize of the snooker table. She looked round the huge space, noting the sign over the swing doors, the photographs of Spurs players, the scarves, the trophies, the testimonials, the letters of thanks.

The Blacksmith's Arms was more than just a pub and their regulars knew it. It was a way of life and Martha read that knowledge in the eyes of the men drinking. It was worth defending. She stopped by the short flight of steps to the upper level and then strolled out into the garden where she repeated to her customers what her husband had said.

Back in the main pub, the talk had started. The screen was back on offering wall-to-wall coverage of the rioting. As she returned to the kitchen, Martha felt triumphant.

*

Dolly Pilgrim and her friend Cathy had not moved far from the River Heights Apartments. The crowd was so dense they could barely see what was happening further along the road but they could see the fires from the burning police cars. Other school friends joined them and the girls were quite happy to enjoy each other's excitement: an excitement shared is more than doubled – it's quadrupled when there's four of you and hundreds of times more in a crowd. To the girls it was still a crowd, a crowd out of hand maybe but still a crowd.

There were other fires – some people said in shops but it didn't seem likely to Dolly that it was her dad's grocery store. She hadn't been born at the time of the Broadwater Farm riots; they were not even a distant memory but simply part of history like the six wives of Henry the Eighth. Nevertheless, she'd been fly enough to text her mum to say that she was at Cathy's, just as Cathy had said she was at Dolly's; both sets of parents were now satisfied. As long as they didn't phone each other the girls were safe, and the girls never seemed to remember the other set of parents' phone number and so could never pass it on.

Cardinal to this careful planning was the fact that a friend's car had arrived with the news that things were happening at Wood Green. BlackBerry texts told someone – Dolly was unsure who – that shops were being broken into; she didn't want to do this herself but needed to be able to talk about it when her friends did.

"I don't plan to rob anything," said the youth driving the car, "Someone came up with the idea: if we spread this, can the police like control it? So, like, let's go to Wood Green. I've called as many people as I can. I hear everyone's going to Wood Green. Call as many people as you can. Go to Wood Green."

They arrived to see people breaking into jewellery shops and a man running out of Holland and Barrett's with protein milk shakes. He called out to them and the youth pulled over. The man tapped on the window until it was opened and stuck his head through.

"The phone shop next to JD Sports is ripped apart. Get as many things as you can to sell on. We're bigger than the police! We're bigger than the police!"

"But you're breaking the law," cried Cathy, much to Dolly's embarrassment.

"Fair enough, we are breaking the law and everything but there's more of us than there are of them. If we want to do this, we can do this and they can't stop us."

"I don't want to be part of this, Dolly," said her friend to a silent Dolly, who always, but always, had to be part of the crowd.

"You're in it now, Like it or not," said the driver.

He drove on further and parked the car in a back street, reckoning that it was less likely to be damaged if out of sight: his dad wouldn't want the car returned in anything but a decent condition: not that his dad knew he had borrowed the car.

There were lots of cars, too many to count. People rushed from them in a hurry to reach the High Street, by now a hive of animation, restless young people freed by the events of the past few hours.

*

Gabriel Pilgrim and his wife, Martha, decided to shut up shop. They'd had shutters fitted long ago, memories of Broadwater Farm forever fresh in their minds. They were not really expecting trouble but better safe than sorry. When Dolly got back from her friends, they'd let her in the back door.

"I'm going to go and meet her", said Martha, "There's some rough kids out there tonight. Let's hope the police get them under control quickly. If they don't, I'm going to fetch Dolly. You never know what might happen …"

Gabriel knew what his wife had in mind but didn't think it would happen. Martha liked to worry; women were like that always. He carried on listening but his mind was elsewhere.

*

Miggs had found Simon Tippet by shoving her way, and being shoved, through the crowd. Half of them she didn't know but everyone was together tonight; everyone was helping everyone. Only the police were the enemy. Simon and his mates were wearing masks and carrying weapons – hammers and knives, big knives. She hadn't expected anything like this; Simon – or Sim, as she called him – had never seemed bigger in her eyes. He was a little bloke, really, and some of her friends laughed at how thin his legs were, but they wouldn't be laughing tonight.

"All the police came running down," he shouted, "I just see the bottles flying. I've never seen police so scared before. It's like they've got no control whatsoever. Like even the police cars. We turned them over. Here, cover your face. You don't want to be recognised, do you!"

Miggs pulled her coat up round her chin. The road at her feet was spread with broken bottles, rocks and all kinds of debris. Miggs bent down and picked up two half-bricks. Well, why not? Sim would be pleased.

*

Emma Hare had had law and order running through her veins since she was a child: both her grandfathers and also her father were police officers. It had never occurred to Emma that she might consider another profession.

The force was still chauvinistic to an extent: jokes about women officers brewing the tea and making the station look attractive still floated around, especially among the older policemen. None of this banter had ever bothered Emma: perhaps because she was used to it from her grandfathers, although her own father had never indulged in that kind of humour, and her grandfathers had never really meant what they were saying. Put their comments down to tradition, to saying what was expected. Only once, when referring to the Broadwater Farm riots, had her mum's dad wondered whether women officers should be involved in something so violent. Her dad had corrected him but the old boy had meant what he said kindly with no disrespect to women; he was, quite simply, of that generation who saw men as the protectors.

Emma had just holidayed in the Adirondacks. She and a group of friends had been trekking – hard walking up to twenty miles a day and don't complain about the blisters: you should have toughened your feet before you set off! It was a good holiday, a good getaway with friends she'd made at university when she took her degree in law and criminology. Talking round the campfire at night several of them had asked why she didn't go in at the top of the force. Emma had said she knew the contempt felt by ordinary officers for those who marched in with a degree and had never pounded the beat. Respect couldn't be learned; it had to be gained. Unless she knew what it was like doing the job on a day-in, day-out basis how could she lead those who had that experience?

She was tall and a natural blonde and "as fit as a fiddle", as her dad's dad used to say. It was true: Emma kept herself in trim at the local gym and she'd run a few marathons in her time, all for charity.

She was due to accompany an older officer, John Chase, on patrol tomorrow and like him, was watching the rioting on television. She, too, lived in Ealing and decided to take a quiet walk, take a quiet look around. Emma didn't share John's view that all would be well in Ealing: youths were youths wherever they lived and news travelled fast these days.

She found it was peaceful. Outside Ealing Broadway police station, she saw a small group of them, perhaps eight or nine, their hoodies pulled up. They all smiled when she walked over to talk with them.

"We're not expecting any trouble here, are we boys?" she asked.

It was always good to be positive.

"No. It ain't happening here," replied one of them

"I'm pleased to hear you say so," said Emma, throwing each one a look and a broad smile.

As a woman, she'd always found that youths were attracted to her: her being older, if only in her twenties, appealed to them. She could remember a time when she felt attracted to older men, but the feeling had stopped naturally and she'd been careful not to get involved with anyone at work, old or young, on her dad's advice.

She walked slowly away from the Underground station towards the town centre. All was calm, all was still, and Emma went slowly home.

*

Alex Willet and his comrades soldiered on pushing their way along the Tottenham High Road. Fires were now an added danger. A double-decker bus ablaze, threatening the officers with its flame, its heat and its potential as an explosion, was edged past quickly.

The rioters, too, now had the measure of the police, could see the tactics they were using and the slightness of their numbers. Emboldened further, they leapt from alleyways and houses, attacking the lines of officers.

Ahead, motorbikes, high-powered and threatening, revved into view across the road, their riders shrouded in the thick, black smoke from the fires, silhouetted by the fires from the burning shops and vehicles. The bikes moved back and forth, criss-crossing the road.

"They're trying to intimidate us," said Andy Warner, calmly, "Hold steady."

The riders revved once more, veered off and disappeared through the smoke. Alex felt the relief run through him. How many people, he wondered, had been threatened or injured this night.

Ahead, he saw more flames shooting, spurting into the night sky. A small, Aldi supermarket was ablaze, its roof collapsing inwards. A line of shopping trolleys barricaded the road. Behind them stood the rioters attempting to provoke the police. They were defiant: with their verbal abuse came the usual bricks and bottles. Some brandished sticks; others, knives and hammers.

And then the order came that they were to charge the barricades. Alex tightened his grip on the shield and lowered his visor.

Chapter 8
A SERIES OF PICTURES

Daniel Solomon was narked: Mabel Willet had no business speaking to him in that way. He was a good father: none better. He was sure it wasn't his son, Charlie, on the television: *Love Island* maybe, but not on the news setting fire to police cars. He'd see Vanda. What the hell was she doing letting the boy out among a crowd of yobs?

"Doing? What do you mean what was I doing? What were you doing in the pub at 6.30 on a Saturday night, especially as you hadn't seen Charlie all week and let him down this morning!"

Vanda was a big woman: not fat but firm muscled and large. It was one of her attractive features as far as Daniel was concerned. He'd seen her lift a table clear of the crowd at one of their rock combo evenings when a bunch of men stood around open-mouthed wondering where to put it out of the way. Vanda had told them! She was fiery, it was true but then all redheads are, aren't they? And they got on well, provided they stayed out of each other's way.

"Well?"

She could put so much emphasis into a single word, thought Daniel. Most women can, of course, but it was only Vanda who'd ever managed to get under his skin so easily. He supposed it was because he loved her.

"Have you phoned him?" asked Daniel.

"Have you?"

"I've only just got here."

This time, Vanda didn't even have to speak: the excuse was so lame, a look sufficed.

"Get out there and find him and bring him home before he gets into real trouble."

What Vanda might have considered 'real trouble' when, clearly, setting fire to a police car failed to come into that category, Daniel wasn't sure and wasn't foolish enough to ask.

"Where is he?"

Again, the look.

"Well, when the BBC were kind enough to video him for us, he was on the High Road, just up from where you were sitting in the pub. Where he is now, the Lord only knows. Find him, Dan!"

"OK, OK, no need to get excited, Vanda. Leave it to me. I'll see you later, darling."

"Don't bank on it!" snapped Vanda, who was not in the girlfriend mood.

*

Phil Meadows was at an even greater loss than his friend: he had no idea where his son was living or who the boy's mother was with, if anyone. His sister might know; he'd give her a ring; most women were a mine of information on family matters and Phil was soon knocking at a door in Hackney, a quick trip on the Overground.

When his former lover opened her door, Phil barely recognised the woman he'd been with at that Christmas party sixteen years before. She'd aged: an inevitable condition Phil had never related to himself.

"Hello, Lynn," he said, as though they'd passed the time of day only yesterday morning on their separate ways to work.

Lynn, now a teacher, had always kept the door open for him as far as their child, Carl, was concerned: she was never giving the boy or his father a chance to say she'd been difficult and kept them apart. She was tempted to ask whether he'd come to make good the sixteen years maintenance he owed but Lynn contained herself.

"You'd better come in," she said, feeling hospitality was the order of the day.

She'd been told he'd married eventually but knew nothing of the woman or his circumstances: how many children they had, whether it was a second marriage – that sort of thing. She did know he'd always been in work of one kind or another: friends who'd tried to persuade her to get what she could from him had kept her informed out of their own interest. The idea that a man 'might get away with it' was high on their list of vexations.

"Would you like a cup of tea?"

She remembered him leaving empty cans of beer lying around after he'd been drinking when they lived together for a while; she'd arrive home from a hard day at work and he'd be sitting in the easy chair his mess all around him. Always a smile on his face, always a welcome but no meal ready and waiting for one.

"Yes, that'd be nice."

For a strange moment, he felt he was returning home: not that he'd mention this to his wife.

"Is ... Carl all right?"

Lynn almost exploded at the question. Could he really be interested after sixteen years?

"Why don't you ask him? He's up in his room."

Phil was taken aback. True, he'd come to see what was happening, whether Carl was involved with these riots, but he hadn't thought ahead far enough to visualise actually meeting him.

"He's in his room?" he asked, feeling ever so slightly foolish.

"Yes."

She wasn't going to be more helpful; she wasn't going to call her son down to meet a man he didn't know. There was something cowardly about Phil Meadows and Lynn expected him to skedaddle sharply; but while he sat indecisively and she went to the kitchen to fill the kettle, Carl, hearing voices, entered the room.

He'd used the name 'Meadows', although his mother kept her maiden name, because it gave him a link to his biological father. Carl thought those matters to be important. Somehow it acknowledged his mother was a woman who'd been let down by this man, and he loved his mother.

"Hello," he said, in the easy-going manner his mother loved.

Carl was liked by just about everybody; he was never short of a friend and he was a boy who needed friends, desperately – any friends. He was also intelligent in an incisive way and knew without having to ask why this man had appeared at this time. Unlike his mother, he wasn't interested in watching Phil Meadows sweat. In a way, he admired him for taking an interest.

"You work in Tottenham, don't you," he said, using his words as a statement rather than a question.

"Yes," replied Phil.

"Have you seen these riots first hand?"

"They were just up the road."

"From the Blacksmith's?" asked Lynn, coming in with a tray of tea items, unable to resist the taunt.

Carl looked at his mother. He wasn't used to her speaking in that way and wondered what she knew of this man, and whether she felt anything for him. He could see she was uncomfortable and that was enough: Carl launched into his attack.

"The police had it coming," he said, "The police are looked upon as a gang by many young people like myself. They enforce laws that they themselves play fast and loose with. One of the things that really gets to us is this stop and search law and the way the police do it. They are not civil. Young people feel they cannot walk down the street without the police stopping them. They will approach you for no reason and then its 'take your hat off, 'take your hood off', 'what are you doing', 'empty your pockets', 'there are four of you', 'you've got to split up', 'you can't go round in a gang' even when you're just out with your friends."

"Has this happened to you?" asked Lynn.

"Once, when I was out with friends."

"What were you doing?"

"Nothing, Mum – that's the point. The police just class you as someone who's bad. It really irritates me because I'm not that kind of person. We get frustrated at the police thinking they can talk to us as though we're some kind of hoodlum, as though we're stupid and don't know what we're doing, as though we're five years old. Their attitude is 'we're the police, so you listen to us'."

"Who were you with?" asked Lynn, quite shocked because Carl had never opened up in this manner, ever.

"Shekhar, Elijah, Kiran and one or two others."

"Did they think you were doing drugs or ..."

"That's not the point, Mum."

"No, of course not. I can see that, Carl."

"Sorry, Mum. I didn't mean to upset you," he replied, walking over and putting his arms round her.

Phil Meadows looked on – at the exchange, at the tenderness – feeling excluded and wondering what he was doing in their home.

*

Tom Drane's attempt to find his son met with an even briefer encounter. His ex-girlfriend was at work, called into the hospital, where she worked as a nurse, at short notice, and the new boyfriend had no idea where Lewis might be.

"He's been out all day," he said, "Went off when he got up at coffee time. We haven't seen him since."

"Hasn't he phoned?"

"What do you think? These kids don't like you knowing where they are. Did you when you were their age?"

"I suppose not."

"Anyway, I can't help you, mate. Your ... you know – she'll be home soon, I hope, and I'm supposed to have a meal ready."

As the new boyfriend shut the door, Tom realised that having a meal ready was something he'd never done.

※

Mary Rudge was terrified. Finding him in her home was one of those recurring nightmares she experienced regularly, and there he was, sitting there when she returned from a quick trip to borrow some eggs from a neighbour. She hadn't wanted to go to Gabriel Pilgrim's general store on the High Road, not with what was going on there, but Ben liked scrambled eggs on a Sunday morning and she'd run out. So, after the film finished, Mary had gone to ask her friend.

Mike had never handed his house key back. She'd insisted but to no avail: after all, technically, they were still married.

"I came to see Ben."

"Why?"

"I'm his dad."

"You were his dad. You left us years ago. Where is he?"

"He's in his room."

Mary gave the man she considered an intruder one look, up and down, and made for the stairs. She didn't want to disturb her son, just see if he was alright. Opening the door, Mary found him sitting at his computer. He was transfixed on whatever game was playing itself out on the screen and never noticed her peering into his room. This was his sanctuary, his safe place in the world. No one entered Ben's room uninvited – unless, as in Mary's case, it was to change his bed linen. She toyed with the idea of speaking to him, knowing his focus on the game was an escape from what might have passed between him and the man he preferred not to acknowledge as his father. She decided, instead, to get rid of the intruder.

"Go now," she said, arriving back in her living room, "Ben's upset and the sooner you go the better."

"He's all right. He's playing on his computer."

"No, he's not. Believing that to be so just shows how little you know about him. Please go, now, Mike. We don't want him to hear us arguing."

"I'm not arguing."

"We will be if we're not careful, and Ben doesn't need that."

"We were close once."

Mary knew that was true but long ago: before the drunken brawls with Spurs opponents' supporters, brawls that were never Mike's fault: before the nights in the police cells and the drunken arrival home when he was turned out the next morning: before Mary decided she and Ben had had enough and kicked her husband out.

Yes it was true, father and son had been close, closer than any father and son she'd seen. For years, he'd carried the boy around and taken him everywhere. And that was what had hurt the boy – the sudden change, the quick descent into alcoholism. The father lost his job and grew dirty and slovenly in his habits until Mary decided he was doing her son more harm than good by the constant comings and goings.

Once, he'd actually taken the boy away. What an horrendous time in her life were those few weeks when this man she had once loved was turning her son against her and leaving him with a woman he'd taken up with while he went boozing. The woman had turfed him out, of course, realising his talk was just bullshit and nothing was coming of his promises; and Mary reclaimed her son.

Watching the wretch in the chair watching her, she just wanted him out of the house so that she could coax Ben down and let him talk if that was what he wanted. She knew what would be happening now in her son's mind. It was called looping by his counsellor: round and round his concerns would go, always coming back to the same point of worry that obsessed him, a worry that would drive him deeper into his autism rather than ease him from it.

And it was this man, this intruder, who would be the cause of the boy's distress. Mary went to the front door and opened it. She didn't need to say anything, she knew her strength would drive him out, but she did, just to be sure.

"For Ben's sake, please. You loved him once."

"I love ..."

Mike Rudge didn't complete the sentence: he might have been full of bullshit but even hypocrisy had its stopping point. He didn't look back as he walked up the path and disappeared into the night, a night lit by the fires of the High Road.

When she was sure he had disappeared completely, Mary went quietly up to her son's room. Ben was no longer at his computer; and with his coat gone from the wardrobe, Mary knew with her heart sinking that Ben had left the house.

*

"GO! GO! GO!"

Alex Willet sprang forward, spurred on by the shouts of his comrades who were also storming the barricade. Once, twice, three times they tried to take the ground held by the rioters; each time they were driven back, pummelled and pounded by the now familiar barrage of bottles, bricks, paving stones, masonry – any weapon on which the mob could lay its hands. The officers' bodies were punished time and time again as they tried to regain the road. The ferocity of the assault against them was like nothing any of them had ever experienced.

Alex's body was in pain in every limb: his right shoulder was smashed, his knees broken where he fell. The will was there, the determination to see this outrage through but he was now seriously injured: his shield hung from his left arm, his baton held in his damage right.

And yet it seemed pointless, this repeated attempt to drive back the rioters. In front of him he could see three pairs of officers with long shields and beyond them one man moving through the mob. There was a smile on this man's face, discernible even through the acrid smoke, and his comrades moved aside for him. The man was holding a milk bottle, a rag hanging from its neck. In his other hand, a lighter. The lighter sparked, the man panicked, the bottle dropped and smashed on the road. Alex sighed with relief: the last thing the mob needed were petrol bombs.

Beyond the Aldi store, now well afire, was the new property development providing the rioters with their weapons. As the police, trying to advance, received one battering, the building site supplied enough ammunition for them to receive another on their retreat. Looking about him, Alex realised that all his comrades had been injured in one way or another. How could they not be facing such an attack! For a minute or two, he found his professionalism questioned by his realisation that their attempts were futile. And then the horses arrived.

Trained along with their human counterparts, the animals cantered in pairs, protected by shin and leg guards. With fires raging around them and the rioters' weaponry crunching under their hooves, the horses stood steady in a line across the High Road, waiting. Their riders patted their necks reassuringly, their breath steamed from their nostrils, and then they charged, leaping the barricade, disappearing into the hellhole of smoke, fire, flying weapons and screams, driving the rioters further and further back. The mob was on the retreat; for a time, at least, the police held the ground and the fire engines moved in.

SUNDAY, AUGUST 7TH

Chapter 9
UNFORTUNATE ON THE ROAD

Mary Rudge had little idea where she was going. She knew only that she must find her son. Mary always worried when Ben was out alone, although accepting that this must now be the pattern and she must get used to the idea; but in his present state of mind his running off was more than just a mother's worry. Benjamin was vulnerable; he was at risk.

Her first thought was the pub. Ben would not have gone there – he didn't really like company unless he'd learned beforehand who he might have to meet – but Keith Willet was a kind man and if he'd seen Ben pass by he would offer to help her. Partway there, Mary realised The Blacksmith's Arms would be closed by now and was surprised on turning the corner onto the High Road to see that it wasn't.

"Not tonight, Mrs Rudge," said Keith Willet, "Me and my locals are guarding the place. What we have in here would be tempting for that lot up the road. I haven't seen Ben but I'm sure, thinking about it now, that your ex came into the pub earlier."

"He may have done," replied Mary, "and he's upset Ben. I must find him."

"I don't think he'll be far, will he? He's not a boy to want to get involved with the crowds. He's likely to be watching from a distance somewhere. Let me come with you, Mrs Rudge. You don't want to go up the High Road alone."

"I can't ask you to do that, Mr Willet," Mary replied, but immensely relieved the landlord offered.

"No, it's all right – for a short while. There're enough tough-looking characters in the pub to ward off any troublemakers. I'll just let Martha know."

Within minutes the two of them, distraught mother and friendly publican, were making their way along the back streets towards the police station.

Keith Willet had forgotten about Mike Rudge until the man entered his pub earlier that evening, and even then barely noticed him. Sometimes the past is best forgotten; no good ever came from harbouring some memories. Rudge hadn't been a violent man under normal circumstances but was easily aroused when in drink and in conversation – if conversation was the right word – with the opposing team's supporters. He remembered the incident – well, several incidents – when Rudge landed up in jail for the night. They'd all happened out on the street. Keith wouldn't have rival camps in the bar: his pub was for Spur's supporters and he always made that clear to avoid trouble; but those out for trouble always managed to find it on their way to the Underground station.

He'd always felt sorry for Mary Rudge – although his wife, Mabel, said that the two of them had been happy enough in the beginning – and was pleased to help her now.

As they reached what Keith considered a relatively safe spot off the main road, he and Mary saw just how seriously the rioting had turned: buildings were burning, some shops and houses now blackened skeletons of what they had once been; fire officers crouched low to the ground, directing jets of water upwards into the openings that had once been windows; police officers guarded them because the mob was actually attacking the firefighters.

"They want the buildings to burn," said Keith to Mary, quietly, "Can you believe it? What's going on in their heads – they live here, these are Tottenham kids!"

A dozen fires were now burning along the Tottenham High Road; the heat from the flames and falling timbers and masonry wreaked their destruction on adjacent premises: shops, homes, malls all burned wildly, beyond the control of those who fought the flames.

Mary's terror grew as she watched. It seemed to her that there were no what she'd call 'normal' people on the main road through Tottenham that night. She heard glass shattering; she saw a bus as well as police cars on fire. A bus! The very bus she and her neighbours used every day! And the rioters were without faces; they all wore masks and looked like some alien invasion force. They were jumping around crazily, as though caught up in some terrible, communal ritual, creatures purging themselves of hate. She'd seen that frenzy once but in a science fiction film, and not in real life and not by human beings.

From where they crouched hidden, it was difficult for Mary and Keith to be sure of what was happening but through the thickening smoke they caught glimpses of police horses charging the mob. Bottles and bricks careered into the animals but they pushed on driving the rioters back.

Keith touched Mary's arm lightly and signalled her forward. The look he gave her, one of fascinated terror, suggested he needed to know more, since he couldn't believe what he was seeing; and Mary realised for the first time since he'd offered his help that Keith's son, Alex, would be right in the middle of the rioting.

From their new position, Mary saw the old River Heights building ablaze. People lived there above the Carpetright store! She knew some of them – one, a teacher, had been especially kind to Ben when he was at school, a place he found it difficult to handle. Flames now billowed from windows and doorways. It was an old building, three storeys and attractive. Art Deco someone had told her; and now it was gone, past saving, and somewhere out there, among the deafening noise and the madness and the terrible fires was her autistic son, driven from their home by his father, frightened, alone and beyond her help.

Suddenly, she felt at one with Keith Willet, a man she spoke to whenever they met but who she really did not know. 'Together in adversity' was the phrase, wasn't it?

*

Alex Willet was, in fact, not in the middle of the rioting at that moment: he was flat out in Tottenham police station, together with his comrades with whom he had fought against the mob that night. They were exhausted but the station was secure and saved.

Alex's shoulder was one huge bruise and the rest of his body was covered in similar bruises and swellings. He and his fellow officers had taken a hammering and they were relieved to be handing over to the next shift. It would be good to get home, whatever the state of their bodies, and take a few hours rest before being back on duty in a few hours' time.

*

Emma Hare watched television during the day, along with the rest of her off-duty colleagues, waiting for her shift to start. Last night, she'd felt reassured – just – but Ealing had had an edge to it all day. She'd been out and about once or twice just to get a feel of the place, and the feel was different. The groups of kids hanging about were waiting. Emma knew that was so. Waiting! The sense of impending trouble was in the air all day. Nothing on which she could put her finger: the kids weren't masked or anything like that but ...but they were out of place. That was the only way she could express what she felt.

*

Edward Andrews, still hungover, stood in his uniform at Lewisham police station along with five other officers, waiting for orders from his sergeant. He didn't have long to wait.

"Nice to see you, Ed. You managed to get here, then?"

Ed nodded: he was used to the banter of discipline. He knew he was being ticked off but in the nicest possible way.

"Now, lads, thanks for coming in. You'll all have seen the news, I'm sure, and have a good idea of why we're here. We're being deployed to Edmonton tonight. So, let's get our riot kit together and get to the carriers."

"Where are the rest, Sarg?" asked Ed.

"The rest, son? We are the rest."

"Just you and the six of us, Sarg?"

"Just me and the six of you. That is correct."

Once in the carrier, the sergeant informed his men that groups of youths had been seen gathering in the Edmonton area and had made their way to the main shopping street where they were attacking businesses. Looting! It wasn't a word familiar to Ed or any of the other young officers.

"Our local colleagues who attempted to intervene have come under attack and they are outnumbered," explained the sergeant as the carrier, blue lights blazing, got underway. It was fifteen miles from Lewisham to Edmonton through heavy traffic.

On the main street they found a burnt-out police car and saw smoke rising from somewhere ahead. The radio told them that other units were being summoned. They waited. The area was silent; one officer commented that it might have been a ghost town. Eventually, their order came. Guard the high street.

"But there's nothing going on here," exclaimed one of the officers.

"Orders are orders! We guard the high street."

Fully kitted in their riot gear the seven policemen began patrolling the street. They heard the sound of sirens and saw the flashing blue lights; police cars whizzed by, heading in different directions; more carriers arrived and waited.

Ed walked by smashed-in shop fronts, saw burnt out vehicles, nodded to a TV camera crew, heard on the radio that a youth had been stabbed, heard the youth's friends cursing the police. Eventually he paused by a Carphone Warehouse. A call came through:

"URGENT ASSISTANCE!"

His unit remained where they were, patrolling the high street. A group of locals approached.

"What are you doing? They're burning our cars down the street and you stand here guarding burnt out shops!"

Ed didn't like it any more than the frustrated residents but orders were orders: guard the shops. His instinct was to help these ordinary, decent people: their homes, their way of life was under attack and he was doing nothing about it. It went against the grain; it went against the very reason he was a policeman.

*

Neil Stagg, whose friends all called him Spike – he liked it: you can guess why! – was at a friend's birthday party in Brixton when the call came through on his Blackberry. At first he thought it was terrible and then thought how everyone was just getting the stuff they wanted. He didn't mean to nick anything, not really, and he stopped himself for a few hours but then more and more messages came through and he saw people running down the street with their arms full of stuff. Before he knew it, he'd left the house.

He took phones from a T-Mobile shop and then joined his friends battling the police. Bricks, bottles, cans, anything: just chucking them at the feds. And then the call came:

"Currys! Currys!"

A girl ran past in her bra and shorts: she had her T-shirt pulled up round her face. She was about thirteen. Spike was that excited. There were like thousands rushing to Currys, tearing at the shutters, some with bags ready to fill.

A van passed and the driver, a commuter, stuck his head out and called:

"Get us a TV. I'll give you a hundred quid."

Spike almost wet himself with excitement, raiding Currys for over an hour: TVs, Canon lenses, PlayStations, anything. Anything worth money. Back and to from the estate.

*

Benjamin Rudge was confused and frightened. Hearing the row, as he saw it, between his mother and the man who said he was his father, Benjamin had left his home quietly. He didn't want to go. He didn't like being out at night by himself but felt he had to get away. He had to think through what he'd overheard; he had to get things straight in his head.

He found a quiet place where he could watch what was happening. Had he known at the time, his mother and Mr Willet were only a few streets away but further along the High Road near the Carpetright building, whereas Benjamin chose to stay near the police station.

He knew one or two of the policemen – but you shouldn't say policemen because some of them were women – because they came to talk to the children in school. Benjamin had his own special teacher and was sometimes taught in a room with a few other children but that day they had all been in the hall together. He had asked a lot of questions and one of the teachers said he should give the other children a chance but Benjamin said he couldn't learn things if he didn't ask. It was always right to ask if you didn't understand something: that was what his mum and his SenCo had told him.

He didn't like what he saw at the police station. People – some of them children from his school – were throwing bottles and bricks and paving stones and pieces of metal at the line of police. Suddenly, he heard the roar of a car and the people in it drove straight at the police. The ones throwing the missiles leapt out of the way and began to laugh and dance about like mad people. They were excited.

It was good to be excited but you mustn't let it get out of control, otherwise you would begin to shake and make booming noises. His mother didn't like him making those noises. Once, in the cinema, he had got out of control and started to shout at his mother. She told him never to embarrass her like that again or it would be the last time she would take him to watch a film.

Suddenly the throwing stopped. Benjamin didn't know why but the police looked tired and he was glad the missiles stopped hitting them. He saw some of the police move away when it was quiet. They went to a corner shop and Ben wondered why and followed them. They bought chocolate bars and bottles of water and that made Benjamin feel hungry, although he didn't usually eat so late at night.

Usually, he was asleep by now and would wake up in time for breakfast. On Sunday morning, his mother always made him egg bread to use up the bread left over. Egg bread was better if the bread was older. But seeing the police enjoying the chocolate bars, he felt hungry and thought it would be all right if he bought one for himself.

He was standing at the counter counting out his money – he was careful with money and had saved a lot from his pocket money for when he and his mum went on holiday, which was what they hoped to do at the end of August – when the man spoke to him.

"Hello, Ben," he said, "I'm your dad."

Benjamin thought it was unfortunate that he should meet this man who he was trying to get away from just as he was about to enjoy his chocolate bar.

Chapter 10
BITTER ANIMOSITY

Benjamin didn't recognize the man, but he did recognize the voice. It was the man who had been arguing with his mother earlier. Benjamin knew he shouldn't speak to strangers but this man wasn't really a stranger, although he was a stranger to Benjamin, who hadn't liked it when the man walked into the house earlier that evening when his mum was out shopping.

"You needn't be frightened, Ben. I'm your dad. Don't you remember me?"

Benjamin did, but the memories were fleeting and they weren't memories he wanted to return.

"You came to live with me for a time," insisted the man.

Benjamin did remember that time. The man had been living with a woman that Benjamin didn't know, and she gave him spaghetti to eat and he didn't like spaghetti and, anyway, it was red. It was red because it had tomato sauce. Benjamin didn't like spaghetti and he didn't like the colour red. He'd thrown the food against the wall when the woman tried to make him eat it; and he'd screamed and screamed and screamed and the man had taken him to his room to calm down but he didn't want to calm down even if it was wrong to scream.

"Would you like another chocolate bar, Ben."

Benjamin knew what the man was doing: he was trying to get round him. Grown-ups always tried to get round you if they wanted you to do something for them. They didn't really do it to be kind but to get what they wanted. Benjamin wasn't sure what this man wanted but he didn't think he'd like it.

"I shouldn't eat after I have cleaned my teeth," he replied.

"Another chocolate bar won't hurt."

Without waiting for him to reply, the man bought another chocolate bar and also one for himself.

"Shall we get away from here?" asked the man, "Somewhere quiet where we can talk."

Benjamin didn't want to talk; he wanted to think and he could only think when he was alone. The trouble with grown-ups was they never stopped talking. They were always asking you questions or offering advice; and advice wasn't always helpful, especially when you were trying to think things through and clear your head. He wanted to curl up in a ball and for everything and *everyone* to go away.

He'd stopped hearing the awful sounds around him: the shouting, the fires, the sirens, buildings collapsing. All he could hear was the sound of this man's voice in his head.

"I'm not like your mum, Ben. She's a much nicer person than me. But that doesn't mean I don't love you. Do you remember I used to carry you around all the time when you were a little boy."

Benjamin did remember but didn't want to do so. This was what the man had started to say when he walked into the house. Benjamin felt he couldn't listen and wanted to go to his room.

"Your mum and me we had our differences and I don't blame her for what she did when she threw me out ..."

He'd started to say that, too, and that was when Benjamin put his hands over his ears and went to his room. He sat looking at his computer but not really seeing it, but just hoping the man, his father, wouldn't come up the stairs.

"Your mum felt she couldn't take any more and ..."

Benjamin felt he couldn't take any more. The chocolate bar, which he wanted to enjoy, was going soft in his hands and his father hadn't started to eat his yet. If you hold chocolate in a warm hand it softens very quickly and then you can't eat it and it melts in the wrapping and goes all over your hands. Benjamin hated getting his hands messy. He hated being messy. One of his uncles had always said what a sharp dresser he was and his mum had to explain what 'sharp' meant when you were talking about clothes.

"We had a lot of arguments …"

The man's voice – his father's voice – was still going on and on. Benjamin didn't want to hear about arguments. He and his mum never had arguments. Sometimes she said she had to be firm with him but she always understood what he wanted to do and let him do it … usually. Not always and he found it difficult to understand why she sometimes stood against him.

"I didn't get into fights because I wanted to …"

Then why? Why did you do it if you didn't want to? Grown-ups were very confusing. They would talk about not wanting to so something and then go and do it. They didn't always tell the truth and you should always tell the truth because … because if you don't … if you don't what happens?

Benjamin had never quite understood why his mum and dad were not together. No, that's not right! Never understood why his mum had thrown his dad out because his mum never talked about it. And he was glad she didn't. And he didn't want to understand it now.

Benjamin screamed, a sound that rose in pitch high above the bays and screams of the mob. The man, his dad, was holding his arm as he spoke: only gently but Benjamin didn't like being touched in that way. He pulled free and ran.

"Ben come back!"

He heard his dad's shout but didn't want to stop. Quite the opposite: he needed to get away from that voice. Benjamin ran and ran onto the High Road, through the mob and away, not knowing where he was going.

*

David Lammy, the MP for Tottenham, stood in front of a group of TV cameras on Tottenham High Road. He was determined to convey one thing above all: the chaos had been caused by a few hundred people but there were 40,000 people under the age of twenty-five living in the area: this violence was not the true face of Tottenham.

He and his wife, Nicola, had left a few days earlier for a short holiday.. They'd been looking forward to a summer break without the stresses that had followed them during his time as a government minister: piles of briefing papers would always follow them on a summer holiday. With Labour defeated at the recent election, it was a chance for some family time.

And then came the call from the borough commander in Tottenham. Calls from junior officers were not uncommon if there had been an incident, but this one was from a most senior policewoman. David listened as she explained the circumstances of Mark Duggan's death. When the call concluded, David turned to his wife.

"Nicola," he said, "I have to get back to Tottenham."

He spent some time talking to local residents, especially young people. Rumours were rife: 'Mark Duggan had been executed', 'local kids had been ushered away from the scene by police', 'camera-phones had been confiscated'. David spent more time talking to the IPCC, urging it to publish their report quickly. He put out a statement for the media:

I am shocked and deeply worried by this news. There is now a mood of anxiety in the local community but everyone must remain calm. It is encouraging that the Independent Police Complaints Commission has immediately taken over the investigation. There is a need to clarify the facts and to move quickly to allay fears. It is very important our community remains calm and allows the investigation to take its course.

Now, facing the cameras on the day after the first night of violence, his plea seemed to have fallen on deaf ears.

*

Dolly Pilgrim's night of rioting had left her bewildered. She didn't know why she'd joined in with the looting at Wood Green or what she was going to do with the clothes she'd taken. Her mum and dad were going to go nuts.

It had all been so exciting. People running round like headless chickens, her friends with arms full of stuff and everybody laughing.

"Oh my god," she yelled, "You lot are absolutely mad!"

It'd all gone wrong when H & M got smashed in. It was surreal. They put the clothes they'd taken and some creams from Body Shop into a wheelie bin and pushed it along the road. They passed a supermarket someone set on fire.

"What are they doing that for?" Cathy asked, "They go shopping there. Why are they setting it on fire?"

"I know Asda's there," said someone in the crowd, "but we go to Aldi's – it's cheaper. My friend's got kids."

Dolly, excited but nervous, looked away as the first police car passed them, followed by another and another; she later reckoned she'd counted ten.

"They see a group of girls pushing a big wheelie bin along the road and they don't stop us," she said to Cathy, "They're not doing their job!"

But Dolly wasn't sure what they were going to do with the wheelie bin; they couldn't take that back to Tottenham; and where was their driver, the one who'd brought them here, wondered Dolly.

"He's left us!" cried Cathy, who felt she'd been coerced into the looting and hardly dare help with the wheelie bin.

And she was right. The driver was on his way home with a boot full of phones.

*

Miggs hadn't left Simon's side all day, much to his annoyance but she was unaware of that fact. It was enough to be with him, cheering him on. He'd shoved her aside when his gang met, but Miggs was used to his ways and didn't mind because she knew he was planning the next raid.

And the next raid was going to be Brixton. Getting there would be easy: London Transport were still laying on buses and tubes. They spent most of the day at the Brixton Splash Festival: smaller than Notting Hill but fun and always good to be with friends. It was a celebration of African and Asian culture; they'd been told that at school when the teachers had been worried about racism. There were loads of food stalls, music stages, reach-out stuff for the younger kids. It was great; Miggs had always enjoyed The Splash. It was a fun day for the family.

All right, the gangs were there and they usually caused a bit of trouble but the police kept their eye on them, quietly but it kept things safe. Miggs had gone with her mum and dad and brothers and sisters when she was young but now it was with her boyfriend, Sim.

*

In Wood Green, where Dolly and her friends had looted local shops, Turkish and Kurdish shop owners were out in force to protect their businesses from the kids who they knew had already stolen from shops on the High Road, stolen from shops and set cars alight. This wasn't going to happen to them and their families; they were going to do what the police seemed unable to do – protect their livelihoods. They'd come to Britain for several reasons, one being to give their children a better chance in life and gangs of thugs were not taking away their hard work.

*

Jim Brown had been a copper in Brixton for several years and like his colleagues in other London boroughs felt a definite sense of duty and loyalty to what he called his 'patch'.

He especially enjoyed The Splash, which gave him a chance to mix and mingle with the people he served.

He wasn't expecting anything other than the usual trouble: the gangs turning up later in the evening to strut their stuff and look for a fight. He and his colleagues could deal with those lads; only a small force would be needed. Move in quickly at the first sign of disorder and the situation could always be contained. Whatever might be happening in Tottenham and elsewhere, any trouble in Brixton could be controlled.

It was only when the first brick went through the windscreen of the first car that Jim Brown knew tonight would be different. Other missiles followed in rapid succession: shop windows, police cars. And the gangs didn't scarper when Jim and his colleagues moved towards them. They turned on them.

The youths gathered across a large grassy area in front of the Somerleyton Estate. Jim could see that the gangs were mixing among themselves; there was confusion and disorder, a lack of understanding about what was to happen. Kids who would have normally turned on each other were puzzled; some clearly had not got the message, whatever that message might have been. They ran around brandishing knives and threatening each other. It was during this disarray that the boy was stabbed, the stabbing Edward Andrews had heard about on his police radio, while patrolling the streets of Edmonton.

The boy was lying in the gutter. Officers were trying to reach him. He was alive and conscious but could be bleeding to death internally. He needed to be reached quickly. As the officers, still in their beat uniforms, moved in to help the boy, the bottles and bricks were heaved upon them, landing with force on their bodies, arms and legs.

"What the hell's going on? "cried Jim, "We're here to help."

His appeal made no difference; the intensity of the assault with anything the gangs could find only increased. Jim moved forward, determined to push the mob back, to give the officers a chance to help the injured youth.

As he and his colleagues shoved in on the gangs, one of them, struck by a bottle on the head, fell. The policewoman, injured and unconscious, lay face down as bottles and bricks cascaded upon her. Shattered fragments of glass and stone lay all around. Jim noticed her metal hat badge was twisted as he covered her body from the assault, while police medics moved in to retrieve the stricken officer.

Jim and his colleagues continued to ease the mob back until there was sufficient space around both the officer and the stabbed youth for the medics to help them: the boy was taken away to be examined, the officer dragged clear of the missiles.

But the mob advanced, missiles pounding into the line of police, knives out. Still the line of police officers moved forward, batons at the ready; knives or no knives, this was not going to be a night for the gangs to crow about. Hand-to-hand if necessary but they would take the day. At the sight of this determination, the gang members backed down and a state of calm held sway.

Jim caught his breath, waited and watched. Other police units arrived, some in carriers, others in minibuses; some officers looked fresh, others were bruised and bleeding. Many were still in their beat uniforms, their riot kits still bagged. No time to kit up and another fight on their hands. Where the hell had these officers come from, what had they seen and endured?

Now, here in Brixton, it would be different. Kitted up they stood a better chance. Orders were to stop the mob getting to the town centre where most of the shops were situated. There were at least two hundred in the mob that came upon the lines of officers, the usual missiles at the ready – traffic bollards, blocks of wood and chairs among the regular bottles and bricks – and a burning bin, flames licking from it. But the bin was too heavy to move far and the rioters, realising the bin would not stop the police, paused in their attack.

The officers charged; the mob retreated; the officers held their ground under the now usual barrage. The officers charged a second time and a third; ground was retrieved from the mob and held, once, twice, three times. The numbers of the attackers began to dwindle as some broke away and disappeared down surrounding streets. The officers returned to the crossroads and waited.

Jim found it hard to understand what was going on. At times, his police radio suggested that the gangs were re-grouping; at other times it seemed that small groups of police were chasing looters through alleyways and streets. Eventually, an order came to move from the Coldharbour crossroads to the main Brixton Road and the officers prepared themselves for a further battering, but no; they found, instead, the usual traffic they'd have found on a normal day – taxis, buses, private cars trying to negotiate their way through lines of riot-clad police officers.

The counter-order came – return to the Coldharbour crossroads. Once there, it became clear that nearby shops were being looted and Jim wondered why they did nothing to prevent this outrage.

"Our orders are to secure the junction," said their inspector, "and that's what we do!"

Only a few yards away could be heard the cries of looters and the smashing of shop windows: also, the calls for help of officers who were trying to prevent the looting; but all Jim Brown could do was stand and wait.

Chapter 11

PROUD CONSCIOUSNESS

When it happened it all happened so quickly: and that showed how clever Sim's planning had been. One minute they were sitting, chatting, on a grassy mound and the next everyone was putting on masks and pulling out weapons.

And they took over the high street! People snatched fags from counters, while Miggs watched. While she stood admiring Sim's planning, a man dashed passed with an armful of trainers.

"Where'd you get that lot?" she asked.

"Foot Locker!" he called back, "Everyone's running for Foot Locker."

The shop was being ripped apart when Miggs arrived, and not only by young people: an old man – he must have been seventy – snatched a hat and ran for his life. Miggs took out her Blackberry and began filming: a teenager grinning beneath a stack of eight shoe boxes, the store in flames.

The police were nowhere to be seen. It was a free for all, and Simon led the attack on H & M. Using bins, bricks, rocks and their feet their smashed their way in, yanking at the metal security shutters. A big, hooded youth – one of Sim's gang – climbed through the broken glass and lifted the shutters from the inside. Others – people Miggs had never seen before – waited for their moment and then charged through, grabbing anything they could lay hands on. She didn't want to go into H & M because it was dark, and she didn't like the dark.

Shop alarms rang out all around them but no one cared. For once, they had so much power it was unbelievable. The police had no control whatsoever; they'd been shafted good and proper. The crowd were proud of themselves, sharing a common consciousness.

*

Alex Willet, having returned home to Katy and Louise at ten o'clock that morning, was back on duty, battered and bruised, this time in Brixton.

The place looked like a village or town might look after it had been used as a battleground, subjected to enemy fire. Ahead, Alex could see the now familiar missiles flying through the air and falling onto other officers as they advanced with their short shields. Hundreds of masked looters rained weapons down on the police as others continued to smash their way into the shops.

Alex's unit was ordered to cordon off the street in order to prevent the mob being reinforced by like-minded thugs. Truth to tell, he and his colleagues, exhausted from the battle of the previous night, were relieved not to be in the thick of the fighting yet again.

Overhead, the police helicopter circled, illuminating the scene, and Alex could see that his colleagues were winning the day: the looters were beginning to fall back.

As he watched, the order came for his unit to redeploy elsewhere: a Tesco supermarket was under attack. When he arrived, the dog handlers were already in position: the German Shepherds sounded angry, glass and goods were scattered across the car park, the police moved in covering all entrances and exits. No one was going to escape if they could help it.

And then the weather came to their aid. Heavy rain poured down, calming the situation: the looters, not wanting to get wet, dispersed, and the fire crews moved in. The streets had been retaken. Where next, he wondered; when the order came, it was Peckham.

*

Hugo Battersby was exhausted: looting was tiring work but a matter of principle. He'd been back and forth between the shops and his parent's house so many times, he'd lost count. Only from 'major consumer brands' was his mantra but his bedroom was looking more and more like J D Sports, Foot Locker and PC World than he really wanted. Sooner or later, he'd have to sell the stuff on, hide it or get rid of it. Looting on this scale was only possible if you had somewhere to stash the loot or someone to handle it for you. He hadn't thought about that when he started. It was just as well his parents were away for the weekend.

*

Carl Meadows left soon after his absent father, Phil, drifted away. 'Drift' was the word: one minute he was in the house listening to Carl and his mum, Lynn, talking about the riots, and the next he was gone.

"Much like he just disappeared after you were born," Lynn commented, unusually because she'd never run the boy's father down – at least not to him.

"I'm just off out, Mum," said Carl.

"You're not going to join those rioters, are you, Carl?"

"What do you think, Mum? Hmm?"

"Well, I ..."

"Do I look like a rioter?"

"No."

"There you go, then."

Lynn responded to her son's hug by kissing him affectionately on the cheek. She was frightened for him: knowing his need for friends, she felt he might be easily drawn into the riots.

Carl had no such intentions. What he'd said to his father on their brief acquaintance was how he felt: the police were looked upon as a gang by many young people like himself, but he wasn't about to start throwing junk at them.

He was more interested in seeing what was going on in Brixton. Going to The Splash hadn't bothered Carl but messages were coming in strong and fast about what was happening now. The Overground and Underground were still running nicely: a quick trip on the Overground to Islington and then the Victoria Line all the way. It was very convenient.

He saw a group of kids he knew from school reaching in over the smashed glass of the Foot Locker window. There weren't enough police on the streets, were there? And he could do with a new pair of trainers. He could probably find his mum a pair but that wouldn't be a good idea. Still, taking a pair of trainers wasn't the same as heaving bricks and bottles at the police. He'd draw the line there.

Carl felt good in the trainers. It wasn't often his mum could afford to buy him anything anywhere nearly so expensive. A friend of his was parading up and down the road in a Nike tracksuit.

"I feel good, Carl. I feel like people with money, like good families. When I get new clothes I feel better. People don't look down on me no more. They can look down on somebody else. My clothes are always ripped and dirty. Now I feel good."

On his return to Hackney, Carl noticed that gangs were gathering on the streets, the roads were covered by broken glass and lumps of concrete, some of the commercial bins had been set alight and a barricade of shopping trolleys blocked the road. It was eerily quiet, thought Carl as he made for a group of friends.

"We've got the police under control," said one of them, "We've got them under manners for once. They've never had us under manners. We'll have them on lock, on smash. We're not running from them. They are the criminals now. You'll see, Carl. We'll be enforcing the law, getting them out of our town because they ain't doing nothing good for no one."

Looking around him, sensing the menace, Carl thought that things were certain to get worse. There were no police around at the moment but when they arrived, were they going to be in for it. His friend obviously felt empowered by what was happening; for him and for others, attacking the traditional forces of law and order was a form of catharsis.

*

Martha Pilgrim had never seen her daughter, Dolly, look so dishevelled; usually, she was so fussy about her appearance that they often left late for whatever event they were attending, much to Gabriel's annoyance.

"Where on Earth have you been?" she asked, "I thought you were at Cathy's."

"Don't go on, Mum. It's been a long night," replied Dolly.

It was the kind of evasive answer Martha was used to from her daughter when the girl – and she was still a girl, whatever she might want to believe – had something to hide. Martha guessed that Dolly had intended going straight to her room when she got back to avoid any questions.

"Where have you been?"

"I said."

"You said you were at Cathy's."

"So?"

"So why weren't you?"

"Who says I wasn't?"

"No one, but you weren't were you?

Dolly remained silent, stubbornness in every line and frame of her face and body. She wasn't going to tell her mother: that would have meant a gating of weeks and no money.

"Well, where were you?"

"We came back on the tube."

"From where?" snapped Martha, tired with the line of evasion being pursued by her daughter.

"From Wood Green."

"Wood Green! You've been to Wood Green? Was Cathy with you?"

Dolly hesitated. She was in trouble. No doubt! But she didn't want her mum phoning Cathy's people.

"Well? I'm getting tired of this, Dolly."

"Yes."

"Did her parents know?"

"We got a lift."

"Are you telling me her dad, a schoolteacher, gave you ..."

"No."

"Then who did?"

"A friend."

It was going to be a long, long morning and Martha had been up all night with Gabriel and their regulars guarding the pub.

"I'm tired," she said, very, very quietly, "Go to your room and get cleaned up. I'll be up when I'm ready and I want the whole story just as it happened with nothing left out. Do you understand me?"

"Yes."

"Louder! I want to hear it. Yes?"

"Yes, Mum."

The girl had fallen asleep – or pretended to do so – when Martha first looked in and so it was late morning before she had the whole story, including the bit about the wheelie bins.

"And so, you left all you stole in the wheelie bins?"

Dolly nodded. She didn't know whether she felt like a criminal or a fool.

"And so, what are you going to do now?"

"What?"

"Don't start that again – Little Miss Sullen. What are you ... let me rephrase that – what *should* you do now?"

Dolly looked at her mother, unable to believe what the other was suggesting.

"You don't mean ..."

"I do mean."

"What does Dad say?"

"Don't hide behind your dad. It'll make no difference.

Gabriel, Martha knew, would side with his daughter. He was weak when it came to Dolly and would want to protect his child; and when he heard the news, later that day, Martha was pleased to find she was right.

"But Martha ..."

"'But Martha' nothing. We both love our daughter and will do whatever we can to help her. *However*, any good parent – and we do try to be good parents, Gabriel – would find the courage to do what's right. These riots are happening because good parents do nothing. If parents keep their mouths shut these kids will keep rampaging through our streets."

"Dolly will be made an example of ...," protested Gabriel.

"That is a bit unfair – I grant you. She should be accountable for her actions but not everyone else's."

"Are Cathy's parents doing the same?"

"I haven't asked them. It's none of our business. But I should imagine so – he's a schoolteacher. How could he talk about good behaviour and shield his daughter from her crimes."

"They're not criminals."

"What would you call looting, Gabriel?"

The honest shopkeeper was silent. He knew his wife was right but it broke his heart to acknowledge the fact. Quietly, almost timidly, he said:

"Dolly was going to be a youth ambassador for next year's Olympic Games in London."

"I know," replied Martha, just as quietly, "We'll have to see what Mr Johnson, our mayor, has to say about that."

MONDAY, AUGUST 8TH

Chapter 12
THE DESPISERS OF MANKIND

Edward Andrews, tired and angry after a long night doing next to nothing as far as he was concerned, was now also hungry. He and his colleagues, guarding the shops in Edmonton, had not eaten or had anything to drink all night. The catering arrangements seemed to have been side-lined. He wasn't amused, a feeling that deepened when he saw a group of local residents approaching. More complaints like those last night, he wondered: but no, these people came to thank the police officers, grateful for their presence.

And then another sight met their eyes. An elderly lady approached with a tray of tea and toast. Again and again, she came, delivering by the time she'd finished twenty-one cups of hot, sweet tea and round after round of warm, buttered toast.

*

Benjamin knew he should be running home. His home was in Tottenham; he knew his way but not from where he was now. He was hungry and in a few hours it would be time to get up and have his breakfast. But first he had to sleep. He had his phone with him. He could call his mum. She would come and find him. 'Always call me if you feel lost, Ben. You know I will find you.' But he wasn't lost.

Benjamin switched on his phone. It was a Blackberry and there were lots of messages. One was from his bestie, his best friend, Angus. It was with Angus he had gone to see the latest Spiderman film, *Spiderman 3*. That was four years ago when he was only twelve. His mum had been worried about him going without her, but he had been all right with Angus. The next Spiderman film, *The Amazing Spiderman*, was not due out until next year, 2012. It was a long time to wait. It would be good to talk to Angus. It would calm him down.

*

Edward sighed in exasperation. Only four hours had passed since he came off-duty and the phone had called him back; he was wanted in Lewisham. It was midday, just midday; he hadn't had a wink of sleep!

"Pick up your kit and get your backside over here!"

When he arrived at Lewisham police station the place seemed deserted. A young woman constable, crouched over a computer in the Integrated Borough Operations office looked stressed and looked up, puzzled.

"Is there a briefing?" asked Ed.

"No. Just go out and deal with whatever you see," she replied, returning her attention to the pad on which she was making notes. "Oh ... and help yourself to a bottle of water from the stack in the corner.

Ed looked at the young officer who clearly had more on her plate than she needed. Was he really to go out on his own? He stood thinking for a moment, and then picked up his riot kit.

Outside, on the pavement, he looked up and down the road; the direction he chose didn't seem to matter. Ed jogged off.

*

Benjamin, relieved to hear his bestie's voice on the phone, listened.

"Go to Tottenham Hale Underground. You know where that is?"

"Yes," replied Benjamin, and he did because it was the tube station his mum had taught him to use. The Victoria Line always took you to Oxford Circus. His mum liked getting off there because there were lots of shops. Benjamin liked it, too, because then he could go to Hamleys where he could spend hours just looking at the models "But I don't know how to get there," he added.

"Where are you?" asked Angus.

"I don't know."

"Look around. What can you see?"

"The school! I can see the gates. I'm outside the school."

How he arrived there, running from the man who called himself 'Dad', Benjamin had no idea. Instinct maybe? Running from the smoke and the flames and the noise to somewhere familiar?

"Right. Go to the end of the road ..."

"Which end?"

"The one that leads to the main road."

"Which way is that?"

"What?"

"Which way do I go?"

Benjamin crouched against the brick pillars of the school gates and panted. Right or left? Up or down? You couldn't go up a road. Up was up. Right or left depended on which way you were facing.

Suddenly, Benjamin heard a woman's voice on the end of the phone..

"Benjamin, this is Angus's mum. Stay where you are. I'll come and get you."

It was more than Benjamin wanted to cope with: he was to stay the night at Angus's house. Angus's mum had phoned his mum and they thought it was safer than trying to get home through the riots but Benjamin didn't like staying in other people's houses. He liked his own room where he knew where everything was; and he didn't like using other people's toilets. His mum had shown him how to wipe the toilet seat before he used it but he didn't know where the surface cleaner was in Angus's house. It was an uncomfortable night sleeping on the settee but his mum had said he should be grateful and polite to Angus's mum.

*

Geoffrey Dale arrived at Ealing police station full of questions: he couldn't understand why he had not been called in earlier. Riots! Looting! Fires everywhere! What the hell was going on?

Standing in the station yard along with other officers who shared his feelings, Jeff felt that, at last, he was being put to good use. The only problem was the lack of a riot carrier. Beside them in the yard was what amounted to a minibus: no lights, no sirens, no grills.

Jeff was a sergeant with fifteen years' experience and he knew the other officers in the yard, all younger than himself, would be looking to him for leadership. Jeff nodded towards the minibus and nodded to the others that they should stow their riot gear. Riot gear, including flameproof overalls, but no shields. Great! Nevertheless, they had to get going with or without shields. Hackney was their destination. The word was that they could expect real trouble in Hackney on what was the third day of the rioting.

*

John Chase, arriving at Ealing police station for the late shift was hoping for a normal day's policing: after all, Ealing wasn't Hackney and normal policing had still to be done. He and his colleague, Emma Hare, set off in their Ford Mondeo, heading towards Ealing Broadway. Both lived in Ealing; both loved the place.

They noticed groups of youths loitering but not, apparently, with any specific intent, some lounging around, others sitting on railings outside the shops. Both officers noticed that these were not local youths, not ones they recognised. Slight doubts began to stir. Further on, outside the railway station, they saw another group, hoodies pulled up despite the hot, August evening.

On their way back to the town centre, text messages poured in on their own phones: rumours of trouble. The kids were using BlackBerry Messenger as a means of communication: 'Ealing's going to kick off tonight'. No, thought John, still sanguine, not Ealing.

"The feel's different, John," said Emma, "Odd groups – not wearing masks for sure, but ..."

She left her question hanging.

At that moment, one of the groups charged towards their car and leapt onto the bonnet. It was sudden and, in a flash, the youths cleared off, but it was a declaration of war. No doubt.

They drove on. Ahead was Acton police station. And then the call came:

"WE'RE UNDER ATTACK! URGENT ASSISTANCE!"

John spun the car round and headed back towards the town centre, blue light flashing, siren screaming. Word came through on the radio that smash and grabs were in progress inside the Broadway Shopping Centre; jewellers were being targeted.

"I know where they will come out," said Emma, "Pull back. Head for the High Street."

As they did so, twenty hooded men charged out of the centre and ran across the front of the car. John reached for the car door.

"Leave it, John," cried Emma, "There are too many for us to handle."

"Right, but we'll stay with them."

He began to follow the sprinting looters.

"Feds! The Feds are chasing us!"

Emma laughed, a hollow one, one filled with disbelief as well as amusement.

"Feds," she said, "Where on earth do they think they are?"

John stayed with the looters and both officers saw, lining the road ahead, four or five cars, engines running, doors open.

"They're waiting for the looters," said Emma, "This has been carefully planned. These people are taking advantage of the mayhem."

The looters leapt into the passenger seats and slammed the doors. The getaway cars sped off down the narrow streets. As he gave chase, John nodded to Emma, who put out a pursuit call on the police radio. A reply came immediately, and Emma felt the exhilaration of the chase. They'd catch these people who represented everything she detested about the criminal world, the people her father had called 'the despisers of mankind'.

The getaway car swung sharply into a side road, determined to shake John off but, at once, saw ahead the police van Emma had summoned on the radio. More blue lights, more sirens. The getaway driver panicked and swung back across the junction crashing into a metal bollard on the pavement corner. The jewel thieves were out in a flash: their only hope now was to outrun the police. But that wasn't going to happen.

Emma was on him before one man had run ten yards and brought him down, struggling and kicking, to the pavement. Gripping his arms behind his back, she brought the man, a young man in his early twenties, to his feet, as one of the officers from the police van strolled over, handcuffs at the ready.

"Arrest him for burglary," said Emma.

John nodded towards the crashed car; the footwells were festooned with stolen jewellery.

"And the others?" asked John Chase.

"We'll have them. You were quick off the mark."

As the officer spoke, two more handcuffed men were seen being led up the road.

"We'll leave you to it," said John to the officer in charge of the van. "We need to keep our eye on what's going on."

He was right to be worried: back in the town centre, groups of youths were gathering, sullen in their movements, determined. And then they began to kick at the plate glass windows of the shops.

John Chase sighed: this was Ealing, his beloved Ealing and the looting he thought couldn't happen had just done so.

*

Edward Andrews continued to jog the streets of Lewisham, still alone, the streets deserted. It was a situation his friends would describe as 'surreal'. He thought of his wife: it seemed an age since they were dancing at a friend's wedding. An age, and it was just two days ago! His breath was coming fast; he knew he was frightened. And who wouldn't be, he thought, alone on the streets now ruled by the mob. He'd heard the older officers talk of PC Keith Blakelock, hacked to death in a stairwell on the Broadwater Farm estate during the riots of 1985.

Ed paused for breath and to still the thumping of his heart. He lifted the visor, misted up, of his riot gear and looked about him. There was someone, a solitary person up ahead, someone who was jogging towards him. Doreen Manners, a police sergeant. He knew her; it was a relief. Not that one more officer would make any difference if they came across a gang of thugs, but the company meant everything to Ed.

"Fancy meeting you here," said Doreen with a grin, "Alone are you?"

"Yes."

"Join the club. Fancy a jog?"

The two officers had not gone far when they came across a police minibus, its windows shattered. There were four officers inside the vehicle, on edge, battered.

"Fancy a lift?" asked the driver as he opened the door.

"What's going on?" asked Ed.

"It would be nice to know, wouldn't it," was the reply from a policeman who was bloodied and sweating, "No one's been briefed, no one's spoken to anyone of rank, no one's been told what the hell is going on!"

"But we've found each other," laughed Doreen.

Her optimism, and maybe her rank, quietened any further comment and the minibus moved on; but not far before the now familiar but no less terrifying call came through.

'URGENT ASSISTANCE! URGENT ASSISTANCE1'

The call came from Bromley Road Retail Park.

*

At the park half a dozen police officers were facing a mob of around fifty youths. The officers wore their normal beat uniforms, with only two small, round shields between them; the mob, shouting angrily, held an armoury of bottles, bricks and fence posts.

"We're gonna hit PC World and there ain't nothing you gonna do about it," yelled a voice from the mob.

The officers did have a choice: they could run, but that wasn't going to happen. This was their patch and it would take more than fifty yobs to make them yield their ground. To reach the store they wished to loot, the mob would first have to kill the officers.

The mob, emboldened by their anger, moved closer; the officers raised their batons. It was the only show of strength they could muster; the mob didn't seem bothered, and the first brick was thrown. It landed a few feet in front of the very thin blue line. The mob were out of range; they moved closer. The missiles now slammed into the officers' legs and bodies. The pain was intense. The mob saw they had the advantage and charged.

Since to flee wasn't a professional option, the six officers decided to charge the mob, and the two forces met, the officers swinging down with their batons. The mob retreated. The officers stopped and took two steps backwards, holding their position.

The mob, arming itself afresh, charged again; their excitement was infectious. They had the upper hand, fifty of them against six coppers made good odds. Again, the thin blue line was slammed with glass and masonry. The battering was fearful: bruises and cuts on arms, legs and ankles; and they knew in their hearts that another charge would be fruitless. The mob wouldn't be intimidated a second time. The situation was desperate. How long could they possibly hold out?

*

This was the sight that met the eyes of Edward, Doreen and the four officers in the minibus when they arrived. Ed stared, not believing what he was witnessing. Doreen gazed, tears in her eyes. Was this what the world had come to: an anarchy, a new reality, where the streets were to be ruled by criminals? Watching the six police officers, she realised they were making a last, brave stand; and then they amazed her – they charged, six against the mob.

"LET'S GO!"

It was her own voice she heard, almost in disbelief. The six of them from the minibus made a third charge, ready for what must end as hand-to-hand fighting: batons against missiles. The rioters splintered: some running off along side streets, others turning against the police, still so few in number.

The officers continued their charge straight into the mob, striking them back with their shields. All around her, Doreen heard the shouts, heavy breathing, and saw the anger in the rioters' eyes. Men with gritted teeth and hate in their eyes pushed against her and her companions. As some of the mob was forced back, others, freshly armed, came forward, charging the shields. Batons rained down; this was policing in modern Britain, and it wasn't why she'd joined the force.

Beyond the immediate fighting, Ed saw rioters returning from where they'd run down side streets at the first sign of resistance from the thin blue line of the six officers; they were freshly armed, this time with estate agents' signs and the pointed posts that held them. The signs were flung at the police, whistling through the air, followed by the posts as javelins. Ed leapt aside, dodging a stake.

"GO!"

At his command, those from the minibus charged into the mob. The rioters scarpered and the police found themselves in a side street littered with broken glass and shattered masonry. Again, they charged, eager to root out the mob from the warren of side streets and onto the open road.

All the time, urgent messages were coming in on their police radios: other units calling for assistance. It was confusing: information suggested that some rioters were brandishing knives, others held guns. Thin blue lines of police officers across the city were in fear of their lives.

And then the order came through to leave the rioters they'd been battling for an hour: a Halfords store back along the road needed guarding. Ed looked at Doreen and the companions who'd fought with him. Was this true? Was this even sane? Police officers calling for help and they were told to guard a store?

*

Simon Tippet was overjoyed: his strategy had proved successful: the gangs had refrained from attacking one another in favour of venting their anger on the police.

Strictly speaking, the strategy hadn't been Simon's alone, even if he took the credit with his own gang, The Blades, but that didn't trouble him too much. There was joy among the gangs in general that mayhem reigned and police officers were being injured, hopefully killed. Brixton was in the hands of the gangs and they were going ahead with what needed to be done: looting, arson and violence were the order of the day and Hackney was just waiting to be given a dose of the same treatment.

The message had gone out earlier on good old BlackBerry Messenger:

Hackney everyone. As soon as it comes 5 o'clock start rioting

Hackney was the place and Simon and his gang were heading there from Brixton: Underground and Overground. Dead easy!

Chapter 13
GREATLY DISTURBED

Greatly disturbed describes very well the state of mind in the Pilgrim and Rudge households: Mary Rudge with regard to her son, Benjamin, and Gabriel, Martha and Dolly in relation to each other.

*

Mary had reluctantly agreed to let Benjamin spend the night with his bestie, Angus Wilson, but took consolation in the fact that she would fetch him home later in the day; this had not worked out as she hoped.

"I'm sorry, Mrs Rudge," explained Angus's mother, "but they went off this afternoon and haven't returned."

"Don't you know where they are? Haven't they phoned?"

"I didn't think. I expected them back before dark and now ..."

"It's 7 o'clock! I know! I should have come earlier but Benjamin seemed so pleased to be with his friend, I thought I'd let him stay as long as possible. Oh, it's been an awful two days."

"Come in. We can wait for a call over a cup of tea."

Mary Rudge, with no one she could talk with except her oldest son and that was mainly on the phone, was only too pleased to accept the invitation. It was the nearest she was going to get to her son: since he was with his friend, it didn't seem likely he would return home.

*

The exchanges in the Pilgrim home were fraught: Dolly accusing each of her parents of not caring about her, Martha adamant that exactly the opposite was true and Gabriel wavering between the two.

"You know how much I wanted to be an Olympic Ambassador," cried Dolly

"I can't imagine that Mr Johnson will even consider you now," replied her mother, "You should have thought of that before you went looting."

"Cathy's parents ..." began Dolly.

"Cathy's parents are of exactly the same view," interrupted Martha, "Your dad and I spoke with them earlier."

"Dad?" appealed Dolly, looking pensively at her father.

Gabriel coughed and muttered something inaudible.

"Your dad agrees with me!" said Martha.

Judging from the fact that Gabriel left the room at that moment, it cannot be safely assumed that his wife was correct in her opinion.

*

Greatly disturbed, also, was the Mayor of London, Boris Johnson, who had, belatedly some said, decided to return from his summer holiday on August 8th, the third day of the riots. Mr Johnson had yet to express his opinion on his Twitter account but was of the view that anyone involved in the rioting was not fit to represent the city of London as an Olympic Ambassador or in any other capacity.

*

He was not the only politician hurrying home that day. David Cameron, the Prime Minister, was also on his way, shamed no doubt by an article in the Daily Mirror, which had a headline shot of Mr Cameron against a burning building and asking the question 'Where is the PM? Posing with a waitress on holiday in Italy?'

＊

It might be said that Jeff Dale was more greatly disturbed than any of them. He and his colleagues had been warned to expect trouble in Hackney on the third day of the rioting and the warning had not been exaggerated: on that night they became direct targets of the mob.

"Kill the police! Kill the police! Kill the police!"

It was the sole chant of the rioters who prowled the streets of Hackney. Debris was scattered everywhere, barricades of supermarket trolleys had been set up, bins set alight, the air was thick with smoke and the yobs were marauding the narrow streets, out for trouble, out for the kill.

There was no slow build-up to the attacks: a barrage of the usual missiles met them on arrival, crashing into the minibus. A side window shattered, the officers ducked and the bus drove on. In a side street the police officers got out but, although in riot gear, they were without shields: walking into the violent streets would be tantamount to walking to their death.

One of the officers mentioned that they had passed a number of unmanned carriers on the road into Hackney and the police made their way towards them. It was the case: the police who abandoned the vehicles had done so in a hurry. Among the scatterings of food and drink, Jeff's colleagues found riot shields. Once fixed to their arms, the shields made the officers feel better, more confident of avoiding serious injury.

Out in the streets, they came across a line of police horses facing a crowd of rioters. Flames licked the air, absorbing the oxygen around them; the horses champed at the bit, restless, hoofing the ground. The presence of the animals seemed to make no difference to the attitude of the rioters: usually wary of horses, the mob now picked up bricks, bottles and paving slabs that they hurled at them.

Jeff was confused; as to what they might be expected to do when the order came to follow two police dogs along back streets he did not know. The German Shepherds pressed on followed by the officers until they emerged onto a main road. The plan was to box the rioters in but on the main road they came across traffic: buses and cars seemed to be taking people about their usual business, business suddenly interrupted when the mob turned their attentions to the vehicles on the road and the passengers found themselves to be the targets of scaffolding poles and lumps of wood.

Along the road, looting continued unabashed. The mob controlled the streets and did as they wished. It was down to Jeff and his comrades to regain control. They moved forward, riot shields in a line, forcing the mob backwards to create a clear area behind his unit where more officers could gather to prepare for an assault.

The long riot shields now took the bashing from the missiles with the police officers crouching low behind them. Time and again the shields took the brunt as the line of police moved forward a few steps at a time.

As one blue line gave way to another so Jeff found himself on the front line and for the first time looked into the eyes of the mob they faced. There he saw real hatred in their faces, the faces of all ages from eleven-year-olds to thirty-year-olds. These people are mad with loathing, he thought, do I really want to be a police officer? But the thought passed as the need to fight for his life took over.

Lumps of paving so heavy it took two rioters to lift and throw them were now hurled at the police and they faced knives strapped to posts and broom handles. If Jeff had had any reason to doubt the hatred of the mob, it went from him now.

His unit needed to push forward but all they could do was hold the ground they'd gained. The shields took the impact but the officers' arms took the weariness. And then the first petrol bomb was thrown: the smell, the bright orange light and the heat. Rioters had managed to get behind the police lines and the bombs were coming from the rear, aimed directly at their bodies. As Jeff watched, his comrades were going up in flames. Using their personal extinguishers and gloved hands the officers tried to help each other.

"The only way to deal with this is to rush the bombers," yelled Jeff, "Drive them back out of range."

In twos they ran, leaping over debris, driving the bombers back. The rioters aimed their bombs at the officers' feet. They exploded and the police found themselves charging through a wall of fire before returning to their lines, their uniforms alight. As the bombers reformed, the officers charged again and again until the groups of bombers were pushed out of range.

Jeff looked about him, trying to get his bearings. Across the door of one of the buildings that had been looted were the words 'FUCK DA POLICE', painted in large red letters. In charging forward to push back the mob, the police found themselves in a courtyard surrounded by flats, corridors and balconies. As they watched, the mob began reappearing, flames rose from bins, smoke and dark shadows obscured their vision. The intensity of the attack now reached a point where it was impossible to avoid being hit. Try as the officers might to shield themselves and deflect the hurled masonry, they were struck time and time again.

Jeff caught sight of a huge slab flying through the air. It was too far to the left to hit him but before he could shout a warning it struck his sergeant. The officer fell, his helmet split. He lay prostrate, motionless, out cold. The rioters on the floors above became mad with excitement; they roared their delight. The barrage of missiles grew even more intense.

Jeff grabbed hold of two other offices urging them backwards, seeing their long shields as the sergeant's only chance of survival. A slab of concrete struck his shield. He fell back and the slab ricocheted onto his face. He retreated, stunned, tasting blood, but he was conscious and his sergeant was still flat out, missiles crashing into his body.

Jeff reached for the man's overall, hoping to pull him back out of range of the missiles. The two officers he'd grabbed moved to help him, their shields offering some protection to the sergeant's body, while their own became targets for the rioters. Slabs of pavement, bottles and bricks continued to slam into them as they tried to drag their sergeant clear. The rest of the officers also began to pull back, and the rioters, realising that the police were retreating, surged forward. Jeff looked about him. No one was attacking the mob that would soon reach them.

'KILL THE PIGS!' 'KILL THE PIGS!'

Why wasn't anyone attacking the mob? Jeff looked about in dismay.

"HIT THEM," he yelled, "HIT THEM!"

The order seemed to jolt the line into action and they moved against the mob, batons striking downwards. But it wasn't enough.

"ATTACK FROM THE REAR!" came the cry.

Jeff turned. The mob had got behind them: more bricks, more petrol bombs coming from all angles – front, back and above, wave after wave of violent assault. Jeff looked down at the sergeant they were trying to save. How badly was he injured? There was no telling and the ambulance had no chance of getting through the mob.

*

Richard Mannington Bowes had had enough. He lived in a flat on Spring Bridge Road in Ealing. A 68-year-old retired accountant, he was used to what were regular issues such as drunks urinating against his front door but this time it was a full-blown riot: yobs attacking the police, looting, arson.

Wearing a blue and white plaid shirt and shorts, he went outside to deal with a fire in his street, a fire in a supermarket bin taken from the nearby Arcadia shopping centre.

As he tried to put out the fire, a 16-year-old youth ran to stop him. He punched Richard on the jaw, felling the older man to the ground. His head hit the pavement. He lay unconscious on the concrete.

"No, no!" cried someone, "He's just an old man!"

As Richard lay on the ground, rioters and burning bins around him, he was robbed of his wallet and mobile phone. Some of the rioters began dragging the man's body onto the pavement. The youth who'd felled him watched and then left, heading off to where the shops and restaurants were being looted.

Meanwhile, a line of police advanced along the Spring Bridge Road, a line that included John Chase and Emma Hare.

As they did, a 60-year-old neighbour of Richard's, Peter Firstbrook, rushed out to see what was going on. Some of the youths approached him.

"There's one of your lot over there," one of them said, "and he's injured."

Peter Firstbrook forced his way through the mob and saw his neighbour prone on the pavement, his legs dangerously close to burning debris. He tried to pull Richard away but the man was a dead weight. He called to the youths who'd spoken to him and three came over. With their help, Peter dragged Richard's body clear; they then scarpered. Peter tried to rouse Richard but there was no response. He checked his airway and his pulse; there was nothing, and then he noticed blood coming from his neighbour's ear. It could only mean an internal head injury.

The line of police, slowly forcing the rioters back, arrived on the scene and saw Richard on the ground surrounded by the burning rubbish. Still under attack from the missiles, the police stopped to help, kicking away the burning litter, but it was already too late; Richard Mannington Bowes never regained consciousness and died later in hospital.

"I'm shocked," said Peter Firstbrook, "very shocked. The whole neighbourhood is shocked. Ealing is one of the most peaceful parts of London."

Chapter 14
DEVIL MAY CARE

John and Emma joined the line of local officers engaged in a pitched battle with the mob involved in the looting. As far as they could see, every business was being attacked; restaurants, with customers still inside, were having bricks thrown through their windows; gangs of masked youths hurried past, arms laden with bottles of alcohol; hooded men were kicking at the plate glass window of a Bang and Olufsen shop and striking it with a metal bar. The glass had started to crack. Behind the group, three cars were burning in the street.

John, Emma and their colleagues drew batons. An order was shouted. They charged. The group fell back. A few missiles were thrown. In the centre of the road a car – now a barricade – burned. The rioters slowed their pace and beckoned to the officers. More rioters appeared from the side streets, perhaps thirty or forty in number, and advanced on the line of police. John raised his baton and the police charged once more. The mob fell back; the officers regrouped.

But the mob knew they outnumbered the police; it was only a matter of summoning the nerve to push forward again. Bottles and bricks continued to fall upon the officers. John and Emma, together with other colleagues were without helmets, shields and riot overalls.

"We'll get back to the car," said John, "and try to get behind these people. It's our only chance."

Once in their Mondeo they drove on towards Ealing Broadway. Passing the Ealing Green supermarket that was burning furiously, they watched masked looters dashing in and out of the store, despite the fire, arms laden with loot. Residents from the flats above were leaving with what belongings they could carry. Smoke and darkness permeated the air.

John drove on further towards the film studios. They passed a wrecked bus, more burning cars and hundreds of masked rioters and came to a single, much larger group at the centre of which a tall man was wielding a machete.

"He must be seven feet tall," said Emma.

"At least," replied John, grim humour in his voice.

The machete man – as he came to be called – was clearly directing the rest of the group. He pointed towards the film studios and several of his gang scuttled towards them and clambered over the metal gates.

As they watched the excited group following machete man's orders, Emma heard the sound of a diesel engine behind their car; a police carrier was coming towards them. She leapt from their car and waved the carrier down: the last thing they needed was to attract the attention of the gang around the giant with the blade before they were ready to charge. The carrier was loaded with officers. Emma flashed her badge at the driver.

"We need to tackle this lot," she said.

The driver looked at the masked mob.

"Sorry, darling, can't stop," he replied and drove off into the darkness.

John Chase couldn't believe what had happened. He looked back at the mob of looters. Machete man had seen them and was walking in their direction, followed by some of his herd. John reversed the Mondeo quickly, keen to be out of sight in the dark. Emma radioed for more units.

They waited and waited and, eventually, saw the units arriving on the far side of machete man's gang, pushing the rioters towards them. John revved the engine, reversed rapidly and drove from the chaos at the studios to the quiet of Mattock Lane.

*

Benjamin and his bestie, Angus Wilson, were as curious as anyone else about what was going on and sitting at home watching the riots on the television was not the same as being out there in the action. Not that either of them wanted to be involved personally but they did want to see for themselves. In truth, it was Angus who was keen and it was Benjamin who did not want to lose his friend; he'd found that people soon dropped you if you didn't fit in with what they wanted to do. A very close bestie had no more to do with him after Benjamin wouldn't "go and get smashed" with him; but Benjamin didn't like alcohol – it made him feel sick – and the idea of being 'smashed' was unappealing.

They decided on Croydon because it wasn't Hackney where Angus's other friend – who Benjamin didn't know and didn't want to know – said all the violence would be; they also decided on Croydon because Benjamin had been there several times to see a friend of his mother's and he knew the way. You went to Tottenham Hale Underground station and took the Victoria Line to Highbury and Islington, where you got off; you then followed the signs to the London Overground that took you straight to Croydon without having to get off, but you had to make sure you got the southbound train.

Angus told his mum that they wouldn't be long, and the journey went according to Benjamin's plan. Angus, who'd never been to Croydon, was impressed.

Croydon wasn't as Benjamin remembered it: youths – some he thought he recognised from school – wearing masks and hoodies were running round the town centre; there were policemen in what the television people called 'riot gear' standing in lines and they held long batons in their hands.

As Benjamin watched, he saw groups of the masked youths going in and out of the shops stealing things, and the policemen did nothing about it, just as though they thought it was right. They looked stoical, thought Benjamin, choosing a word his grandmother used.

"Why are the police just standing there?" he asked, turning to Angus.

Angus shrugged his shoulders and Benjamin knew this meant he didn't know. Then, one of the policemen called out "HOLD THE CORDON!"

Benjamin understood; it was a clear instruction. Then, something very strange happened: the youths who were stealing from the shops stopped, came up to the line of policemen and began to dance and make faces in front of them. The policemen did not move. Angus laughed and Benjamin joined him: it was funny, like a cartoon film he'd seen where Tom, the cat, did a daft dance in front of the bulldog, Butch, thinking the bulldog was chained to his kennel. Only he wasn't.

And then things got nasty: the youths who were dancing began to throw bottles, rocks and wood at the line of policemen. The police raised their shields to protect themselves but they still didn't do anything.

After a while – Benjamin thought the youths might have got bored – they stopped throwing things and went back to stealing from the shops. The police stood still. This went on for at least ten minutes because Benjamin looked at the time on his watch: the youths would throw things at the police and then go back to smashing windows and stealing from the shops. Throughout, the police did not move.

"Come on then," said Angus.

"What do you mean?" asked Benjamin.

"Well, the police aren't doing anything so it must be all right."

"What must be all right?" asked Benjamin, now frightened.

"It's a shopping mall. There're lots of shops. We could get what we liked ... and go."

"It's not all right," replied Benjamin.

"They're all doing it! Everybody's doing it."

"They're stealing. Stealing is not right," said Benjamin.

"It is if nobody minds," urged Angus.

Benjamin stood irresolute. His friend was confusing him. People didn't mean what they said: sometimes they meant just the opposite. But Angus seemed angry and when people were angry they often did mean what they said or they got angrier. And there was always the truth. You must tell the truth and how would he tell the truth if his mum asked him what he had done?

"Don't be soft, Ben. Be like everybody else," said Angus.

But he wasn't like everybody else: he was autistic and that's why they kept him in a separate class at school with the other children who weren't like everybody else. But he did know right from wrong, and stealing was wrong because his mother had said so, and so had his teachers.

The masked youths were still dancing and making funny faces in front of the police and then throwing things at them; and the police did nothing. Some of those people in masks were looking at him and Angus.

"I'm going," said Angus, and he ran into the shopping mall.

All around, buildings, where Benjamin thought people lived (he could see them waving from the upstairs windows) were on fire; roofs were collapsing and falling into the street; black smoke was everywhere he could see, rising into the dark night; further away, he could see flaming bottles being thrown through the air and exploding on the road; and then someone drove a car into the line of police as if they were trying to kill them; overhead, a helicopter, its blades whirring loudly, shone a horrible light onto the crowds; and Angus had disappeared into the mall.

Benjamin ran. He didn't know where to go except his mum had taken him to Reeves Corner to show him a very old building that had been a furniture shop for 140 years she said, and he would find it and then know the way back to the London Overground.

*

Melanie and her friends were walking along one of the streets in Peckham when they came across the abandoned police car. Peckham was quiet as far as they knew but it wouldn't do any harm to liven things up, would it?

They smashed the window and one of her friends stole the police radio; then, they tossed in a petrol bomb.

"Don't it feel good!" yelled Melanie, as they ran from the burning car, "Say something on the radio, Sharon. Anything. Confuse the police. It's fair to do that."

And it did feel good, the police not knowing what was going on.

At the police station, gangs had already gathered, petrol bombs in hand, when Melanie and her friends joined them. It was one thing to burn a police car, another to set fire to the station. They tossed their bombs, which crashed into the protective shutters on the windows. The building, an old Victorian one, three-storeyed with a solid wood door, had already been shut and locked.

In the front office, a young officer with just two years' experience, Wendy Rackham, waited and wondered. Her superior officer, the borough commander, was sitting calmly at his desk, completing paperwork. He seemed oblivious to the shouts and screams from outside as the petrol bombs hit the building.

"It might be a good idea to move out, guv," she said.

He collected his things and left, leaving her with a smile. Wendy remained, fire-extinguisher at the ready. She approached the windows and peered through the shutters. The gang of youths seemed clueless with regard to how the bombs might be used effectively; they just continued to throw them against the walls and shuttered windows. After a while, they gave up and wandered off, sulkily.

In the station yard, behind its high walls, Level 2 riot officers were kitting up. They were excited. It was time to go and teach those bastards a lesson. Uneasy yes: there was nothing some of those kids would like more than to see a dead police officer and the station burnt to the ground, but that wasn't going to happen: already, other Level 1 officers were on their way in armoured Jankels to throw a protective ring around the station.

Chapter 15
SEIZE THE DAY

Alex's unit drove into Peckham to find shops burning, shattered windows strewn across the roads and officers chasing after small groups of rioters. Gangs of people – some watching, some filming – stood around. They'd been told that the police station had come under attack by petrol bombers but there were no signs of that now; the local police must have done their work. The pattern adopted in Tottenham and elsewhere was to be adopted here: short shield advances against groups of rioters, pushing the thugs backwards, away from the main places of trouble.

Take the junctions and hold the ground. The missiles they now thought of as being 'all in a day's work' continued to smash into them but they were gaining ground and holding it. Peckham, crushed and broken, would soon be back in the hands of the forces of law and order. And then where, thought Alex, and what's happening back home? How are Mum and Dad at The Blacksmith's Arms? And how are Katy and Louise – safe?

*

Jeff Dale stood in the hospital corridor waiting for news. An ambulance had managed to get through, as the gangs fell back from fighting the police to looting. As far as the doctors could tell at a brief examination, the sergeant was suffering from concussion and what they termed "compression of the neck". What that might imply, health-wise, remained to be seen, thought Jeff. His own injuries had been photographed and bore witness to the horrific attacks he and his fellow officers suffered in Hackney.

Now, they waited. Jeff guessed that they would be called back out: there was no suggestion the riots would suddenly stop and the police were stretched, pushed to the limit. When the order came, it was no surprise, and Jeff had already looked along the corridor for any protective gear that might be available. He hoped an injured officer may have abandoned a shield but there was nothing. He felt for his baton. He wasn't looking forward to facing the killer mobs with that alone but what were his choices?

Only a short time later they were entering an attractive residential square of townhouses, the line of officers at one end, a mob at the other, dancing and laughing. Smoke, spreading from a fired Portakabin, shrouded everywhere and through the blackness came the expected barrage of bottles and bricks. Bottles and bricks, bottles and bricks! Jeff thought someone, one day, might write a song around the phrase.

Attached to the Portakabin were gas cylinders. Wonderful, thought Jeff, and the arsonists have no idea what will happen if the cylinders go up.

"We need to get the fire brigade here quickly," he said.

"Through that lot?"

Rioters appeared through the smoke, hurling abuse at the police officers.

"Then we must clear the area," said Jeff, "and quickly."

The line advanced closer and closer to the Portakabin. Missiles continued to pelt them and the intensity of the heat grew ever fiercer. Jeff felt he might choke on the fumes. Around and about them, people watched from what they saw as the safety of their homes, homes about to be blown to pieces if the cylinders caught fire.

"Keep pushing the fools back!" yelled Jeff, knocking missiles aside with his baton as though he was swotting wasps aside at a summer picnic, "If the cylinders blow, they blow. We have no choice."

With each hit from a bottle or a brick, the officers felt their energy sapped just that bit more, energy already at a low ebb; but they advanced.

"Stay calm," said Jeff, "Let's keep it methodical. Let's drive them out of the area, foot by foot, yard by yard."

And at last, the mob was driven far enough back for the fire engines to enter and deal with the blaze and the cylinders. Bottles and bricks continued to be tossed at them but the job was getting done and the mob turned its attention to the residents' cars, dragging and bouncing them across the road to form a barrier and then firing them.

"Hold the line," commanded Jeff, "Hold the line," as he breathed the smoke, blacker and more acrid than ever, into his lungs

*

Alex didn't have long to wonder about his mum and dad or Katy and Louise: with Peckham back in the hands of the police, Alex's unit was directed to Walworth. When they pulled into Walworth Road, the atmosphere in some respects resembled a carnival: people were everywhere, running and laughing or fascinated by the spectacle, some with their arms full of goods. Shop windows were smashed and bins set alight, buses had come to a standstill, looters had forced their way through the shutters of Argos, a man was swinging a fire extinguisher against the windows of a betting shop.

Among this chaos, the general public gazed in a kind of wonder: an elderly lady stepped gingerly from a bus, her eyes fascinated by the looters; several businessmen stopped briefly to watch the burning shops and strolled past; dogs were being given their regular walks; cyclists whizzed by, braked, stared and then carried on; cars, unable to progress further, reversed slowly from the trouble; a number of people, irritated by their inability to bypass the police lines, pushed aside riot shields.

"Get back, madam!" suggested a policeman.

"You can't tell me where to go," she replied, "This is a free country."

The defiance of authority wasn't limited to the rioters and it seemed at times that the police were in danger of losing control of the streets. Shop alarms blared out, looters whooped with joy, police carriers waited, engines running, blue lights flashed.

"It's like Christmas," cried one girl who had travelled from Lambeth to be involved, "It's weird."

"You can have anything you want, anything you've ever desired," her friend responded, "It's laying around like it's in your own home."

"Everywhere – perfume, knickers, bras just there for grabs."

"It's like a trick. You know you shouldn't do it but you do."

The girls kept their eyes on the lines of coppers, ready to make a dash for it if they had to, but they didn't seem to be doing much, just standing there watching like everybody else.

*

Among the looters in Walworth was Tom Drane's son, Lewis. He'd gone home after Wood Green but the new boyfriend was there – he'd be there all weekend – and Lewis slid out quietly. He'd been at Brixton on the Sunday and then joined friends he'd made when the BlackBerry messages came in loud and clear, ready for the Monday.

Lewis didn't think he'd ever been so excited in his life. During the rioting he was angry; during the looting he was excited. It was all money-motivated, really – nothing else, just money motivated. Get what you could while you had the chance because it wasn't going to come again.

"It's exciting isn't it," said one of the girls he'd met, "like driving a fast car."

"And it's our city and I can't believe it's happening in our city."

The boy who spoke stood holding five packets of crisps in his hands along with a bottle of Pinot Grigio. He'd never drunk wine before and wondered what he was going to do with it.

*

Then the order came and Alex's unit, together with other groups of officers, moved to push back the looters and clear the main road. As they pushed against the mob, police carriers followed them. Some people cleared out of the way, others stood on the pavements, wondering what the police were going to do. An order was shouted; a charge was made and the various units broke away, moving into junctions, forcing the mob back with their shields. There was resistance but the sudden charge had taken the looters off-guard.

Alex's unit held one of the junctions, soaking up the abuse thrown by angry looters deprived of their thieving. Some in the crowd were crying, others screaming. Fear was in the air, uncertainty as to what the police intended dominated. One man rushed at the line of officers, thought again and retreated. The crowd dispersed through the maze of backstreets.

*

Having left machete man and his followers at Ealing Studios, John Chase and Emma Dale were ordered to make their way to Southall Broadway: word was out that the gangs – presumably the professional gangs with whom Emma and John had already had dealings – were to 'hit up the jewellers'.

Southall had not been ignored by the rioters but damage there was far more limited than elsewhere in Ealing. Sikh men – in order to protect their businesses, homes and gurdwaras – had armed themselves with hockey sticks, baseball bats and their long, traditional swords, the Khanda. Gathering together, they stood quietly, presenting a deterrent; it was enough.

Emma and John drove past down South Road, looking into side streets as they went. This was a busy shopping area, full of Asian stores and fast-food outlets. Behind the shopping areas were small, residential streets, lined with Victorian houses. It was down one of these streets that John noticed a group of youths – forty in number, he estimated – kicking at the doors of private houses. Several cars and a van were parked in the street.

"They're forcing their way into people's homes," he said.

"Taking advantage of us not being around," replied Emma, "burgling."

"It's sickening," said John, quietly, "our patch and this is happening – on our patch! I'll have to report this to control."

The main road was empty of cars and their Mondeo was noticed almost immediately. One of the group of burglars cried out:

"Feds! Feds! Fucking Feds!"

Emma laughed but quietly to herself, realising John was in no mood for humour, however dark. Have these louts been to the States, she wondered, do they actually know what a federal agent is? She didn't have time to wonder long, however: the gang was running at them, led by the man who had called out, a man wearing a scarf over his mouth and a hood pulled down over his head; they were waving sticks and lumps of wood.

"Time to go!" said John

As he revved the car, the hooded man dropped to his knees and pulled a gun from his jacket pocket. He was only sixty feet away. Gripping the gun with both hands, in the style made famous by so many television shows, he aimed it at John.

John froze. He'd never experienced anything like this in his entire career. Violence was not part of British policing. He recalled with horror a friend's tale of being mugged at gunpoint in Leipzig many years before: he'd found the friend's story hard to believe – he hadn't wanted to believe it. And now, here he was, a gun pointed at his head.

"Let's go!"

It was Emma's voice calling him to action. John shook himself and drove off sharply, turning left onto The Broadway. A hundred yards or so along the road, he parked the car and radioed:

"All officers need to be aware there are guns out here."

"Are you able to describe the gunman?" came the reply.

"Dark clothing, a hood and a scarf round his mouth," replied John, thinking that could apply to just about anyone in the mobs he'd seen.

Before he could complete the call, a van followed rapidly by several cars tore out of the street where they'd seen the burglars.

"They're heading off towards Southall," said Emma.

"Dead right they are. I'll inform control."

And suddenly it was not only silent but still. The streets were empty, nothing was happening; bedlam had been replaced by peace and quiet.

Chapter 16
GRIEF AND SORROW

At The Blacksmith's Arms in Tottenham, where Keith and Mabel Willet with their regulars had maintained a vigil throughout the nights of Saturday and Sunday, a discussion was in full swing as to whether a third night's vigil was necessary. At the centre of the discussion were Daniel Solomon, Phil Meadows and Tom Drane.

*

Daniel had no success finding his son, much to the exasperation of Charlie's mother, Vanda. It was at moments like the one when he arrived at her house to wonder if the boy had returned home that Daniel realised for the umpteenth time the wisdom of them not living together. The question of marriage had raised its head occasionally during their relationship but the thought that it would involve their sharing the same house soon drove the idea away. It was better by far that he stayed away except, perhaps, at weekends when he might take the boy to kick a ball around, if he remembered to do so, and have a nice evening with Vanda afterwards.

'Yes, he had been home', was the opening salvo of Vanda's spleen, 'but like his father soon disappeared again *and*' – she emphasised the word – 'didn't feel the need to let her know where he was going or when he might be back'.

It was a long verbal ordeal for Daniel and he was only too pleased to get out to the pub where he'd 'been helping Keith and Mrs Willet guard it against the rioters'. Vanda's response to this show of neighbourliness needs no recording since it can be well imagined, although it may be worth noting that it referred to the duties of a father as a role model, a role Daniel had always supposed to be fulfilled by an interest in football and his playing in a rock combo.

*

Charlie Solomon, after setting fire to the police car on that first night of the riots in Tottenham had had what he thought of as 'a right old time'. He'd been involved in fighting the police at Hackney and also in Brixton, after which he'd caught up with a group of friends who'd made their way to Clapham Junction

Clapham Junction was a real disappointment: there was hardly a copper in sight. All right, there was plenty to nick and Charlie saw the chance to make some money afterwards – 'cause the riots couldn't last forever' – by selling stuff on, but really he'd come to fight.

He arrived just after the rioters had chased away the police and taken over the High Street. He stood gobsmacked: people were running down the road with TVs on their backs saying:

"Do you want this?" as though the free-for-all had engendered a spirit of generosity.

Others ran by with a pile of T-shirts making the same offer; there were TVs on the floor, smashed up, wires everywhere, trainer boxes, trainers, tags on the floor, smashed bottles, cigarette packs. People were hiding looted items underneath cars and in skips. Charlie supposed they intended returning for them later. It was madness gone riot.

Charlie met a friend of his, Kath, standing outside a pawnbroker's shop. She offered him a bag she was holding: one she must have looted and didn't really want.

"Here, Charlie, just have it."

"OK," he said, not wanting to offend her.

Further along the same street he came across another kid – he was only fourteen – who he'd met in Hackney.

"When did you get here?" he asked.

"I came straight from Hackney. I got here at five o'clock, and I'm in a bit of a moral dilemma."

"Go on," replied Charlie.

"Wow, I was just thinking I might, yeah, get a new computer, get my little brother his birthday present. That kind of wore off and I'm thinking just forget it for now."

"Where did you tell your mum you were going?" asked Charlie, suddenly reminded of his mother by his friend's concern for his little brother. Charlie had never had a little brother: his mum always said one was enough.

"I said I was going to the skate park with friends."

Charlie gave the kid a friendly punch, assuring him that to get the new computer was the only sensible thing to do and then wandered off down the road himself. With the police out of the way, there didn't seem any point in sticking together and he wanted a new pair of trainers he'd seen in JD. They were easily come by: Charlie ditched his old ones, put the new ones on and then took another pair for the future.

Feeling the new kid on the block in his new trainers, Charlie walked on. There was a real sense of freedom in the air: police gone, no one to tell you what to do. And then he saw, about fifty yards ahead of him, a mate in trouble. This was one of the kids who'd gone with him to throw bricks and stuff at the police in Hackney. He was holding an Xbox and some bigger kids were trying to take it off him. Charlie wasn't sure whether to run and help his friend or not and then the decision was taken from him. One of the big kids punched his friend in the face, grabbed the Xbox and ran off with it. Decision made and Charlie felt relieved: he hadn't fancied a punch in the mouth.

"You all right?" he asked, running up to his mate when the big kids had gone.

"Yeah, thanks Charlie. I've had a bad night."

It turned out that Charlie's friend, Brad, had arrived before the police were chased off and a woman in a car had urged him to throw a brick at one of the coppers.

"Dash it at them, she said, Go on, dash it at them, and I looked at her and I looked at the policeman and he ran up to me and I went 'What?' and I threw the brick but it didn't hit him and like went over his shoulder."

With the police out of the way, it was to prove a rough night in Clapham Junction: with the forces of law and order stretched beyond their limits, mob law became supreme.

A man who'd fallen to the ground had his wallet and Blackberry stolen and then was repeatedly kicked by the woman who'd thieved his belongings.

As soon as the shopfront of Debenhams was smashed the looters poured in yelping with excitement: clothes rails toppled to the floor, tills were smashed, alarms wailed, people ran up and down escalators grabbing what they could. It was pitch black in the store and this added to the sense of danger, lifting the looting to a frenzy of exhilaration. The looters felt that the rules no longer applied, they imagined they were in their own homes just picking up stuff they needed.

"A few women, yeah, just having a little shop," said one woman, a twenty-year-old, to her friend, "but Debenhams is empty, it's empty."

Charlie felt vindicated as he watched people filling up their cars, holding shutters up to help others get what they wanted, running down the road, their arms full, breaking into TK Maxx and stuffing the suitcases they'd stolen elsewhere. Not that he felt he needed vindicating: he and his mates, from the moment he torched the police car, had come to humiliate the coppers and they'd succeeded, but the looting added icing to the cake: these people were getting their just rewards in a greedy society that didn't give a stuff for people like them.

*

At home in Guildford, a police officer friend of Edward Andrews couldn't be said to share Charlie's feelings. He'd been sitting at home on his sofa all day, having been told that police officers weren't needed. He still hoped the phone would ring and he'd be ordered into work. It didn't ring and he felt frustrated beyond measure. Right now, he was watching Clapham Junction going up in flames: Currys had been looted and Ladbrokes had had a window shattered, residents were standing round wondering what the police were going to do. As the officer watched, he saw Party Superstore, a local fancy dress shop, being looted. The thieves were running out dressed in masks and wigs and then, to the officer's horror, he saw the flames. Some idiot must have set light to one of the costumes. In no time, the store was ablaze and the officer watched, tears in his eyes, as it was gradually gutted.

"I might as well have a beer or two," he said to his wife, "I can't get into work now even if they want me. I can't get the train and there's no way I could drive through these mobs. I may as well watch it on telly like everybody else."

His wife said nothing; she'd never seen him so desolated in his life and never ever seen him cry.

*

Phil Meadows hadn't gone back to see Carl's mother when he failed to find the boy: there didn't seem much point since he didn't really know either of them: and, anyway, they seemed happy enough without him. 'Go with the flow' was one of Phil's mottos.

*

His son, Carl, witnessing the violence in Hackney and being concerned for his mother, returned home. He didn't want to stay long but felt obliged to make an appearance. When he felt she understood that it would be a good idea to stay in that night – the night he knew the violence would come to Hackham, where his mum had bought her house – Carl made his excuses and his promises and set off to find some friends. He'd no intention of getting into the violence himself; he might take a thing or two but he wasn't going to be throwing bricks and bottles at the police; but – and it was a big but – he wanted to see what was going on.

It was nearly midnight when he found his friend, Raymond, in Peckham. He admired Ray; Ray was just twenty and a student at university. Ray was on holiday and pleased to be home at what he called 'the right moment'. Ray was intelligent and into 'moments', and this was a 'moment' no one was ever going to forget and that university types would be talking about for decades. Ray was proud to 'move with the current', and that made sense to Carl; it built a kinship between them.

"I've just had the biggest adrenalin rush of my life, Carl," he said as soon as they met, "We were tossing petrol bombs at the police station! Can you imagine that – can you! Man, if we'd have got in there, what wouldn't we have done! Broke into their files, burnt all their documents, cracked open their police helmets – we'd have given them law and order. We'd have been running round in their yellow vests."

"But you didn't get in?" asked Carl.

Ray looked at his friend sharply, sensing he didn't approve but dismissed the thought. Who wouldn't approve of burning down a police station?

"It was like a dream, man. There's no other word for it. I felt alive. It was like it will always be the best day of my life forever. It's Catford next and then Clapham. You coming?"

"Yeah, yeah of course," replied Carl.

They moved on through the early hours and eventually came to Croydon where the arsonists had had a field day. Roving around among the burning buildings, Carl was captured in the glow of the fires. It reminded him of pictures he'd seen of Hell, where the devils danced with delight. He couldn't help himself, he said afterwards. They already had bags full of stolen goods, goods they'd collected on their way round, but there was the bike and it was too good a chance to miss.

Carl rode around on it, feeling devilish himself as he weaved and tracked his way among the looters, gathering the laughter and approval of his friends, until he saw the kid with the new iPhone – 500 quid's worth of up-to-the-minute iPhone. He snatched it from the kid and rode on.

It was when he returned to the group with the iPhone that one of them intervened. It was the big bloke, Stuart, who worked in Tottenham.

"We can't be seen with this lot," he said, "Best to stash it in the graveyard and come back for it in a van."

Carl wasn't sure where they were to find a van but went along with his friends.

✳

Tom Drane, Lewis's father, had not approached the family home again; after all, it was no longer his home and he was no longer a member of the family – not since his girlfriend threw him out and, especially, since the new boyfriend moved in. Tom had been disenfranchised, and not only as a dad.

He spent some time wandering aimlessly around before deciding to phone Lewis's mum, Jenny.

"You know his number. Haven't you phoned him?" she asked.

"He won't answer."

"Well how do you expect us to know?"

It was the 'us' that choked Tom, the knowledge that the mother of his child and some other bloke were now an item, 'in a relationship' as the saying goes, and with his son. He knew none of his son's friends and so there didn't seem to be anyone he could phone.

✳

Lewis Drane, after that first night at Wood Green, had moved on with friends. One of them, Hugo, seemed to be the boss. Hugo had everything organised. His parents were away for the weekend and he said they, his gang, could stash the stuff at his house. Only from big brands, he'd said, but they hadn't stuck to that: taking stuff was so easy, you couldn't say no. 'Foot Locker, PC World, JD Sports, Currys ...'. It had been like a chant at first and they'd gone backwards and forwards. It was all building up at Hugo's parents' place and Hugo reckoned they had £5000 worth of stuff they could sell on.

Lewis phoned his mum several times but there was no answer except once when the new boyfriend picked up the phone, and Lewis didn't want to speak to him and so he just said, "Tell Mum I'm with friends", and switched off.

*

Mary Rudge had stayed only a short time talking with Angus's mother: it soon became clear that she knew nothing that would help Mary find her son. She was given a few phone numbers of Angus's friends and both women made the calls, calls that produced no information. Mary knew that teenagers were good at keeping from their parents what they didn't want the parents to know but that had never been the case with Benjamin. Benjamin needed to talk, often over and over again about the same issues, and she was the one in whom he confided.

Mary Rudge knew that her son was out there, somewhere among the rioters, arsonists and looters, alone, very vulnerable and was at a loss as to what she could do to find him.

Chapter 17
FITS AND STARTS

Mike Rudge had been unable to find his son: the boy simply disappeared into the crowd. Mike was unsure what to do. There was no good asking a policeman: they were all too busy. Mike laughed at his thought: there was dark humour in the fact that there were no bobbies on the street to ask for help. Mike had nothing against the police, although he'd come up against them a number of times, especially when Tottenham were playing at home. He didn't approve of what was going on but it was none of his business and it was best to keep his nose out of it. There was nothing he could do, anyway.

There was nothing he could do to find his son either. Perhaps he should tell Mary, but she'd know: she'd have gone to the boy's room after she turfed him out. Mike didn't blame her for that: Mary had put up with a lot from him – the brawling, the drunkenness, losing his job. He'd been a good painter and decorator – none better – and his business had been thriving until he took to drink. He wasn't a drunk: he didn't have to have a fix like some druggie, but he did enjoy a drink and the company it brought. He didn't drink because he had problems; he drank because he enjoyed drinking.

It was through drink he got involved with that other woman – he couldn't even remember her name now – and that had been the final blow for Mary. She gave him his marching orders and divorced him straightaway. Never mind! Things would turn out OK. But where was Ben? He'd always been a little devil for running off when he was young. Mary would find him: she always did. He'd best get home.

Mike lived in Ealing. Lived might be putting it a bit strongly: he had a place there, a little flat. It belonged to a painter and decorator he sometimes did work for if the bloke, a mate, was pushed to get a job done. 'Stay off the bottle, Mike, or I'm finished with you.' He always said that. If he'd kept off the bottle before, he'd still have his own business.

It hadn't been the bottle, though, so much as the brawling and ending up in the police cells. Customers didn't like to think they were hiring a criminal, however good he was at his job. But best to get home, out of this mayhem.

Mike had driven over in the company van. His boss let him use it because it was kept near the flat and he knew Mike would keep an eye on it. Best to get it home and out of the way of this mob. He could see a crowd of the rioters dragging bins into the road and setting light to them. The rubbish, commercial rubbish, burned with a black smoke, thick and choking. Some of the bins had been tipped over and the burning rubbish spilled out across the road, melting the tarmac.

Best out quickly. He'd parked in a side road, off the main thoroughfare: the van should be safe from the mob. They were even tipping police cars over and setting light to them. Best out.

The van was safe and Mike was soon on the road out of Tottenham. Thirty or forty minutes and he'd be out of it, but he'd need to pick up some petrol on the way. He had the boss's card: it shouldn't be a problem.

As he approached the petrol station, all seemed quiet: the lights were on, some cars were filling up. He pulled in by the pumps. It was as he was getting out of the car that the kid approached him.

"We need your van, mate."

"Bugger off!"

"And we need you."

Mike looked at the youth. He was only a boy, perhaps sixteen or seventeen, the same age as Ben, but he was holding a gun and laughing.

"It's not my van," replied Mike – lamely, he thought afterwards but it seemed sensible at the time: he was responsible for it, after all.

"We ain't gonna torch it," replied the youth, "We need it to move some property of ours."

The youth laughed when he said 'property', as though owning property was some kind of joke. Mike declined to ask.

"Whose 'we'?"

"You'll see."

As if the youth had signalled in some way, a gang of them rushed from the petrol station, making for a line of pumps on the far side from where Mike intended to fill up. He looked over. The gang was trying to pour petrol from the pumps and setting it alight.

"Bloody hell. Stop them!"

"We're off, mate, unless you want to burn."

Mike didn't. As the youths piled into the back of the van, tossing out the equipment and paints stored there, Mike turned the ignition key and was away. It hadn't occurred to the youths that Mike may have stopped for petrol and with reason.

"On your way, mate. You're going to pick up some property of ours," said one of the youths, laughing, like his friend at the idea of 'our property'.

Looking into his rear-view mirror, Mike saw staff rushing from the station shop and kiosk. Flames were licking across the forecourt threatening the very safety of those attending to the vehicles. Had these kids any real chance of blowing up a petrol station because if they did the catastrophe didn't bear thinking about.

He drove on with no idea of where these youths were taking him or what their 'property' might be. He lost track of where he was driving. They seemed to be in the Notting Hill area but he wasn't sure; and then he felt the gun poked into his cheek, making a quite unnecessary threat since the youths knew they had him where they wanted him.

"Turn next right."

The road ran along the side of a store. There was still other traffic about and no sign of any rioters. His kidnappers seemed to have arrived ahead of the mob. The back of the store was in darkness except for two lamps that lit what must have been a customers' car park.

"Park here."

The youths clambered from the van, tossing out any remaining paints, spirits, oils or equipment and looked around. It was very quiet and none of them seemed bothered about being discovered: there was no attempt to hide their faces by pulling up their hoodies despite the certainty of cameras recording their every movement.

The back doors of the store were made of thickened glass and the youths set to work at once to smash their way through. A shopping trolley was raced into the doors, followed by two commercial waste bins, a leaping yob, a barrage of bricks and bottles and, lastly, a scaffolding pole. The youths seemed in no hurry. Traffic was still passing along the main road, their headlights occasionally illuminating one side of the car park.

Eventually, the gang managed to drive one of the scaffolding poles through the jamb of one of the doors.

"Time to load up."

Mike heard the youth and smiled: while they were pilfering whatever this store held, he'd make his escape and phone the police.

"Come on, mate."

"What?"

"You're going to help us. You don't think we'd leave you out, do you?"

Mike's heart sank. He might have got away with being kidnapped at gunpoint but if the cameras showed him loading his van he'd be done for, especially with his record.

It was an electrical goods store and Mike soon found himself running backwards and forwards across the customer car park, laden with television sets, computers, mobile phones, Xboxes and – as he put it – 'Christ knows what!'

*

Simon Tippet was having a good night and a good morning: early, but nevertheless, morning. Who'd have thought, three days ago – or was it four: Simon had lost track of the time, but he guessed it was now Tuesday early – that Hackney would be in the hands of The Blades – well, The Blades and the other gangs, and that the biggest gang of all, the police, were on the run. All it needed now was a killing.

He was tired, mind you, and looking forward to a break. He'd met one of his mates in Hackney and his mate had said they could crash out at his place. He hadn't mentioned Miggs but that was her problem: no one, especially him, had asked her to tag along.

"We'll have a shower, chill, smoke a bit and then off out again. Everyone's going to Ealing now. Best get there before everything gets looted."

It seemed a good idea to Simon.

*

John Chase and Emma Hare drew up outside the pub in Ealing. The window was smashed, glass scattered over the street. John gave a friendly wave to reassure the people in there and the landlord welcomed the pair of them: he knew both Emma and John as local officers.

"They've gone now," he said, offering the two police officers a chair, "but it was touch and go when those louts were outside. After they'd smashed the window, they heaved petrol bombs in. Lucky we were here to put out the flames. We locked ourselves in, see. Been here ever since these riots started."

John was thoughtful. All night, he and Emma had been criss-crossing Ealing, their own patch, trying to keep calm and restore some kind of order – the situation was a nightmare – while other officers were also fighting for their lives in other places across London. He looked up at the giant TV screens in the pub. Everywhere was a war zone: Hackney, Croydon.

The landlord brought across mugs of steaming hot coffee and a pile of fresh sandwiches. He gave them a grim smile.

'What the hell is going on,' thought John, as he watched screens.

It wasn't just the borough of Ealing, and it wasn't just London: across the country, cities were burning, while dedicated police officers fought rioters, looters and arsonists. Lines of fellow officers were stepping forward in the face of vicious onslaughts with nothing to protect them except riot shields. There was hope only in the fact that these men and women were pulling together, he thought, fighting to save their cities and their homes.

Emma nudged him. Her radio was talking to them: trouble had broken out again. It was time to go. They thanked the landlord and made for their car.

*

Keith and Mabel Willet had decided to shut up The Blacksmith's Arms, Keith willingly but Mabel with a degree of reluctance. She acknowledged that Tottenham was now quieter, that the mobs had moved on, but wasn't ready to acknowledge that they might not return. Keith could see the sense of what she was saying but his regulars, those who had stayed with him to protect the pub, needed to get home.

Besides, everyone was tired. In the morning, early, they could open up again and be ready if necessary, but a good night's rest, a real sleep, would benefit all and sundry.

*

Alex Willet was sitting in a police carrier outside Peckham police station eager for orders. He and his colleagues were desperate to do something, anything but sit and wait.

Chapter 18
HIS VEHEMENT NATURE

Benjamin Rudge found Reeves Corner easily because it was what his mum called a 'landmark'; that was why she'd chosen it as the place to meet if they were separated, and from there he knew the way to London Overground.

Benjamin wasn't really interested in old buildings but this one was a landmark and, therefore, important. Once at school the class he was attached to had been looking at old buildings in Tottenham, but Benjamin had wanted to study dinosaurs and so the teacher let him because it was 'easier that way'. Benjamin heard the teacher say that; he wasn't sure what it meant but knew it had something to do with the time he'd rolled up into a ball like a woodlouse in the corner of the classroom and screamed and screamed until his mum came to take him home. His mum had been very upset; he didn't want to upset his mum but he did want to study dinosaurs.

Outside the furniture shop at Reeves Corner a gang of people were running in and out of the shop. They were looting like the ones at the mall where Angus, his bestie, had disappeared. One of the looters ran out with a laptop and then ran back inside. Benjamin wondered why he did that instead of running away.

"Who's got a lighter? Let's torch the place!"

The man in the shop was shouting to his friends and jumping up and down like a madman. He looked like the Joker in the Batman film. Benjamin's uncle said that the Joker was one of the best examples of a psychopath in comic films. This was the uncle who'd told him he should go and see his older brother in Manchester because otherwise his mum couldn't go because she couldn't leave him on his own. Benjamin didn't like his uncle saying that because he didn't want to go but he knew his uncle was telling the truth because his mum said he always did, and he'd been truthful about the Joker.

As Benjamin watched, he saw the man in the shop set fire to a sofa. It was terrifying to see how quickly the fire spread; soon all the furniture – nearly all the furniture on the ground floor was burning and the flames were climbing up the walls. The looters drew back as the fire took hold of the building and Benjamin was frightened. He didn't like noise; in particular, he didn't like shouting and these people were screaming at the tops of their voices. Not only screaming but dancing up and down, waving their arms and throwing their legs about at funny angles like demons Benjamin had once seen in a painting. They were all excited but some, like himself, were also frightened.

And then the police came. Somebody must have told them to stop standing still like they had been doing because they were running at the rioters in lines, and the rioters were hurling bottles and bricks at them.

Benjamin moved away. He didn't want to go far from Reeves Corner because then he'd not know the way to London Overground but he was scared stiff as the bottles and bricks and sticks crashed down around him. On the other side of the building, further along the road he saw the fire engines, but they couldn't get to the fire because the rioters wouldn't let them. The rioters were throwing everything they could lay hands on at the firefighters as well as the police.

Blue lights were flashing, sirens were wailing, and both these horrible sights and sounds Benjamin saw and heard through the flames that were now ferocious. Benjamin had seen scenes like this in films and thought it would be exciting to be there, but it wasn't.

Benjamin looked about him; he wanted to get away, but where could he go. He looked up. People were jumping out of the upstairs windows. People must live above the shop; he didn't know that was so. He couldn't believe what he saw; he knew he'd never have the courage to jump out of a window. He'd be crushed on the ground where he fell. People were frightened because they were trapped, and that was why they were jumping. If they didn't jump they would burn to death; and the rioters wouldn't let the fire engines get through.

And then the police charged into the rioters. They were using their shields to push their way through to the fire engines and using their batons to hit the rioters who attacked them. The police kept together in a group but when they got separated from the group the rioters surrounded them, grabbing away their shields, tugging off their helmets. One policeman had his helmet snatched and one of the rioters held him in a headlock and repeatedly punched him in the face and tried to pull him down to the ground until the other police rescued him.

Benjamin turned to his left and then his right; he must get away. He was now really terrified and if he didn't get away he would fall and curl himself into a ball and he didn't want to do anything of the sort. He knew none of these people and if you don't know people they don't care about you unless they are your teacher or your counsellor, and sometimes they don't care either. To his left a gang of youths were brandishing knives – real knives, knives that glistened red in the flames, red like blood. Benjamin didn't like the colour red. He didn't know why but it scared him. He knew he mustn't scream because if he did a crowd would gather round him and they might laugh; and these youths might push their knives into him; they looked nasty, as nasty as anyone he'd ever seen, because they were waving their knives about in the flames and laughing.

As he wondered what to do, the crowd took Benjamin with it, jostling him along across the front of the burning building. He could feel the heat of the fire on his face, on his arms and legs, all over his body, even through his clothes. He felt in his pocket for his notebook in case it had got lost in the rush. He didn't want to lose his notebook: he always carried his notebook and wrote down things he didn't understand so that his mum could explain them later.

The police, some of them, had reached the furniture store building and were kicking in the doors. The wooden doors were alight, fire was running down them as the police ran into the building.

"Is anyone here? Is anyone in here?"

They were all shouting at once telling the people trapped in the building that they must come out to face the rioters or burn to death. Some people did come out, some crying, some screaming in fear but some seemed too frightened to be caught up with the rioters. Benjamin was caught up and he didn't like it but he thought it might be better than dying in the fire.

Kicking and shouting and screaming: the sounds were deafening to Benjamin as doors caved in, youths cried for the blood of the police and petrified residents ran from their homes. Benjamin usually had difficulty seeing something from someone else's point of view but even he realised that these frightened people would never set foot in their homes again; never set foot in them because they wouldn't be there. Walls were giving way and falling into the street, ceilings were collapsing and their plaster and woodwork was spilling out onto the street. If there was one place Benjamin loved above all others it was his home and especially his room, his sanctuary from the world.

*

At home in Tottenham, worried to death about her son, Mary Rudge had received a phone call from Angus's mum. Angus had been arrested by police for stealing a watch from a jeweller's shop in the Croydon mall. Before Mary could ask the question, the other mother answered.

"No, Ben wasn't arrested with him."

Mary had been watching the extended 10 o'clock news. She saw on the screen what was happening in Croydon. Police were baton-charging the crowd, trying to reach the buildings, trying to make it possible for the fire engines to get through to the flames and the trapped people.

And then she'd seen that awful moment when the woman jumped from the upstairs window through the flames on to the street. Mary later learned from the newspapers that the woman was Monika Koncyzk, a Polish shopworker who lived in the flat above the shop. Burning debris from the furniture store at Reeves Corner had blown across the road to the opposite line of shops, setting them alight. Terrified – no doubt, Mary knew – Monika was seen leaning out of her window. Others had jumped; now, it was her turn. Police officers were holding out their arms on the street below, while the fires raged around them. There was screaming, missiles were careering through the air and she was being asked – no, told – to jump. Mary easily put herself in Monika's place, then and in the nightmare nights to come. The police were waiting for her; they would catch her, but how could she be sure.

And then she jumped. It was a sight Mary Rudge never forgot.

And Benjamin – her beloved son who she'd nursed, not without great difficulty at times, however much she loved him – was there, somewhere, at the mercy of his vehement nature: but, at least, now she knew where he was and she would go and she would find him, come what may.

*

Gabriel Pilgrim, having made a quick visit to The Blacksmith's Arms for a swift half, was standing outside his general store checking the shutters for the umpteenth time when Mary Rudge, hurriedly dressed and carrying a tote bag, rushed past.

"Mrs Rudge?"

"Oh hello, Mr Pilgrim. I can't stop – don't mean to be rude but I must get to the Tube station before the last train goes, and I don't know when that is."

"What's your hurry? Benjamin?"

"Yes, he's in Croydon and ..."

"Oh, my word. You can't go there alone. Have you seen the news? Just a moment."

Gabriel disappeared inside his store and then, as though having second thoughts, came out again and waved Mary in before him."

"Martha!"

It was the first time Mary had heard the shopkeeper raise his voice. Martha Pilgrim, followed by a sheepish Dolly, came down the stairs from their flat above and Gabriel outlined Mary's plight.

"You'll go with her, Gabriel, of course," said Martha without hesitation.

"I thought you'd say that, my dear."

"I'll fetch your coat, Dad," offered Dolly with an eagerness Mary didn't understand.

"You be careful," said Martha, "I don't want you coming back half dead."

"Wholly dead would be better, would it," replied Gabriel.

It might have been amusing at another time, a standard marital parry, but not then, not with Martha seeing the look on Mary's face and knowing the anxiety in her heart.

In less than twenty minutes after receiving the phone call from Angus's mother, Mary was on her way to Tottenham Hale Underground station in the company of Gabriel Pilgrim, wondering why she hadn't protested at his coming with her but pleased she'd not done so.

Chapter 19
THIRSTY BY THIS TIME

Edward Andrews, Doreen Manners and their team, relieved from guarding the Halfords store, were waiting for further orders at Lewisham police station. They were exhausted, following their battle with the rioters and looters at Bromley Road Retail Park, but eager to be out there doing something. Thirsty by this time, Ed took a long swig of water; revived, he felt his adrenalin returning that had continued to drain away with the waiting.

The restlessness was infectious: the officers would glance at each other, anger in their eyes, knowing other colleagues were out there on the streets fighting for their lives. Every now and then an URGENT ASSISTANCE call would come in but they'd been ordered to wait. Community meetings were being held by senior officers and community leaders to discuss the best way of dealing with the riots.

"Community meetings!" yelled one officer, "What good are they now? The time for those is long gone! We need to retake the streets. We need to stop the rioting and looting!"

Doreen, who was a sergeant, felt the pressure: any decision to disobey orders by doing something rested with her as the senior officer present.

"Sod it!" she said, suddenly, "I've got an idea."

She'd realised that 'doing something' involved the need for transport and they possessed none. As the indecision ran through her mind the idea occurred.

"We'll commandeer a bus. The bus station's not far from here."

The others looked at her in astonishment. Among them were male officers who had, however jokingly, looked upon women police officers as mainly decorative and yet here was one who was anything but: if the scheme fell apart, she'd be for it, discipline-wise.

"Come on, Ed, you and I will approach the drivers."

At the bus station two drivers, wiping their hands after cleaning their cabs, looked up as Doreen explained her plan: looked up and then at each other. Silence followed, followed by more silence.

"We know it's a lot to ask."

"Do you know how to drive a bus?" replied one of the men, a short, dark-skinned man with a distinct Turkish accent.

"No," answered Doreen.

"Hmm!" said the man, with a faint, teasing smile behind his dark eyes, "Come on, I'll drive you."

It was only minutes later that the bus pulled out of the bus depot and arrived at the police station much to the amazement of the waiting officers.

"It's a double-decker!" cried one.

"Would you prefer a single," replied the driver to a round of laughter that increased as the officers climbed aboard.

"Where to?" asked the driver who introduced himself as Mehmet.

"Sydenham, please, driver," Doreen replied.

The bus moved away, only to stop a few minutes later at a set of traffic lights.

"Why have you stopped?" asked Ed.

"The lights are red," replied Mehmet, the faint smile behind his eyes.

"Go through them!"

"Through a red?" questioned Mehmet, "It goes against all my training."

His manner and voice were deadpan: there was no knowing whether or not he was serious, and then the lights changed and the bus moved away.

Heading along Sydenham Road, they came across a group of sixty youths raiding a Costcutter supermarket; cigarette packets and bottles of alcohol had dropped into the road as the looters nipped back and forth between the cars and buses slowly making their way.

"We're as good as invisible," said Doreen, "These louts will be looking out for police cars. Go slowly, Mehmet, and park up at the side of the road."

Tense, the officers waited until the bus had stopped, waited by the middle doors of the bus ready to charge; there was no knowing whether the youths were armed, but it was known that knives and even guns were on the streets.

Ed led the charge, eager to get at the looters, and a hooded youth, a bottle in one hand, turned to face him, shock in his eyes at seeing a policeman. He raised the bottle – to throw or strike, Ed wasn't sure, but it didn't matter; he slammed his riot shield in the youth's face, taking him off-balance and sending him backwards down to the pavement.

The police officers now had the advantage; despite the readiness of the youths to fight they'd been taken by surprise.

"Let's show the bastards we're in charge," yelled Doreen.

The officers surged forward, determined to clear the road by forcing the looters back onto the estate. After a very short time, the mob, running towards the Hazel Grove estate, were in retreat and it was strange to see the normal flow of traffic returning, almost as though nothing like a riot had happened.

"We should have done this hours ago – days ago," said Ed, "This was real policing – firm, assertive. They didn't like it when we took the initiative."

"Brazen sods," replied one of his colleagues, "Doing what they liked while we were ordered to stand and watch."

Back on the bus, the ambience was jovial, the officers laughing and joking, the driver with a broad smile on his face.

"Where can I drop you lot off?" he asked, as though making his regular run.

"Catford, driver, if you please," replied one of the officers, a young policeman, his confidence restored.

Once again, the driver was able to take the bus in close and the contingent of police officers emerged from the bus. In no time they were piling into the rioters who'd gathered at a retail park. Some ran, others felt riot shields rammed into their bodies or batons brought down onto the weapons they held; and they skulked away, forced off the streets, prevented from damaging any more buildings.

All the while, the driver had been ignoring orders to return the bus to the depot; instead, he chose to continue bravely into the thick of the rioting. It wasn't something the police officers involved were going to forget and for Mehmet he was always to recall how once he "drove a busload of coppers" into the midst of the fray.

Chapter 20

WITH A KICK AT THE DOOR

Dennis Batterby was anything but jovial; there was no laughing and joking among him and his friends as they sat smoking and chatting in the ruins of the Carphone Warehouse in Southwark: from their point of view a golden opportunity had been wasted.

"An opportunity to change society lost," wailed one, "We should be revolutionary against capitalism."

"They fucked up big time, the opportunists," replied Dennis, "If they'd gone to parliament and stood up for what they thought was correct, they could have brought down the government with a kick at the door. We could have changed the everything, the whole government, but people wanted Nikes, crap on their feet."

*

Hugo's idealism had also suffered a setback: his intention to concentrate on the big-name brands had gone by the board once the fever of looting set in among his gang and those he had influenced along the way through the three nights. He and Lewis Drane stood in Hugo's parents' house wondering what to do with the thousands of pounds worth of loot littering every room, piled in the hallway and obstructing the stairs.

Lewis thought of his dad and what he would say if he found out what he'd done. It wasn't like him; he wasn't himself. He still liked his dad even if he didn't see much of him these days, and he'd be upset – but then, he was never there for him, not when he was needed most. Lewis wasn't sure why what had happened had happened. He was a thief now, and he'd never be a probation officer like he wanted.

*

Simon Tippett was in a better frame of mind: not only had the attacks on the police been more than successful but so had the looting. Once he'd got the gangs to stop fighting among themselves for a change, he'd been able to organize the looting better. It was the way the police attacked them that gave him the idea. He'd seen that the pigs worked in lines – the thin blue lines they keep boasting about – and so he'd got the rioters and looters to work together in the same way. While the frontline kept the pigs busy, the backline looted the shops. It was sort of formation planning. And Miggs was just wetting herself all the time; he'd never seen her so worked up.

*

Driving slowly along The Broadway, following their radio call at the public house, John Chase and Emma Hare saw an Asian couple standing outside their looted jewellery shop. The couple were crying. John knew them from his patrols: a decent couple who'd come to Britain for a better life, and there they were, all their hard work ruined by a mindless mob in just one night. John was ashamed. Couldn't the police have done more to protect working people?

The radio kept them alert as they drove on towards Southall. The streets were starting to fill again; reports came in of a group of about two hundred people. John pulled up alongside a group of men; they were holding cricket bats, hockey sticks and swords. Emma got out of the car and approached them. The men were Sikhs.

"Is everything OK, gentlemen?" she asked.

"Yes, thank you, constable," replied one who was either their leader or their spokesman.

"You're sure?" questioned Emma, holding her ground, knowing the law was being broken: the swords were illegal on the street and the sports items didn't suggest an interest in the games.

"If those rioters come back here, damaging our businesses and our lives, we'll deal with them ourselves," replied the man, without smiling, "and so, yes, everything is all right, thank you."

"I see," replied Emma.

"It's not your fault, constable, we know that, but no one is protecting us and so we must protect ourselves."

Emma smiled and returned to the car.

"Is everything OK?" asked John, needlessly, he thought, since he'd listened to every word spoken from his position behind the wheel.

"Yes, I think so," replied Emma, "they're reasonable people living in unreasonable times.

Chapter 21
SHADOWS OF THE NIGHT

Mary Rudge and Gabriel Pilgrim made it to Croydon. It had not been easy: the Underground system was packed with people, some simply returning home from a day at work or out for a night in the city, others hell-bent on reaching their next place of riot. It was a strange experience for both of them, but particularly for Gabriel.

His Pickwickian proportions pressed him up against all and sundry, some who passed less than complimentary remarks about his size; his hard stare at a lout occupying the seat for those who had difficulty standing, were elderly or pregnant produced nothing but a leer; at the same time, a young Asian woman immediately offered him her seat, a gesture that both delighted and embarrassed him. He insisted Mary took the seat, at which gesture another young Asian woman offered him hers.

Nothing prepared either of them for their arrival in Croydon – not the attitude of the young people who poured off the train with them or what they had seen on their television screens. Police officers seemed to be running everywhere, in and out of burning buildings, calling loudly 'Is it clear? Is everyone out?' over and over again; heat and smoke billowed from the houses and shops; in the streets, police officers fought rioters and looters, fire-engines pressed their way through the mobs.

Mary went immediately to Reeves Corner, knowing it was from there that Benjamin would make his way to the Underground station. She hadn't found him at the station and was hopeful he might have simply waited. She'd always said to wait if he felt lost and that she would find him. It was hopeless: no single person could be seen amidst the mob. Benjamin would have been terrified once he'd left Angus – and Mary assumed he'd done just that once Angus started looting.

If anything, the streets around Reeves Corner were worse than the corner itself: small groups of looters seemed to be roaming freely while the police tackled those at the centre of the rioting.

"I don't know what to suggest, Mrs Rudge," said Gabriel, "You're sure the lad's phone is off?"

Of course, she was sure: Mary had tried Benjamin's mobile dozens of times, dozens and dozens of fruitless rings to receive no answer at all.

They found themselves in a narrow street overlooked by a block of flats. Looters were all over the place, dashing back and forth to parked cars, carrying stolen items; young men passed them by, not bothering even to wear masks or hide their faces with their hoodies. Gabriel was furious; Mary urged him to say nothing. Two men carrying a large television set were set upon, beaten and robbed.

"The robbers robbed!" commented Gabriel, remembering that his own daughter, Dolly, was to be recorded among the thieves.

Mary didn't know who to ask for help: the police were busy, too busy to be concerned about the whereabouts of one, autistic boy. The looters, looting from each other, would suppose she was mad to be worried – mad and maybe worth robbing. Mary wasn't a nervous woman – life with an autistic son and a drunken husband had toughened her sinews. She laughed at the thought, remembering how much she'd enjoyed her schooldays, especially Shakespeare: they'd studied *Henry V* at 'A level'. It all seemed so long ago now, more than a lifetime. And, somehow, it seemed to have nothing to do with the life she'd led.

*

It was here in the very street where she and Gabriel now stood that Benjamin had first asked for help. Confused by the flames, by the choking smoke, by seeing policemen collapsing as they helped people out of the burning buildings – in Benjamin's world, policemen never collapsed but were always available to ask the way – he had been unsure where he was; it should have been easy – he knew the direction to take but had always taken it with his mother. Always he had waited until she arrived if they got separated, but tonight he knew she would not be arriving. And so, he'd asked for help.

The man seemed all right. He was sitting in his car waiting for someone.

"Is this the way to the Overground Station?" he asked.

"What?"

"Is this the way to the Overground Station."

"Bugger off!"

"I need to get to the Overground station because it is the way home to Tottenham."

The man gave him a sharp look. He was a short man with scruffy, blond hair. Benjamin always kept himself very smart. His mother liked him smart and advised him about what clothes to wear. He wondered whether this man had been the right person to ask. He had looked OK through the windscreen of the car but Benjamin had seen only his face

"Is this the way to the Overground station, please?"

Benjamin found that repeating himself could be annoying to people but, at the same time, they usually got fed up and told you what you wanted to know.

"It's that way," the man replied, waving his arms nowhere.

Benjamin knew the man was trying to get rid of him: people were like that when they didn't want you to hold them in conversation. Benjamin liked talking because he had lots to say but people didn't always want to listen, especially when they were not interested in what he wanted to talk about.

It was so dark now, shadows of the night were everywhere he looked, shadows cast by the flames and blackened by the smoke. Benjamin could see that the man was also frightened: he wanted Benjamin out of the way. Benjamin wondered why: he was only asking the way to the station.

And then two men rushed towards the car. They threw open the man's boot and ran off with a television set.

"Get 'em!"

"Pardon?" said Benjamin.

"Get 'em! Run you little fucker. Don't lose sight of them!"

The man was clambering from the car as he spoke, clambering out and yet wanting to wait for someone. Benjamin didn't understand. He was frightened by the man's shouting, unsure what to do. Perhaps if he helped the man, he might tell him the way to London Overground?

The men with the television set ran off through the smoke and got into another car that seemed to be waiting for him. It was only a few yards along the street and even through the smoke and in the dark Benjamin could see easily what happened. The car sped off before the doors were closed.

As he watched, the man who he'd asked for help joined him.

"Where'd they go?"

Benjamin pointed in the direction the car had disappeared into the smoke. The man looked wildly about him and as he did so, another man rushed up. He was carrying a television set.

"What's happened?"

The man Benjamin asked for help explained quickly, so quickly he gabbled.

"It was a silver Peugeot 208," said Benjamin, "The registration was ..."

"You know the registration?"

Benjamin was fascinated by numbers; he only had to see a set to remember them. He was also good at knowing the different kinds of car: that was why he knew the car the men had gone off in was a Peugeot 208. One of his besties had a book with drawings of the different types of cars. He and

Benjamin would look at the book for hours, fascinated by the colours and the designs.

"Get in."

"Pardon?" said Benjamin.

"Get in!"

"I don't get into cars with strange men," replied Benjamin.

The man who shouted tossed the television set into the back of the other man's car and pushed Benjamin into the front seat.

"Let's go!" shouted the newcomer, "They can't be far. It's a one-way and there's a T-junction at the end. Keep your eyes in front of you, son. Keep looking."

"Are you taking me to the London Overground?" asked Benjamin, fearing they were not.

"When we're done," snapped the driver.

Their car, a Ford Focus, shot off along the street swerving and careering between the bursts of smoke. Benjamin felt the heat of the flames that were consuming the adjacent buildings. He was frightened but exhilarated: the chase was like the ones his superhero, Batman, did in the Batmobile.

When they reached the junction the Peugeot was out of sight but Benjamin was too scared to admit he couldn't see it.

"Left!" he cried, "Turn left."

And there it was, ahead but not too far, held fast by a group of rioters and looters. The Focus closed in behind and followed the other car through. Once clear of the rioters the Peugeot gathered speed but Benjamin's driver was having none of it. He caught up with the other car, clipped its wing causing it to swerve and then swung ahead blocking the way.

Two men stepped out of the Peugeot, one holding a gun. He didn't hesitate as he approached Benjamin's car but pointed the gun and fired. The driver grabbed his right arm and jerked backwards. The man fired again and the driver slumped forward over his steering wheel. Benjamin could see the blood running from him and knew the man – the one he'd asked for help – was dead.

TUESDAY, AUGUST 9TH

Chapter 22
WHERE THE DAWN CHORUS SINGS

David Cameron, the British Prime Minister, decided that he must recall parliament. It wouldn't be a popular decision, demanding that politicians should return from their summer holidays to deal with a matter that should, properly, have been the responsibility of the police forces of the country, but it had to be made: the rioting, looting and arson in London had now spread to other parts of the country, and the government of the day must be seen to be in control. First, though, before he faced Prime Minister's Question Time on the 11th, a meeting of COBRA, the Civil Contingencies Committee, was necessary; a statement must be made to calm the public.

His was the burden of responsibility; on his shoulders alone, it rested. The electorate would be looking to him for answers and ideas. Punitive ones were gathering in his head as David Cameron approached the meeting: giving the police the right to remove face masks where they have suspicions, no phoney human rights concerns about using CCTV camera images, rioters could face eviction from social housing, look at whether it would be possible to prevent people communicating via social websites to plan disorder; and homeowners and businesspeople whose property was damaged could receive compensation.

It was going to be a rigorous briefing for the cabinet.

*

Boris Johnson, the Mayor of London, was already on the streets, bristling with anger, broom in hand. Never one to miss a photo opportunity, he wished to be seen, ready to help with the clean-up. He was confronted by those who suffered at the hands of the rioters:

"A brick came through my window," cried the owner of a Clapham Junction hairdressing salon, "and no one was here to defend me. We were in complete shock. They were mocking us from the outside. We were left completely terrified. We could hear them smashing everything. The noise was atrocious. You could hear them cheering each other, screaming. They were young, very young, twelve to fifteen years old. I was shaking for two hours afterwards. It's outrageous! This is a war zone. It's like a scene from a war movie."

Theresa May, the Home Secretary, standing with Mr Johnson facing the verbal onslaught decided to leave. It was important she should return to parliament and try to re-establish her reputation as 'a safe pair of hands'.

*

Theresa May had worked with Ian Duncan Smith on her party's thinking about what had come to be called 'the broken society'. He had set out his ideas ready for the recent election when they removed the Labour Party from power. The 'steady rise of an underclass' were his thoughts on the riots, 'the day the inner city came to call on the rest of society'.

He suspected there would be much talk over the next few days about the 'broken society'; it was part of their pre-election narrative. It was all going to be so much easier relating the rioting, looting and arson to a particular underclass.

*

Edward Andrews, Doreen Manners and the rest of their crew had returned to Lewisham police station once they said goodbye to their bus driver, Mehmet. A carrier awaited them and a call to Deptford.

None of them needed telling about Deptford: it was well-known as a place where gangs held sway, a challenging area. The High Street was lined with locally owned shops: pawnbrokers, betting shops, halal butchers, workmen's cafes, street markets. It was a vibrant place.

Small fires were burning, a small group of youths, about forty, were gathered when the officers arrived.

"Riot shields up, batons at the ready," commanded Doreen, "let's move these youths along."

A brick shattered at Ed's feet; then more bricks and glass bottles came flying through the air; then petrol bombs exploded around them.

The police quickened their pace: seizing the initiative was of paramount importance, they all knew.

"Run!" called Doreen.

They did, guarding their bodies with the riot shields, they charged. It was a brief flurry ending as they'd expected: the mob dispersed, disappearing into the nearby estate.

Ed looked at the rest of the crew. After what they'd been through, this was a bit of a disappointment.

*

Alex Willet and his colleagues sat at Peckham police station waiting for orders. Their radios told them that there were outbreaks of trouble all over London but that Croydon was the worst hit.

"We need to get stuck in," he said, "Waiting is doing nobody any good."

When the order finally came, delivered by their inspector, it was to be Croydon.

"But as a precaution," he insisted, "things are quieter there now."

Driving along Whitehorse Road, the officers saw people running in all directions. The stationery store, Staples, had been broken into; looters were running back and forth carrying an assortment of goods, including television sets, in their arms, not oblivious to the police but not concerned by their presence. Another world had opened up, it seemed to Alex.

Charging out of the carrier with the other officers he made for one man and grabbed his arm. The television set he was carrying fell to the ground. Such was the force of the man's flight that he pulled Alex to the ground and there they struggled together, both bewildered by the temerity of the other: Alex that the man seemed upset at being apprehended, the thief by the fact that Alex had bothered to do so. What was the night coming to? Up to now it had been a free-for-all, no holds barred.

Fights were going on all around them between Alex's comrades and other looters; it was more like a pub brawl than a series of arrests. Piles of stolen goods lay scattered across the pavements and the road.

Alex pulled out his handcuffs and snapped one cuff onto the man's right wrist.

"Now the other!" said Alex.

"I wasn't doing nothing," replied the man.

"'Doing nothing's' right," replied Alex, "You were doing something – thieving!"

"I was just looking."

"Just looking! With a television set in your hands?"

Alex snapped the second cuff over the man's left wrist.

It was strange sight: lines of looters being led towards the carrier by officers, all the prisoners cuffed.

"Where are we taking them? Asked Alex.

"I'm waiting to hear," replied the driver, "the Met's custody suites are full."

"All of them?"

"So, it seems."

"But there are over a thousand cells."

The driver smiled ruefully, his ear on his radio. It crackled.

"Guildford," he said.

"Guildford in Surrey," exclaimed Alex, not really believing his ears.

"I believe that's where it is, son. We're off to where the dawn chorus sings rather than coughs."

The driver was a man from Teesside and his remark an example of Northern, industrial town humour. Alex had heard similar before but had he realized what was happening at home, he would not have been so amused by his fellow officer's remark.

Chapter 23

HOMEWARD BOUND

Keith Willet's decision to stay up all night to defend his pub with the help of his locals worked well during the days rioting took place in Tottenham but things were quieter there now, the rioters having moved elsewhere, and he reflected contentedly that he and Mabel had been right to call off his battalions, as he thought of them. She, of course, had cast doubts on the wisdom of such a move, but that was women for you: always cautious, always hedging their bets so they could blame someone else if events turned out the other way.

It was late in the evening and he sat with three of his regulars, the trio who always shared the same table, although tonight they weren't playing dominoes. The few others in the pub looked as though they might be snatching a drink rather than making a night of it, and Keith was disappointed.

"My message to Londoners is the same," he said, for the umpteenth time, "Go out, have a good time and don't let the bastards grind you down."

Daniel Solomon, Phil Meadows and Tom Drane nodded in agreement, each with his own thoughts about the use of the term 'bastards' but not completely ready to disagree with Keith Willet, a man who welcomed disagreement reluctantly.

Behind the bar, Mabel Willet, polishing glasses with a cloth, smiled quietly to herself. She, too, was pleased with the way their regulars responded to her call – not that they'd have been very welcome back if they hadn't – but she still held tight to her doubts and was pleased she'd persuaded her husband to cancel their usual karaoke night on the coming Friday. You couldn't be too careful. She wondered how long the trio would remain drinking: you couldn't blame men for hurrying home from work and those three had a few things on their minds.

Daniel Solomon heard from a friend that his son, Charlie, had been seen in Clapham Junction, and to be fair to the man he'd travelled there looking – all to no avail. It had been a nightmare: one he could have done without: Debenhams smashed in, alarms blaring, people (ordinary people like him) filling up their cars with looted goods, a man kicked on the ground by a woman who'd then run off with his wallet. Daniel tried to help him and waited until the ambulance got through the mob; and knowing – well, fearing – his son was right there in the mob. It didn't make Daniel feel good as a father, especially knowing what Vanda would have to say – and she'd said it when he phoned. Yes, phoned: he didn't feel like a face to face.

Phil Meadows had fared no better, but he'd not really tried; for him it was a complete silence. Knowing nothing of his son, knowing nothing of the woman, Lynn, who'd given birth to Carl, he ran out of contacts before he got back to Tottenham and decided he might as well see what was happening where he worked at the funfair. You never knew what might turn up. Sitting listening to Keith Willet, he wasn't to know that Carl and his friends had nicked more stuff than they knew what to do with and were desperately stashing it away in a graveyard in Croydon. Phil would come to learn this later and feel he might even have found them the van they needed to carry away the loot after things quietened down. He liked to be helpful, popular, and doing a kindness for his son once in a while would make him feel good.

Tom Drane had fared better: his son, Lewis, phoned him. He was desperate. He and a friend, Hugo, needed a van and they seemed in short supply. Lewis wouldn't explain why (he knew his dad would be disappointed with his behaviour) but did his dad know anyone who might have one? He did, of course: people in the parks department were bound to have a van, as Lewis knew full well, but Tom wasn't sure how it was going to be used.

"I can't get it now, Lewis," he'd explained, "It isn't the right time with these riots going on."

"No, no, all right, Dad," Lewis replied, disappointed but understanding.

The call had left Tom gutted: once more he'd failed as a father.

The three men sat for a while, each with his own thoughts, until the evening darkened into night and then, one by one, the three fathers drifted away. Left almost alone, wondering if his pub would find any more customers that night, Keith Willet pondered the state of affairs in Tottenham. He'd no idea where Alex was but knew his son would be fighting the rioters, right in the thick of it. Mabel hadn't stopped worrying – and talking about it – since the riots started. Worrying was one thing but talking was another: talking never solved anything and got on his nerves.

"If we don't get more customers than this, we might as well close at 9.30," said Mabel, looking concernedly round the virtually empty bar, "I'm off up."

"Umm!" replied Keith, feeling he'd make that decision: he was the landlord: it was his name over the door.

But Mabel was right: the bar did empty gradually, leaving, perhaps, half-a-dozen drinkers, and so Keith called "time" and the remainder of his regulars left for home.

He wandered out onto the street. It was a quiet night, the sounds of rioting no longer deafened Tottenham and Keith breathed in the warm air, relaxed, pleased with himself. He looked along the High Road, wondering whether Gabriel Pilgrim might pop in for a swift half. Keith felt he'd appreciate the company. He strolled up and down and found Gabriel's shop locked and shuttered; there were no lights to be seen. But there was always tomorrow; hopefully Alex would be home by then. He might even give the boy or Katy a ring, just to be sure.

Back inside The Blacksmith's Arms, he saw to a last tidy round, straightening a few chairs, adjusting the placing of a few tables, spreading a few beer mats. Was that a sound in the street? Alex calling in on his way home? Keith went to the door, saw nothing but heard the roar of drunken voices. He was familiar with the sound, welcomed it as any landlord might, especially on match days when Tottenham were playing at home; but this roar had an ugly edge. It was cacophonous. Shut the door, bolt it, turn out the lights! Offer no encouragement!

Keith had barely moved back into his pub when Simon Tippet and the Blades turned the corner, pouring out of an alleyway onto the main road like rats along a gutter. Ealing had been a godsend. Well, everywhere had been a godsend, especially Hackney. They'd come home from Ealing laden with booty, bags of it, to hide away in the warehouse where the gang met. Things were getting a bit sticky at the scene and it seemed shrewd to get away before the police started to gain control – if they did, if they could. Take a rest now, keep messaging on the Blackberry and start out fresh somewhere else, somewhere the pigs weren't expecting you to strike.

It was Miggs who saw Keith Willet retreat into the pub, Miggs who screamed out that she was thirsty and needed a drink, screaming with laughter all the time. For a moment, just a moment, Simon hesitated: this was his local, after all, or would be when he was old enough to drink legally. Besides, he thought he'd shaken Miggs off and, anyway, didn't like being ordered about by a woman. But he couldn't back down now, and anyway it was too late: the Blades saw their chance to create more mayhem.

An iron bar landed on the floor of the pub, shattering a window bearing Tottenham's emblem, a cockerel standing on a football, that had been there since 1882. Under the football was the motto *Audere est Facere*, one Latin phrase all locals knew, 'to dare is to do'. A hesitation of seconds, brought on by the shock, from the Blades and then they poured into the bar.

Keith stood braced, his arms and fists ready to deter the first ones in, but there were too many, and three of the gang bore him back and downwards, legs kicking, into one of the chairs he'd straightened.

"Bind him!" commanded the gang's leader, placing his thin legs akimbo in front of the landlord, "We don't want him interfering."

Keith Willet was quickly bound to the legs and arms of the chair by the gang members using their own belts for the job. Once the man was helpless, they stood back admiring their handiwork.

"Let's get to it!" said Simon, "it's been a hard day's night and we're thirsty."

"It's been a few hard days' nights," echoed one of the gang.

"And we'll need our belts back when we go," cried another, "they're new. It'd be a shame to lose them: they're expensive belts."

This last remark caused a great deal of amusement and the laughter was carried round the pub as they sought for what mischief they could do.

"You're scum," yelled Keith, "Not one of you is up to a decent day's work. Thieves, scum – the lot of you. Get out before I lose my temper."

Simon Tippet leapt down from the bar where he'd placed himself, a position he found commanding and convenient for the pulling of pints.

"You be careful, old man. You don't talk to us like that: we're in charge now. You mind your manners," he remarked, giving Keith an open-handed slap across the face, "Someone gag him. We've heard enough from him for one night."

"That's enough,"

The speaker was Dennis, the nineteen-year-old revolutionary who'd joined Simon's gang on their retreat from Ealing.

"I've said before, we've fucked up proper. We could have brought this government down. We should have marched on parliament. Not spent our time nicking goods."

"Who are you to say?"

"I'm saying – that's all."

Blades were out but none of the gang challenged him. Simon looked him up and down, suddenly realising that being leader of the gang was a tenuous position to hold, realising that this youth, only a few years older than himself, had something. He wasn't sure what but it wasn't worth fighting over.

"Let's enjoy ourselves," he called, "We can't stay here all night."

It was a call to action his gang seemed to understand and their enjoyment began. Each tap on the row of fifteen keg beers was turned on allowing their contents to spill out across the floor, except of course for the ones captured in glasses and poured down the throats of the revellers. Once the glasses had served their purpose they joined the flood of beer, shattering as they hit the floorboards. The bar now looked a little less inviting and Keith watched, holding back the tears that sprang to his eyes: his life was the pub, the pub was his life – these little bastards were killing him in ways they couldn't begin to understand.

Several chairs then went through the windows that gave light to the bar all year, hurled by the more aggressive of the louts while others turned their attention to the plentiful supply of world spirits that adorned the back of the bar and were reflected in the mirror. 'Not the mirror', thought Keith, 'the mirror is as old as the pub. Dickens probably saw himself in that mirror'. Such a consideration didn't seem to enter the heads of the Blade members, however, and soon a competition was in progress seeing who could do most damage before the mirror disintegrated completely. Bottles of spirits flew everywhere.

Many were drunk when they came and could take no more alcohol but this couldn't be admitted lest their manhood was doubted and so they collapsed on the short flight of stairs leading to the upper level, where they pretended to swig from the bottles but were actually pouring the whisky, gin, vodka and tequila down their fronts and onto the floor.

The snooker table, full-sized and one of The Blacksmith's Arms great attractions, was too good to ignore. It was surprising how much fun could be culled from running cues along the surface and ripping up the baize; and even more fun could be had by them attempting a game of snooker and watching the balls get caught up in the tears. Urinating in the pockets saved going to the toilets and brought cries of disgust from those still playing.

It was at this point that Mabel Willet, woken from her sleep, appeared on the stairs that led up to their private rooms. She was an attractive woman, no spring chicken but fresh of flesh and firm with a certain come-hither look in her eyes, not unusual in landladies and barmaids. This was not lost on the drunken youths rampaging around the bar. They stopped and looked, caught between two thoughts: here was their mum come to tell them off and here was a bit of all right I could fancy.

"What the hell's going on?" she asked, not raising her voice but giving her words the emphasis she thought their mothers might employ, if they bothered about their son's behaviour.

"Go back to your room, lady," said Dennis, once again taking charge, "You don't want to be down here."

Mabel looked him up and down: he was the one youth among them she did not know, and he had something about him, a menace the others lacked even with their knives brandished.

"He's right, Mabel," encouraged Keith from where he was tied on the chair.

It was a tense moment, one of those times when events can cool or take a nasty turn. Mabel had seen many similar and thought immediately of her daughter, Dolly, upstairs – Dolly who she'd told to stay in her room. She gave the room another cool gaze, turned, winking to her husband as she did so, and swept gracefully away.

Simon Tippet looked at Keith and then at Dennis; he wasn't sure what had happened except that another had, once again, taken over as leader.

It was Miggs who saw the danger, the threat to their festivities; she ran around the bar and yanked out the phone, including the extension cable that ran upstairs.

"She was going to phone the pigs." she yelled, "Didn't you see what she was up to? The pigsty is just up the road. Her son's a pig."

This set the tone for their final revelries of the night; the sign over the swing doors, **White Hart Lane Stadium** with the arrow was pulled down; photographs of players past and present were torn from their frames and jumped upon; scarves were retrieved from their hangings and wound round necks; trophies that had stood on shelves for decades were balanced on heads and noses or tossed from hand to hand; the framed testimonial from the man who felt the pub had saved him from watching Arsenal was trampled underfoot.

Finally, flags heralding **Spurs on Tour** danced off down the street, accompanied by laughter and song from voices more drunk than when they arrived, led by Simon Tippet himself.

Keith Willet slumped forward in the chair, unaware of Dennis standing behind him until he felt the young man release one of his hands.

"Get some sleep, old man," he said, "and don't be in too much hurry to contact the police. These boys live round here and can come back anytime. You wouldn't want that to happen, would you?"

There was no threat in his voice: it sounded more like a friendly warning.

Chapter 24

A PROUD SIGHT AND A NOBLE DAY

The lack of vans to carry away their booty – a sore point with Lewis Drane, Carl Meadows and their friends – had posed no problems for the looters who had snatched Mike Rudge at the garage they'd attempted to set on fire.

Driving away now from where the gang had forced him to take their loot, the nightmare was still very fresh in his mind. He looked down at the passenger seat of the van: a brand-new television set and a laptop stared him in the face. A present from his 'grateful customers': that had been the gang leader's comment. The rest of them thought it very funny. There they were giving away gifts. What the hell was he going to do with them?

He could still see himself running backwards and forwards between the warehouse and the van his arms full of stolen goods. It wasn't a sight he wanted to remember; it wasn't a proud one.

Get the van home and try to think. It might be best to stick to the truth: that would be easier. Hijacked at gunpoint, I had no choice. Getting rid of the stolen goods would just make him look more guilty. More guilty! He wasn't guilty of anything! But were the police going to believe him?

And there was the problem of all his boss's equipment that the gang had chucked out of the van: hundreds of pounds worth of gear. He couldn't explain how that happened if he tried to wriggle out of the whole business.

Mike Rudge was all of a sweat when he eventually arrived at the shoddy little flat he rented – well, sort of rented – from the bloke he sometimes worked for. Get the van out of the way in its usual spot, get inside, have a quick drink – only a quick one – and think. Think!

He could hear the cops knocking at the door, but it was only in his imagination. Mike found the bottle of whisky he kept for emergencies and medicinal purpose and took a long, grateful swig. Christ! What was he going to say? He sat in the shabby armchair by the window and looked out into the street. They'd have him on CCTV. Cameras everywhere, and they call it a free society.

"They threatened me with a gun. I was terrified for my life if I did not follow their orders. I had no choice. I had to drive them to the warehouse they were going to rob. All I was doing was looking after my boss's van and getting some petrol ready for tomorrow. I was kidnapped!"

Mike could hear himself making his excuses. Excuses! They weren't excuses! they were reasons! But the cops wouldn't see it like that: they'd remember him from his time in the cells. He had a record.

They'd have him up in the magistrate's court with all the CCTV pictures of him running backwards and forwards to his van. It would look as if he was helping them do the looting. And then it'd be bail and the long wait before he was back before the judge. He could hear her now:

"The message needs to get out that this kind of behaviour will not be tolerated. You face a lengthy custodial sentence."

He'd never been in prison and the thought wasn't an attractive one, not if you could believe what you see on television. You never knew who you might get to share a cell with, and there were some funny buggers inside.

Mike stood up and looked out of the window. There was still time to dump the 'gifts', but no, he'd thought that one through: it would make it look worse. Wait a minute – should he report what happened? Go to the police himself and explain? Tell the truth. It would look good and might even convince them not to arrest him. Mike reached for the phone in his pocket. But no. Sweat it out and the whole business might go away. He'd just have to explain to his boss where the equipment went but there was no need to involve the police.

No need at all but he could still hear the ring at the door. He was stuffed.

Chapter 25

RUMOUR OF THE DAY

David Cameron had his speech ready; it was going to be hard hitting as he had planned on the flight back from his holiday. The public would need reassuring before he faced Prime Minister's Question Time on Thursday. First, the press: they'd all be waiting outside Number 10. He stepped out onto the famous street ready to face the barrage of cameras; the equally famous podium was waiting.

"Good morning. I've come straight from a meeting of the Government's Cobra committee for dealing with emergencies where we've been discussing the action that we will be taking to help the police to deal with the disorder on the streets of London and elsewhere in our country.

"I've also met with the Metropolitan Police Commissioner and the Home Secretary to discuss this further and people should be in no doubt that we will do everything necessary to restore order to Britain's streets and to make them safe for the law-abiding.

"Let me, first of all, completely condemn the scenes that we have seen on our television screens and people have witnessed in their communities.

"These are sickening scenes - scenes of people looting, vandalising, thieving, robbing, scenes of people attacking police officers and even attacking fire crews as they're trying to put out fires. This is criminality, pure and simple, and it has to be confronted and defeated.

"I feel huge sympathy for the families who've suffered, innocent people who've been burned out of their houses and to businesses who have seen their premises smashed, their products looted and their livelihoods potentially ruined.

"I also feel for all those who live in fear because of these appalling scenes that we've seen on the streets of our country. People should be in no doubt that we are on the side of the law- abiding - law-abiding people who are appalled by what has happened in their own communities.

"As ever, police officers have shown incredible bravery on our streets in confronting these thugs, but it's quite clear that we need more, much more police on our streets and we need even more robust police action and it's that that I've been discussing in Cobra this morning.

"The Metropolitan Police Commissioner has said that, compared with the 6,000 police on the streets last night in London, there will be some 16,000 officers tonight. All leave within the Metropolitan Police has been cancelled. There will be aid coming from police forces up and down the country and we will do everything necessary to strengthen and assist those police forces that are meeting this disorder.

"There have already been 450 people arrested. We will make sure that court procedures and processes are speeded up and people should expect to see more, many more arrests in the days to come.

"I am determined, the Government is determined that justice will be done and these people will see the consequences of their actions.

"And I have this very clear message to those people who are responsible for this wrongdoing and criminality: you will feel the full force of the law and if you are old enough to commit these crimes you are old enough to face the punishment.

"And to these people I would say this: you are not only wrecking the lives of others, you're not only wrecking your own communities - you are potentially wrecking your own life too.

"My office this morning has spoken to the Speaker of the House of Commons and he has agreed that Parliament will be recalled for a day on Thursday so I can make a statement to Parliament and we can hold a debate and we are all able to stand together in condemnation of these crimes and also to stand together in determination to rebuild these communities.

"Now, if you'll excuse me, there is important work to be done. Thank you."

*

Theresa May, the Home Secretary, was relieved to hear the speech: sixteen thousand police officers on the streets would reassure the public: the Met should have done just that when the riots first broke out three days ago. 'Robust' was the word: that was what was needed from the police forces of the country. She and the Prime Minister were at one as far as that was concerned.

*

Edward Andrews, Doreen Manners and their fellow offices, cheered by their success with the help of the bus driver, Mehmet, on the Sydenham Road, made their way to Blackheath, a pretty village settled between Lewisham and Greenwich.

Across the common, Ed saw fellow police officers stretched out on the grass: they were exhausted, some talking amiably, others sleeping. He stepped down from his carrier and sat next to a group on the grass.

"It seems we're winning the fight," he said, adding, "slowly."

One of the officers resting smiled up at him. Both men were relieved: the past four days had taken the stuffing out of them; it was good to be able to rest if only for a short time, before the next call came.

When it did, the message was from a friend, a fellow officer: a call of concern rather than a call to action on Ed's phone.

"Have you seen the television pictures, Ed? Croydon's in flames. You've got off lightly."

Ed wasn't sure he agreed with his friend, not after what had happened at Bromley Road Retail Park. He put the phone back in his pocket and listened to the voices coming in over the police radio. It was still going on, the rioting: elsewhere there was no let up. Ed looked across at Doreen, still sitting ready in the carrier. Then, he slept.

*

Nancy Mayhew was on her way to work; it was a six-mile cycle ride to Brixton each day and she enjoyed the exercise, which was doing her good, and didn't see why a bunch of hoodlums should stand in her way.

As she passed a housing estate near her home, a rock hit her handlebars. Nancy braked and looked at where the rock had been thrown. A boy whose age she estimated at about seven years, stood grinning at her. He seemed to be alone.

"What do you think you are doing?" she demanded.

The boy continued to grin and immediately threw another rock; this time it struck Nancy on the arm. And then, as though answering the call, a group of what she supposed to be the boy's friend appeared apparently from nowhere. They were all kids: not one of them could be over the age of twelve. Stones and bottles of water smashed all around her, some hitting the road, others her bike, soaking both. Nancy felt quickly through her handbag: her phone would be somewhere and she needed to call the police.

"Call the police, you fucking stupid bitch," they yelled, "they're not going to do anything."

Nancy walked to the street corner, only a few yards, and bumped into a group of teenagers led by about twenty women.

"We're going on the rob," they screeched, "It's a happy atmosphere. Lots of people laughing and giggling, just picking up whatever they like. Running in, running out! It's a happy vibe."

Nancy watched them rush past. The sense of anarchy was palpable.

*

Benjamin wasn't sure what was to happen next. The man with the gun was still pointing it at him and the other man in the car. Was he going to shoot them both? Benjamin wasn't sure but his mum and his counsellor had always told him not to panic if he faced a difficult situation: the sensible thing to do was to remain calm and think things through quietly.

The other man, the one who'd arrived with the second television set, seemed terrified. He was shaking from head to foot. Benjamin remembered that phrase from a book he'd read, a graphic novel where the words were easy to read because there were not too many of them.

Suddenly the man with the gun looked up, over and beyond Benjamin's car, and turned quickly away. In fact, he ran, jumped into his own car that sped off fast. Benjamin wondered why. Why was the man with the gun frightened: he had the gun.

Benjamin's answer came rapidly in the shape of a police officer who tapped on the driver's window. The other man opened his rear door and stepped out of their car. He was telling the policeman something but Benjamin couldn't hear what he said. The policeman opened the boot of their car, the Ford Focus, and looked inside. He smiled and stepped round to Benjamin's side of the car. Benjamin was in the passenger seat because it was he who knew the registration of the car they were chasing.

"Step outside, son," the policeman said, "and keep your hands where I can see them."

The policeman didn't seem perturbed by the driver, dead against the steering wheel.

Chapter 26
PHILOSOPHICAL MEDITATION

Mary Rudge, accompanied by Gabriel Pilgrim, stood silently at Reeves Corner. There was a bus stop there, named after the furniture shop that had been a landmark of the area and that had now been burnt to the ground, and it seemed a sensible place to stand. It was quieter now: the rioters, looters and arsonists had passed on.

The fires continued to burn but now the firefighters were able to reach and subdue them. Scattered everywhere, covering every inch of ground, Mary gazed on broken bricks, shattered glass, torn timbers and crushed masonry. Her nostrils were invaded by the bitter smell of smoke; it was everywhere, clinging to the uniforms of the firefighters and police officers, hanging in the air, rising from the shattered shops and homes.

Many of the residents hung about trying to believe what had happened to their homes, peering through exhausted eyes at the places where, once, they'd sat and watched television or rested after a day's work. Cold and tired they stood, the bitter smoke curling around them.

A group of police officers sat resting against what was left of a burned wall. Gabriel could see that these people – who, he guessed, had been fighting the rioters for days – were spent. They had nothing left to give; some were dozing fitfully, others enjoying a cigarette, one man lay like a corpse along the remains of the wall itself. They seemed nonplussed, as though waiting for further orders from a higher authority that had deserted them.

As he and Mary watched, wondering what to do next in their search for Benjamin, the door of a nearby pub opened and the landlady came out carrying a large tray of bacon sandwiches and mugs of hot tea. She crossed over to the officers who sat up, not only relieved but overjoyed that someone seemed to care.

She looked over to Mary and Gabriel.

"You don't live round here, love?"

"No," replied Mary, "I'm looking for my son. He's autistic and I fear he may have been caught up in all this awfulness."

A couple of the officers looked across at Mary, little sympathy in their eyes: 'caught up' wasn't something for which they had much truck.

"Would you like a sandwich?"

"No, I'm all right thank you but ... a cup of tea would be most welcome."

The landlady caught Gabriel's eye and smiled.

"I'll bring you a sandwich as well," she said, seeing that a man of his Pickwickian build must enjoy his food.

It was while she drank the hot tea, scalding hot and welcome, and while Gabriel tucked into a sandwich, that Mary came to a decision.

"I want you to go back, Gabriel," she said, "I'll stay in case Ben turns up, which I think he will, but there's just a chance he did get home and it would be nice for someone to be there. I'll give you my key and if you or Martha would go round and check it would put my mind at rest."

There wasn't much Gabriel could say: reluctant as he was to leave Mary at a place so forlorn, a place where there was a chance, he felt, that the louts might return; her manner was so cut and dried, he was left speechless. The Tube system was still running – unbelievably, he thought – and so it wouldn't take him long.

"My phone still has some battery left," said Mary, "if you'd give me a ring when you know, I'd be grateful."

"If you're sure, Mrs Rudge."

"Yes, I'm sure, Gabriel," she replied, adding (since she guessed he was uneasy about leaving her), "I'll be all right, and if Benjamin is wandering around lost here somewhere, at least they'll be somebody for him. It's getting towards daylight: I'll be OK."

Gabriel squeezed her arm and set off for the Overground station.

Mary was as sure as she could be that her son was either at home or still in Croydon. If the Overground trains had been running during the night, he might have gone home; if not, he would have stayed where he was because that was what his mother had told him to do. 'If you're ever lost, Ben, stay put and I will find you'; it was like a mantra.

While she stood, considering her position, wondering how long a wait might be – if, indeed, there was a wait at all – an old man – Mary guessed hm to be about 80 years old – came and stood by her side, not to be acknowledged necessarily but just for the closeness, the company.

The ashes were still smouldering on what had once been Reeves Furniture Store and it was into these ashes that the old man stared, into the ashes and the rubble.

"What kind of people would do this?" he asked, quietly, "Our shop was the hub of the community. We've weathered so much, only to have our shop smashed up by people in our own community. I'm shocked to the core. I've been in hospital … and I don't know how I'm here today.

"The shop has been in my family for one hundred and forty-four years. It survived the Great Depression and Hitler's bombs. I began working here just after the Second World War. I was sixteen.

"Children used to be well-behaved then but these days it doesn't seem to be the case. A lot of them leave school without the basic skills. And sometimes parents aren't doing their job. You see police going around town and they're too afraid to do anything. One policeman told me he's not actually allowed to do anything. We need Churchill to come down and sort it all out.

"When I was a boy there was so much more of a sense of law and order in the community. There weren't the troublesome types and we'd all be home by ten o'clock."

Mary didn't think she'd ever seen such sadness cast by anyone's face or eyes. The old man smiled at her, a smile of sympathy and resignation; and she realised that he must be Maurice Reeves, whose family owned what was now the smouldering ruin in front of them.

Chapter 27
TIDINGS EVERYWHERE

Back in Hackney, Jeff Dale watched small groups of rioters ran around the nearby streets; they would need tackling – the night wasn't over. He and his colleagues had been too short of manpower to tackle these rioters as they should have been tackled. Certainly, they'd saved Hackney from a worse fate than it might have suffered but the residences, the shops, the vehicles and the police officers involved had all been damaged by these hooligans; he was only surprised that the police casualties had not been worse.

Jeff was annoyed and not alone in his annoyance; there'd needed to be better discipline and better training. None of his colleagues on the streets had been prepared for what they faced; and why hadn't they been called for sooner? Why had it taken senior officers so long to get to grips with the situation? He'd been kicking his heels for three days before he got the call to action.

But the job was now done – at least for the time being – and later in the day he'd be home.

*

Still at home in Guildford, the police officer friend of Edward Andrews still sat waiting, watching the television and hoping for the call to action; like Jeff Dale, he could not understand why he was still sitting in his lounge enjoying – no, not enjoying! – a beer while his colleagues fought for their lives on the streets of London. What was it with the top brass:

were they frightened to react in case they were accused of over-reacting? It had happened before they'd faced such criticism: do as little as possible and be accused of under-reacting, get stuck in and be accused of over-reacting! The public needed to make up their minds what they wanted from the force.

He heard a knock on his front door as he sat brooding. When he opened it one of his neighbours stood there holding a cottage pie she'd made. The old girl seemed startled to see him.

"Oh, I thought you'd be in London," she said, "I was worried your family might be worried about you and I thought I'd call round with this pie I made."

The policeman stood speechless, looking at his neighbour, a lady he'd known for years. He was unsure what to say.

"Haven't you seen the riots on the telly?" she asked.

"Yes," he replied, slowly, ashamed to be seen standing there in his dressing gown.

"They said on the telly that all police leave had been cancelled," the old lady persisted.

"We weren't called in," replied the officer, "More than that, it was made quite clear by senior officers that if we did turn up to lend a hand we'd never be allowed to work overtime ever again."

"Oh! It doesn't seem to make sense, does it?"

"No," replied the officer, "but thanks for the pie. I'm sure we'll all enjoy it tomorrow. And who knows, I might be doing some good by then."

He smiled: one his neighbour returned. They were grim smiles, suiting the occasion and the times they found themselves living in.

*

"Feral rats!"

The owner of the Ealing baby boutique railed at her neighbours, sharing her misery with them, neighbours – some shop owners like her – who shared her anger.

Behind her, high quality babywear littered the floor of her shop – booties, baby-gros among the debris. Windows were smashed, drawers had been torn form their chests and lay scattered, broken among the clothing.

"It's just mindless destruction. I've spent seven years building up my business and in one night a bunch of thugs tear it apart. What is going wrong with this country? They were mainly young teenagers. What were their parents doing letting them out? Feral rats! There's no other word for them!"

*

'Feral rats' was a cry taken up by many, politicians among them. Ken Clarke lashed out at a "feral underclass" and Boris Johnson, the Mayor of London, caught hold of the phrase, lamenting a "feral criminal underclass".

Many politicians, particularly those attached to the government, complained of the 'steady rise of an underclass'. It was a phrase that captured the imagination and tongues of the press and the public. Ian Duncan Smith, who had done much to develop his party's thinking about the 'broken society' referred to the riots as the day "the inner city came to call on the rest of society".

Others, David Lammy, the MP for Tottenham among them, questioned whether ripping into what political leaders were calling "feral families" provided any real answers.

*

A journalist, fresh from Ealing, sitting at his word processor, was unsure where to start. He'd seen it all and what had struck him most forcefully was that the riots had not just happened: they'd been planned. Many of the looters had agreed through text messages to meet in Ealing after 9 o'clock because they knew riots were being planned throughout the city and that the police would be thinly stretched.

Cars were being filled with stolen goods on a well-organised, relay system. This, he decided, was nothing to do with government cuts or deprivation, which was what many of the thugs were bleating about: this was criminality, pure and simple.

Indeed, there seemed to be a system of hierarchy: senior criminals would wait in their BMWs while gangs of young runners brought them goods to inspect. The gangmasters from all over London were capitalising on the breakdown of law and order 'to steal as much as they could as fast as they could'. The journalist had his sources; he was sure of his facts and what he'd witnessed; it was time to get it into print for next day's papers.

*

Deputy Assistant Commissioner of the Metropolitan Police, Stephen Kavanagh, admitted that his officers "had never been so stretched". He apologised to Londoners.

"It has been suggested that plastic bullets might be used for the first time on mainland Britain," said one journalist, "Is there any truth in this?"

"Non-lethal ammunition will be deployed if considered absolutely necessary," replied Mr Kavanagh, "but the force is not going to throw away 180 years of policing *with* the community", stressing the 'with', "London is bloody resilient and it will get through this. We will get through this together."

*

David Cameron, the Prime Minister, having left his wife on holiday to return to London, invited his old friend, his fellow Etonian, Boris Johnson round to 10 Downing Street to enjoy a meal together. They, were, in fact, in the airy flat above number 11. David was a good cook, a fact little known to the general public, and he was happy to share melon and

Parma ham followed by pan-fried steaks and potatoes with his colleague.

It was important that the mayor did not stray too far 'off-message': these were tense and unpredictable times as the scenes being played out across the country on the television screens showed only too clearly. It would be good to bounce a few thoughts off each other as to what the violence meant and how they might best respond.

*

Social networking sites, official and otherwise, were at work, naming and shaming friends, relatives and neighbours who had taken part in the criminality. The backlash against the rioters and looters had started. 'Catch a Looter' was the call of the day.

Footage taken in Peckham showed a youth running with a large box, a young man with headphones dangling from his neck, a hooded gang running furiously, a boy cycling with a basket of goods, a woman carrying an armful of tops still on their hangers.

From Croydon came photographs of a boy keeping watch as his friend tugged at a shop's security grill, a hoodie-wearing youth, his face clearly visible, a group of young men apparently plotting together, a young woman on the run.

Photographs from Hackney showed a youth laughing as he hurled rocks at the police, a boy poised to swing a plank at a police car, two youths acting as lookouts while their friends looted.

Commander Simon Foy, who is leading the operation to catch the yobs, made his position very clear:

"Those who have or intend to go out and commit violent, criminal acts should be warned. We will have photographs and evidence that we will use to identify you and bring you to justice."

*

Members of The Association of British Insurers were deep in discussions regarding how they might alleviate the estimated £200 million riot damage bill. There was a little known 1886 Riot Damages Act that allowed insurance companies, individuals and businesses to reclaim their losses from local police authorities, funded by the public.

The ABI decided that its members would use the Act to make the maximum possible claims against the police.

"When a riot happens, police compensation schemes are activated to cover organisations and individuals against losses that they could not possibly have predicted," said a spokesman.

Chapter 28

EXCITED BY PORTENTOUS NEWS

Benjamin Rudge had been sitting in the same room for more than two hours, ever since the police took him from the car where the stranger was shot dead. Benjamin answered the questions the police asked him, truthfully, and he did not see why they kept asking the same ones over and over again. He always told the truth. Didn't the police know he always told the truth?

It was a small room and it was bare: there was only the table they made him sit at on a hard chair and he had nowhere to look except at the police officers on the other side of the table. One was a man and the other a woman. The woman had just come in and it was she who was asking the same questions he'd already answered.

"Now, let's go over what you've said again, shall we, Benjamin?"

She was being friendly – or trying to be friendly: he could tell that by the tone of her voice. But she was not being truthful because she did not mean what she said. 'Shall we' was a question. She was asking him if he wanted to answer the same questions again, but she was not really giving him a choice.

"You told us that the man pushed you into the car."

Was that a question? She knew that was what he said. Why was she telling him what he'd said? She sounded like his therapist. Benjamin felt himself getting hot and angry, and he knew he mustn't let himself feel that way because he might have 'one of his turns'. That was a phrase his mother used when she wanted him to feel good about himself and not upset at what he'd done, like that time in the cinema when he'd raved at her.

The policewoman sat looking at him as if she expected him to say something but how could you answer a question that wasn't a question?

"Well?"

That was a question: he could tell by her manner, and she was getting upset. He could see that from the look in her eyes and the way her mouth tensed. She didn't like being ignored. His uncle had told him that women never like being ignored and that it was best to go along with them. Benjamin thought his uncle didn't mean to actually 'go along' in the sense of going with them, but just to agree with them because then there were no arguments. His uncle, like a lot of adults, didn't really mean exactly what he said; language, the way people used it, was confusing.

"Why did you get into the car with the man?"

"I didn't get in. He pushed me in."

"Why?"

"I told you. I knew the registration number of the other car."

"And you'd never met the man before?"

"No."

"Until you asked him the way to the Tube station?"

"The Overground station."

The Overground and the Tube were not the same. There were the Overground and the Underground and the Tube was really the Underground. It wasn't really a tube: that was just the way people described it. And the man had not been helpful when he asked.

Benjamin felt his mind going, thinking about the man. He didn't really understand what had happened. One moment the man was sitting at the wheel of the car and the next blood was pouring from his head. Red blood! Benjamin remembered the redness of the blood and he didn't like red. That was why he'd thrown that plate of tomato pasta at the wall and upset his dad's friend.

He remembered getting out of the car to get away from the colour red and he'd run. Down the road, between the cars: and people had been yelling and shouting at him and then the policeman had grabbed him, hurting his arm and pulling him to the ground.

"There's no use you trying to run away, son! You've got questions to answer!"

He'd been frightened when the policeman grabbed and yelled at him. The police were angry and they were angry at him, and he didn't know why. Questions are all right when you know the answers like in a quiz, but these weren't those-sort-of-questions. They didn't have answers.

"You said the man threw the television set into the boot of your car and then pushed you into the front seat and then your car shot off along the street after the other car," said the policewoman.

Benjamin didn't remember saying that – not in those words. 'Shot off' – did he use those words? No one was shot – not at that moment. 'Shot off' was a metaphor. His uncle had explained that metaphors had an origin in some kind of activity but that they should not be taken literally.

"Do you mind if I write things down in my notebook?" he asked.

The policeman leaned forward, his face full of anger. Benjamin thought he was going to hit the tabletop.

"Look son – can we cut out the comedy. We make the notes – not you! You don't seem to realise that you're in trouble: associating with criminals, driving off with stolen goods. We could be charging you."

"My mum told me to make notes of things I don't understand," replied Benjamin, "and then she can explain what they mean."

The police had tried to phone his mum but said there was no one at home and when they tried her mobile there was no answer.

"What don't you understand, Benjamin?" asked the policewoman with a stern look at her colleague.

"You said 'shot off' but there was no shot until … until …"

He couldn't finish the sentence; all he could see was the red blood flowing over the steering wheel, and he remembered hearing someone scream and it was him.

"We're trying to get the truth out of you," continued the policewoman, "and that's why we keep asking the same questions. Now – you said, and I quote from my notes: *two men stepped out of the Peugeot, and one was holding a gun. He came towards my car, pointed the gun and fired.* Is that true?"

Benjamin didn't like being told what he'd said, and he didn't like people who talked *at* him. He couldn't understand what these police officers were thinking. He had told them what happened. Why did they keep repeating what he'd told them?

"I'm very hungry," he said, "Can I have something to eat?"

People usually understood if he was hungry and it had been a long time since he had eaten. The policeman looked at him with the same expression he had on his face when he didn't want him to get out his notebook.

"We might run to a sandwich, son. Would you fancy a cup of tea to go with it?"

Both police officers laughed when he said that – the man and the woman. Benjamin knew they must be laughing at him. They didn't understand.

"I don't drink tea," he replied, "or any fizzy drinks. They're stimulants and upset my medicine. I only drink bottled water and could the sandwiches be with brown bread, please?

The policeman looked him up and down for several seconds and Benjamin thought he was going to hit the table but he didn't; the policewoman waved her arm just a bit and the policeman went off, Benjamin thought to get the sandwiches.

"How did you feel when the man shot your friend?" asked the policewoman.

Benjamin didn't know how he felt but the man wasn't his friend, just someone he had asked the way to the Overground station.

"Were you frightened?"

"He wasn't my friend. I've already told you that, and I didn't feel anything."

"You ran away because you were frightened."

"No, I didn't. I ran away because I don't like red. I was only frightened when the policeman grabbed me. I don't like being grabbed."

Benjamin could feel the screaming building up in his body. He didn't want to have one of his turns but he was going to do just that if these police officers didn't stop going round and round in circles.

Chapter 29
CONDEMNED THE CIVIL POWER

With the looters dispersed in Walworth, Alex Willet's unit was directed to Lewisham. Reports suggested Lewisham was calm but no chances were being taken: the police were already coming under heavy criticism from those – mainly politicians – who felt the force had fallen down on the job.

In Lewisham, mobile patrols were to be the order of the day, but they arrived noisily – blue lights flashing, sirens wailing – and spent the afternoon driving through streets that were silent and with not a single bottle thrown at their carrier.

Respectable semi-detached houses lined the highways; it was almost as though nothing unusual had occurred until Alex saw, ahead of his unit, a bunch of about one hundred middle-aged men marching up the hill towards them.

"What the hell's going on?" he asked, mainly to himself.

"Football hooligans?" suggested one of his colleagues.

"English Defence League?" suggested another.

"Everyone out! Cordon the road. We need to hold this lot back until we know what they're up to."

His colleagues in position, Alex moved forward to address the men. At once, he smelt the beer on their breaths.

"We're here to help," explained one of the men, a burly character dressed only in a T-shirt (indicating he'd been a student at the University of Minnesota, a claim Alex suspected to be some distance from the truth) and jeans.

"Right," exclaimed another, "We're protecting our neighbourhood."

A laudable intention no doubt, thought Alex, but not one welcomed by him and his colleagues.

"We're on your side," said the man who'd first spoken, "We know you're pushed."

These weren't Sikhs guarding their place of worship or Turkish shop owners protecting their means of livelihood; if any of these men met what they perceived as troublemakers, trouble would be intensified, not mollified.

"We're heading for your town centre," explained Alex, "It's best you make your way there, too."

It was an order but couched in matey terms; Alex had no time for vigilantes but equally no desire to raise their hackles. The bunch of beery men dispersed gradually, making their way back down the hill.

The centre had seen days of rioting and looting and the local people were determined it should stop; if the police couldn't do it alone, then help was on its way. "Protecting our manor". It was a cry the police officers heard throughout that afternoon and evening. Occasionally, someone would break into a run and others would follow, unsure of what they were doing, where they were going or why. It was a situation heading for confrontation, violence and disaster.

Feelings were running high – the quiet majority angry at the antics of the few. What was that Ian Duncan Smith had said about the riots – 'The day the inner city came to call on the rest of society'. Yes, and these men and the other locals were 'the rest'.

The evening wore on and the streets filled with locals, journalists, camera crews and police. It was a tense night, especially after all Alex and his colleagues had been through. These people were prepared to back the police, they were on the side of law and order; but it wouldn't remain so. If the rioters arrived yet again, the outcome would be anything but lawful.

*

David Cameron, along with the Home Secretary, Theresa May, had condemned the civil powers, but Sir Hugh Orde,

President of the Association of Chief Police Officers, was having none of it.

"The fact that politicians chose to come back from their holidays is an irrelevance in terms of the tactics that were by then developing. The more robust policing tactics you saw were not the function of political interference; they were a function of the numbers being available to allow the chief constables to change their tactics," he claimed on BBC2s *Newsnight*.

Sir Hugh's comments followed claims by the Home Secretary that she had told police chiefs to cancel all leave and claims by Mr Cameron that he had been behind the Met's decision to raise its deployment of officers from 6,000 on Monday the 8th to 16,000 today.

"It's the Commissioner's responsibility to cancel leave," said Deputy Assistant Commissioner Stephen Kavanagh, wading in, "and, as I understand, that's exactly what happened. The decision was taken over the weekend before she returned from holiday."

*

While public recriminations raged, looted shopkeepers stood in the ruins of their life's work.

"What we need," cried one man whose Hackney shop had been looted on Monday 8th, "is long term support, welcome though the government's offer of £20 million is. For too long, shoplifting and violence against retailers has been routinely ignored., allowing lawless youths to feel they are untouchable. The appalling scenes we have seen over the past few days are the inevitable culmination. London shopkeepers need the same zero-tolerance policing we've now seen. Sentences given to these rioters should represent a genuine deterrent. If this doesn't happen, retailers will desert London's worst-hit high streets, and this would be a huge loss to everyone: shops are the glue that hold our communities together."

*

His words were echoed in the *Daily Mail* by one of the Turkish shopkeepers who had defended their homes and businesses with baseball bats, snooker cues and chair legs when a mob of twenty teenagers smashed windows and threatened residents:

"We ran after them down the street towards the police line so they were cornered, but the police didn't do anything, and they just let them go."

His words were corroborated by a kebab shop owner:

"The police were telling us to go inside and not to chase them, but it was only down to us that they went away. We can't rely on the police to stop them attacking our shops."

*

Letters to the Editor of the *Evening Standard* joined the general outcry:

In reply to Michael Smith, who suggests the rioters have been led astray by Grand Theft Auto – why don't we just blame games for everything? Perhaps the recession is because of the bankers' fascination with Monopoly? Heaven forbid we should expect parents to try raising their children properly.

David Cameron's 'broken society' is now a 'sick society'. What next – a society in the emergency ward? A society on life support? Luckily, Cameron's brother-in-law is a doctor.

I know everyone is a bit down at the moment, but cheer up, we have got the Notting Hill Carnival at the end of the month.

*

Abroad, the criticism was as vehement: The Spanish newspapers, *El Pais* and *El Mundo*, commented respectively:

Far from reacting quickly, the Government was missing during the crucial hours and has responded with a vagueness which has failed to calm the violence. Cameron's credibility has suffered a new reverse in these days of fury.

That is why the British authorities – in fact, you could say all of Europe – should bend over backwards to stop these violent outbreaks which, if they get worse, would have unforeseeable consequences.

*

At home, well-known public figures made their views known:

People steal and are not punished for it; they do not work, yet receive money ... Those that do want to work at school are held back while resources are directed towards those who don't ... and because young people are denied a decent education, those who should have been leaders at school ... are leaders of gangs. (Norman Tebbit, Former Tory Cabinet Minister)

The kids know what they are doing is wrong, but they don't care because they feel so disenfranchised, so ignored, so marginalised. They see the disturbances as a form of revenge against a society that has neglected them. (Camila Batmanghelidjh, Founder of Children's Charity, Kids Company)

These young people will never be won over by lectures in morality from a political elite that has promoted a culture of rampant greed, commercialism and entitlement as reflected by bankers' bonuses and MPs' expenses. In one sense, the looters of trainers and TVs were simply endorsing the self-centred values of our age. (Professor David Wilson, Criminologist)

*

Alex Willet – back at Tottenham police station where the rioting had started, eager to remove his riot gear and return home to Katy and Louise, where he knew he would find that life was normal somewhere – listened in horror as his friend, Andy Warner (the older, experienced policeman for whom he had huge respect and who held the line with him on that first night of the riots) told him what had happened at The Blacksmith's Arms.

Alex had planned, as always, to drop in on his parents on the way home. It was his daily ritual, done as a duty to visit his parents but also as a pleasure because the pub had been his home for so long and he liked what it represented in the community he policed.

But now, what was he to find and how was he to react? While he'd been away policing his society, his own people had been pillaged.

WEDNESDAY, AUGUST 10TH

Chapter 30
A HASTY BARRICADE

Alex made his decision before he arrived at the pub and saw the smashed window. His father had refused to clear the damage; Keith Willet wanted his neighbours to wake up to what had happened to their local. Tottenham's emblem, the cockerel on the football, lay shattered in several pieces, having fallen outwards onto the pavement. 'To dare is to do. You bastards – I'll do you' were his thoughts as Alex pushed open the familiar swing doors and walked into the bar.

His father was sitting on one of the chairs, streaks of tears on his face.. How long he'd sat in his home, his life, Alex had no idea. Since the early hours? The old man was broken; there was no fight left in him, Alex could see.

"Dad?"

He didn't know what else to say. His father wasn't one for commiserations when things went wrong; he was from the 'get on with it' generation, but his son could tell that the old man had had enough. He wasn't going to be getting on with anything unless … Alex left the thought quietly.

"Where's Mum?"

Mabel Willet answered for herself from the top of the stairs that led to their private rooms. She'd been for clearing up the mess left by the yobs and, normally, would have had her own way, but not today. Mabel knew her husband well enough to leave well alone.

"I'm here," she said, her voice resigned to the destruction of her home, "Pleased to see you, son."

Alex met his mother partway down the stairs and hugged her. The hug seemed to give him the courage to do the same for his father, to overcome the old man's natural reserve. His arms round his father's shoulders, Alex sat in a chair close to him.

"Have you any idea who did this?" he asked, "Any names?"

"What use would it be?" responded Keith.

"Every use."

The old man looked his son in the face for the first time since he'd entered the pub.

"You think you could catch them?"

"I know."

Containment: that was the thing. Don't get angry, get even. Alex had seen so much over the past four days that it was difficult to reach some kind of understanding about what had happened, but seeing his own home in this state cleared his head, focussed his thoughts. Understanding could wait; the law could act immediately.

"There was a girl with them. I've seen her around with Martha's daughter, Dolly," said Mabel, "They sit in the garden sometimes with a coke. Thin girl – plain as you like, with loud laugh. Screams a lot."

"Right," replied Alex, "Time to knock on a few doors."

Martha Pilgrim answered immediately. She'd been up all night worrying about Gabriel and Mary Rudge and when Gabriel arrived, explaining that he was going to sit in Mary's house and wait by the phone in case Benjamin called, Martha just couldn't get back to sleep.

When Alex explained what he wanted, Martha woke her daughter and gave her Mabel Willet's description. Dolly knew immediately who the girl might be. Meghan Marks was plain – some said ugly, but that was unkind.

"I don't know where she lives, Mum."

"Then find out! Make a few calls. You're always on your Blackberry. Get on it now."

Dolly half-tutted, thought better of it and began punching numbers into her phone.

"You say you're dad's pub has been smashed up? How is he and Mabel?"

"You can imagine, Mrs Pilgrim."

"Yes, of course. Is there anything we can do to help?"

"Go round and ask. I'm sure they'll be grateful. There's a big clean up ahead of us all."

"She's not answering, Mum."

"Do you know where she lives, Dolly?" asked Alex.

There was a moment's hesitation but Dolly knew she was in enough trouble already without adding to it by covering for a friend; and within a few minutes of arriving at the Pilgrims house, he was knocking on the door of Meghan Marks' parents.

"She's in bed, constable," the girl's mother replied in answer to Alex's request.

"Just a quiet word, Mrs Marks," said Alex, "I think your daughter might be able to help me sort out a local disturbance."

"I'm sure Meghan will help if she can. She was late in last night and went straight to bed. I'll get her for you. Come in and sit down. Would you like a cup of tea? You're Keith Willet's boy, aren't you? Everyone likes you and your dad."

Alex wasn't sure whether Meghan might share her mother's opinion and when the girl emerged bleary-eyed in her dressing gown, he was sure of the fact. She was one of those plain girls who'd do anything for a boyfriend; feeling like that about herself wasn't likely to lead her into good company. Alex felt sorry for her.

"I don't know nothing," she said before being asked.

"I think you do, Meghan. We have people who saw you in the pub last night. Who were you with?"

"No one."

"You never said you were in the pub! I've told you! You're too young to drink."

"Who were you with, Meghan?" asked Alex for the second time, softly.

"It was that Simon Tippet, wasn't it? I told you he was no good. What did they do, constable?"

"It'll get me into all sorts of bother," wailed Meghan.

"Who's this Simon Tippet?" asked Alex.

"He's a no good," replied Mrs Marks.

"He's not!" screamed Meghan.

"He was with you last night," asked Alex, more as a statement than a question.

Meghan nodded, loath to give a direct answer.

"Where does he live?"

"I can't say."

"It'll be easier for you to tell me now than down at the station, Meghan."

"He'll know."

"He needn't. We'll have other ways of tracing him."

Alex's reassurance seemed to calm the girl and she muttered an address."

"Thank you, Mrs Marks and you, Meghan. We'll be in touch."

It was a sad house Alex left – the mother and daughter at odds with each other. Life wasn't easy for some people.

Out in the street, strolling and thinking, Alex realised he faced a dilemma. He wasn't the best person to pursue this matter: he had a vested interest, a personal stake, in the result.

Less than thirty minutes later, Andy Warner, accompanied by two other officers, was knocking on the door of Simon Tippet's parents.

"He's not here!" snapped Mrs Tippet, part-opening the door.

"And so where might he be, Mrs Tippet?" asked Andy.

"How should I know?"

"He's your son, he's only sixteen years old."

"What's going on?"

A second face appeared beside that of Mrs Tippet, a face full of bluster, a face that spoke of the man's liking for a beer or two at any time of the day.

Andy Warner thought the couple looked well-matched: both, he thought, enjoyed the indoor life. Despite a wonderful summer, both were pale, suggesting they spent little time outside in the sunshine; both had obviously been roused from their bed at an earlier hour than they found comfortable.

"We're looking for your son, Mr Tippet. There was a bit of a disturbance last night and we think he might be able to help us."

"He was in all night," replied Mr Tippet.

"I thought you said he wasn't here."

"He went out early."

Already, a hasty barricade of lies was being erected. Andy liked that: one lie always demanded another and soon the whole edifice of deceit would fall.

"Perhaps we could talk inside?" Andy suggested, adding "We don't want to involve anyone else, do we," mindful as he was of the neighbours.

Once installed in the Tippet's kitchen, Andy Warner began dismantling the barricade.

"You said your son was in all night, Mr Tippet. What time did he get in?"

"He never went out. We were watching television."

"So, the people who saw him in The Blacksmith's Arms were mistaken?"

"Who's told you Simon was in The Blacksmith's Arms?"

"We have a number of people who said they saw him there."

"He might just have popped out," suggested Mrs Tippet, aware that constant denials might be no way forward.

"I said he was in all night," snapped her husband.

"Yeah, but he might just have popped out for a bag of crisps or something," Mrs Tippet insisted, adding "He doesn't drink – at least not in the house. You don't know what they might get up to when they're with their mates."

"He was with his mates, last night was he?" asked Andy.

"He might have been. Yeah, I believe he did pop out for a few minutes," replied Mr Tippet.

"So, who are these mates?"

It was going to be a long morning but Andy Warner had plenty of time and was enjoying himself, enjoying himself far more than when he faced those three men in balaclavas with machetes in their hands four days previously.

Chapter 31

STRONG VIEWS

LOOTERS ARE SCUM

The young woman's summer top said it all. With her blonde hair tied back and her broom in hand, she was ready for the clean-up. She'd written the words neatly with a black felt-tip pen before she left home, accompanied by friends and neighbours.

The people of Clapham arrived for their second day armed with brooms and wheelbarrows. Memories of Boris Johnson, their mayor, arriving the previous day brandishing a broom was still fresh in the minds of many, as were the jeers with which they greeted him. He was not Mr Popularity at the moment, fun though he was at times: according to YouGov approval ratings, the Mayor of London rated only 24%.

"Scum's the word for those louts armed with their bricks and bats," yelled one woman, "We'll show them! The brooms mightier than the baseball bat!"

Her comments were met with laughter. It was a joyful sound. They felt like an army on the march.

"It's the spirit of the Blitz," said one young woman to a Daily Mail reporter, a woman far too young to remember the Blitz, but the spirit was with her.

"Roll up your sleeves and get on with the job!"

It was a chorus taken up by many as they set to clearing the damage and the debris left by the rioters. Twitter had aided the rioters; it was now aiding the clean-up.

"We just came back from a tour," said Ricky Wilson of the rock band, Kaiser Chiefs, "and it was such a shock to see the violence on telly. I haven't got a day job, so I thought I'd come down and help. An army of 500 volunteers with brooms and bin bags is a pretty powerful message. People are out on the streets reclaiming them. That's real community spirit."

Also among the volunteers was Healthcare Assistant, Auriol Harford.

"In a year's time," she said, "we are going to host the Olympics, but we can't even control a few teenagers who want to steal some trainers. A crowd of 200 caused this damage but there are now 500 here to clean it up. That sends out a strong message. There are more of us than them, and we are not going to let them claim our streets and neighbourhoods. I guess it's the Blitz spirit."

Her sister, Elizabeth, a twenty-two-year-old student, chipped in.

"I was absolutely furious that people could attack our community in such a thoughtless way. So many people rallying here illustrates that we will not silently condone this thuggish behaviour."

In Walworth more than fifty volunteers gathered to help businesses with the clean-up. Among those hit by the looters was TD Sports, a small independent sports supplier. The owner, Dave Cox, was devastated.

"I felt numb when I saw the damage. I just wanted to cry. We suffered £50,000 worth of losses on Monday night. I'm far from a wealthy person and without this shop, I will lose my livelihood, my house, everything."

But the volunteers came, even as Dave Cox surveyed the damage. Thirty minutes it took to clear away the smashed glass and restore his shop to what one reporter described as 'a semblance of normality'. Cheery waves and the cleaners were on their way, among them Father Andrew Moughtin-Mumby, rector of nearby St Peter's Church.

"What was really shocking," he said, "was that it was like a carnival atmosphere. But this clean-up is completely spontaneous – here and across London. It gives us some hope. It also shows there's still a real sense of community – the people are reclaiming the streets.

*

Jim Brown, who'd fought the mob in Brixton, put the newspaper aside. He knew what the priest was saying – the community coming together gave some hope – but for Jim the memory of the stabbed youth and the stricken policewoman was too fresh to be put aside.

His colleague had fallen face down, her metal hat badge twisted out of recognition by the force of the blow that felled her, and as she lay unconscious the yobs still hurled bottles and bricks at her body. He recalled struggling towards her and the youth who had been stabbed by the member of another gang. He and the other officers were desperately trying to clear a path to the bodies so that the medics could reach them and yet the rioters still rained potential death and certain injury upon them.

It was sickening. Jim couldn't begin to understand the mentality of the yobs attacking them. In two years' time, he would have served thirty years as a police officer. If decent police officers weren't given good leadership – the kind of leadership needed to deal with these gangs – then it would be time to go. He'd always had strong views about the kind of policing gangs needed. He couldn't speak up while in the force but once outside, clear of restrictions, he'd have his say.

*

Wendy Rackham – the young police officer with just two years' experience, who had watched and listened, fire-extinguisher in hand, as another gang of youths, boys and girls, hurled petrol bombs at her station in Peckham – shared his views. She'd give it a few more years to see if things improved but, if not, she'd be off. There were other jobs out there; she'd always fancied training as an airline pilot.

*

Mike Rudge had sweated it out, hoping against hope that the CCTV cameras might not have been working – that often happened – or the police wouldn't get round to looking at them before they were automatically wiped. Was that after twenty-four hours?

But his luck wasn't in – the knock on the door came the next morning.

"Mr Rudge?" asked the copper, politely but with a smile on his face.

'The bastards', thought Mike, 'they can never leave anyone alone. I'm innocent!'

But his assurances were of no avail. Mike found himself arrested for burglary.

"Burglary? I'm a family man. I've got a son. I've got responsibilities."

The magistrate was no more understanding, and Mike found himself bailed to appear again the following month, warned – as he expected – to prepare himself to face 'a lengthy custodial sentence'.

Perhaps he'd ring Mary. He hadn't been a good husband but she'd understand: after all, they shared a son, Benjamin, and if he hadn't been out looking for him, he'd never have got into trouble with the gang of looters. Mary would know he was no thief; she'd speak up for him – well, not as a good husband but as a father who cared.

Chapter 32

BUFFETING

Mike Rudge's son, Benjamin, was still being questioned at Croydon police station, patiently but with the officers becoming more and more threadbare. As far as they were concerned, the youth didn't seem to understand what they were thinking; he'd been in a car with men who were clearly looters, one of whom had been shot by another man, also a looter and who, it would appear, resented the dead man sufficiently enough to warrant killing him. It suggested to the officers concerned that the men may well have known one another and, if they did, what did the youth know about them, since he was clearly involved.

Benjamin knew how to behave in public: you didn't always show how you really felt because people would think you were strange – odd: that was the word they used, and you didn't want to appear odd to other people. Sometimes his leg would begin to shake violently, and people thought that was odd; once, at the circus, a friend of his uncles had told him off because he was shaking the seat of the person in front of him and his uncle's friend was embarrassed; but he didn't do it to embarrass her. He couldn't help it: he couldn't stop his leg shaking. And sometimes, especially in restaurants when he was excited, he would make what his uncle called a trumpeting noise. His uncle didn't mind but it made other people stare at him and he didn't like people staring.

The police officers were staring at him now and had been staring ever since they brought him into the room. The policeman had brought him some sandwiches but he hadn't cut off the crusts like his mum always did; and Benjamin didn't like crusts. There was something about the way they got caught in his teeth; and then it took a long time to brush them at night.

Staring down at the sandwiches, which he didn't want to chew but knew he should because the policeman took the trouble to get them for him, Benjamin felt overwhelmed. The world was closing in on him and he wanted to be back in his bedroom – his sanctuary – safe and sound. He was tired of shielding how he felt about the questions they kept asking, the ones he'd already answered. He wanted to tell these people how he felt but he couldn't; the words wouldn't come.

*

Dennis scarpered soon after Simon Tippet and the Blades left the ransacked pub. He hadn't liked what they were doing and had stopped Tippet from hitting the old man a second time. He didn't like Tippet and the gang leader knew it; Tippet was just a lout, out for what he could get by doing as little work as possible and making as much trouble as possible. Dennis wasn't sure whether The Blades were involved in drugs or not, but he had his suspicions, and hadn't wanted to be caught if the police found them.

He had a deal of sympathy for how people felt. The kids had felt their feet over the last few days; they'd felt freedom for the first time. Year in, year out, the media kept shoving consumer goods in their faces, goods they could never afford because they hadn't got jobs. In any decent country, like the Soviet Union used to be, everybody had a job, everybody could afford to buy something. But not in Britain. So, when the chance came they took it. They knew the streets; they knew what was going on and they took the chance. They took what the fat cats were shoving in their faces every day. There was enough money around for everyone to have a fair share of what was on offer. People weren't asking for the moon.

They were asking for the wealthy to have their wealth taxed so everyone could live a decent life.

The crying shame was that the kids couldn't see that this was their chance to make their voice heard, their chance to march on the Conservative government in Westminster – a government that protected its own kind – and bring it down.

Dennis felt deflated but the fight goes on, he thought, as he left Tottenham. Back to the *Socialist Worker*. Anger can create new movements and there'd be anger over the sentences the courts would soon be dishing out. Governments have to be seen to be in charge and the sentences handed out for even the simplest bit of looting, like stealing an ice cream, would be extreme. Dennis could imagine the headlines now: **'Feeding Frenzy in courts after riots'**.

*

Hugo's parents arrived home after their few days away to find the proceeds of their son's looting littering every room, piled in the hallway and obstructing the stairs. Angry at first, they threatened to phone Lewis's parents and call the police but they calmed down after a while and began to consider the consequences. What was the point of getting everybody upset and into trouble? What was done, was done and the insurance companies would cover the cost. The important thing was to keep it quiet and avoid their son and his friends going to prison. If they stored the goods in the loft they could dispose of them quietly when all the fuss died down.

"Get yourself home, Lewis, and don't say a word to anyone. You understand? We'll sort this out. The less said, the better!"

Lewis was relieved. It was a weight off his shoulders. Perhaps he could become a probation officer, after all. It was just a matter of working hard at his GCSEs.

It was the following day, after he'd arrived back home and explained to his mum and her new boyfriend that he hadn't been involved in the looting but had only watched that Lewis, flicking through the pages of the *Evening Standard* to see what was happening with the pre-season football matches, came across the following article:

> Westminster magistrates also heard the case of two parents from Wood Green who were alleged to have been found in possession of £2,500 worth of stolen goods from PC World. Martin and Letitia Battersby claimed they had been away staying with friends during the riots and did not know how the electrical items came to be in their home. The couple were refused bail and remanded in custody.

Lewis put the newspaper down; he wondered what had happened to Hugo.

*

Benjamin had suffered enough buffeting. He read the phrase 'buffeted from pillar to post' in a book and liked it. His mum explained what it meant: 'buffet' was to be shaken about by strong winds or waves. His mum said sailors used the word and she'd been buffeted once on an aeroplane when she flew back from a holiday with his dad before he was born. Benjamin always felt he was buffeted at school, buffeted from pillar to post, always being moved from room to room or class to class because he found it difficult to get along with other children.

And now he found it difficult to get on with these police officers. They were telling him that if he didn't answer their questions properly he would be put in a cell for the night. He didn't like the idea: he'd seen police cells on television and they were small, gloomy places where there was no room to move and where you had to go to the toilet in the same room. Benjamin was always careful in the toilet and he didn't want to have the toilet in the room where he was going to sleep.

And the beds were narrow in cells, so that you couldn't move around when you got the cramp.

"There's no good you choosing not to communicate with us, son."

It was the policeman who spoke, and what he said was untrue: he had told them all he knew. They kept going in and out of the room and talking about him with someone else. He didn't like what was happening. He wasn't refusing to communicate; it was them who were refusing to listen.

He wanted to hit the policeman to stop him asking questions but he knew that was wrong and he'd get into more trouble if he did. Benjamin clenched his fists and began to thump the table.

"Stop that, son. It'll get you nowhere."

But Benjamin couldn't stop. He had to hit something and he couldn't hurt the table. He thumped and thumped, but not for long because a policeman standing behind him grabbed his arms and pinned them to his sides. Benjamin struggled against the officer, jumping up and down, lashing out at the table and chair with his feet until the chair fell sideways. All he wanted to do was to curl up in a ball and go to sleep.

He couldn't remember what happened afterwards when he woke up in the cell. There were no lights and he needed the toilet.

Chapter 33
SOME REFRESHMENT AND A BED

Geoffrey Dale, having fought against such odds in Hackney, was just pleased to be resting at home, his wife making a fuss of him, his children playing in the small garden at the rear of their semi.

There had been mistakes by the hierarchy – many mistakes about policing policy that went back years, mistakes forced upon the police by political correctness and the fear of over-reacting – but the police force was basically staffed by decent people who wanted the best for their communities.

Perhaps what had happened over the last few days across London and the rest of the country would convince people that crime and criminals should be handled firmly. Jeff hoped so for everyone's sake, and not only his own family who had been spared this time. He didn't want the riots of the past four days to be repeated when his own children were teenagers.

He didn't expect any recognition for what he and his fellow officers had done, but that was life for you. Nevertheless, he'd stick with the force; he was a good copper and, one day, might even make sergeant.

*

Charlie Solomon's luck ran out after the fun he'd had at Clapham Junction. The Prime Minister's 'No phoney human rights' speech about using CCTV footage had done him no good at all. He'd been caught on camera torching the police car in Tottenham and then again fighting the police and chucking missiles at them in both Brixton and Hackney.

He'd returned home after Clapham and quietly stashed some loot in his bedroom, a place his mum respected as private. The loot was the final proof: even if the CCTV images were blurred, there was no denying he had stolen goods. Charlie could have kicked himself for not wearing a hoodie when he was stoning the police because it was only a couple of days later that there came a knock on the door and a copper wanted to speak with him.

Charlie was embarrassed when he stood in the magistrates' court, his mum crying as she watched. The prosecuting counsel didn't hold back:

"The accused was pictured setting fire to a police car in Tottenham, greeting another with bricks in Hackney and throwing a variety of missiles at the police in both Hackney and Brixton. He and a friend overturned a wheelie bin in the road to block emergency services. They then smashed six windows of Hugo Boss and stole eighty items of clothing. In the accused's bedroom the police found the clothing still with the price tags attached.

"When questioned, the accused said he had not been interested in looting: his motive for taking part was resentment towards the police ..."

The man went on in that vein for some time and Charlie found himself remanded in custody for sentencing at the Crown Court later in the month.

Vanda Solomon left the court in tears. She'd always known that Dan was lightweight but he was fun and she'd chosen to ignore his shortcomings, but this was the end for her. Her husband's lack of interest in their son meant the boy had grown up with no real role model – well, a role model who thought an interest in football and playing rock music was enough. He hadn't been there at those times when Charlie needed firm handling, a bit of serious advice from a father;

and when she'd turned to him for help – like the time Charlie was in trouble at school – Dan just laughed it off. She'd had to cope with the fallout from that incident herself.

And when he got into his teens the boy ran wild. He never knew when his dad was coming or whether he was coming or not to have kick around in the park on a Saturday. So, he wandered off looking for mates and found the wrong sort. Charlie wasn't a bad lad but he'd have a criminal record now and the police would be keeping an eye on him always.

*

"What shall I do, Dad?" asked Lewis, when Tom Drane answered his call and they met up in the High Street.

"It looks as though your friend's parents are taking the blame for his looting, Lewis. Do you think that's a good idea?"

Lewis didn't know what to say: confusion reigned in his mind. He'd thought about it and didn't see how Hugo's parents would be convicted – not once the case was investigated thoroughly; after all, they'd been with friends when the looting took place. Perhaps the police had jumped to the wrong conclusions. Everything was happening too quickly. If he came forward what would happen?

"What's the right thing to do, Lewis?"

"Own up?"

"I'll come with you, son. There's no need to involve your mum at this stage," said Tom, adding hopefully, "maybe not at all."

*

Carl Meadows was angry with himself. He'd had no intention of getting caught up in the rioting: all he'd wanted to do was watch. But then there'd been that daft moment in Croydon when he'd snatched the motorbike and it was too good a chance to miss, weaving his way among the looters, gathering the laughter and approval of his friends.

They already had bags full of stolen goods, goods they'd collected on their way round but nowhere to take them without a van, and they didn't want to get caught with the loot so they hid it in the graveyard, meaning to come back for it later.

Were there cameras in the graveyard? Were they seen?

He hadn't stolen anything himself but he'd helped to hide it. He was what the law would call 'an accessory', but he wasn't about to own up and drop his friends in it.

He remembered his university friend, Ray, and how excited he'd been about throwing petrol bombs at the police station in Peckham. "We were tossing petrol bombs at the police station! Can you imagine that – can you! Man, if we'd have got in there, what wouldn't we have done!" That's what Ray said. He admired Ray but not his behaviour.

Carl thought of his mum, Lynn. What the hell would she think if he was caught on camera? Fingers crossed. He'd get home, now, and reassure her that everything was all right. He loved his mum. Not having a dad worth the name, his mum meant everything to him. Yeah, he'd get home now: he could do with some refreshment and a bed.

*

The Deputy Assistant Commissioner of the Metropolitan Police, Stephen Kavanagh, had no doubts that all those involved in the riots would be brought to justice.

"A lot of people who are seeing these Blackberry images are forwarding them to the police," he said.

'Experts at the GCHQ listening station in Cheltenham had joined forces with Scotland Yard to hunt down hundreds of criminals suspected of masterminding some of the worst looting' wrote a Daily Mail journalist on August 10th, 'Police technical experts may also be able to recover incriminating information from the mobile phones – even the Blackberries – of suspects.

This could include a record of their messages as well as photographs and internet searches. It is also possible undercover agents may be able to infiltrate message networks'.

One such image, a video, caught the public imagination because of its callousness. A young man is beaten to the ground by thugs during the violence in Hackney. He is surrounded by a small crowd and one of them appears to be helping him, dazed and bleeding, to his feet but another circles the victim and proceeds to unzip his rucksack. Soon the thugs are rummaging through the young man's belongings for what they can steal. An opportunity too good to miss. Too late and too weak to remonstrate the victim staggers away, while the thugs examine their thefts.

It was a scene that fuelled the public's thirst for revenge and their support of the sentences handed out by the courts.

*

David Lammy, MP for Tottenham, saw beyond the desire for revenge. Watching the images on the television screen and reading the newspapers the following day, his thoughts turned to remedies rather than recriminations. 'What is needed, more than anything,' he thought, 'in a fractured, anonymous and individualistic society, is a sense of responsibility to one another. This must be nurtured in families, cultivated in schools and enforced from within communities themselves.'

He thought of a man he'd spoken with the morning after the riots, a jeweller whose shop on Tottenham High Road had been looted and burned to the ground, a man caught between shock and defiance. The man had seen 'no link between the loss of a man's life to a police bullet and the ransacking of his shop by gangs of youths'. The businessman, Steve Moore, was looking forward.

"I've had twenty-five robberies in my life," he said, "I've been stabbed, had a samurai through my leg twice and threatened with a gun ... I've survived and I carry on. I want to carry on. To come back from the ashes."

Chapter 34
NO TIME FOR LITERARY FICTION

Gabriel Pilgrim arrived – at last, he felt – at the door of Mary Rudge's house in Tottenham. It had been a long journey from Croydon and Gabriel was exhausted, but he'd kept his promise, reluctant though he was to have left Mary Rudge alone among the ruins of Croydon.

His wife, Martha, had been pleased he'd come home, when he called in on her and his daughter, Dolly. They'd both offered to sit in at Mary's house in case a call came through from Benjamin, but Gabriel was having none of it: he wanted to see this through, dog-tired as he was, until the boy was safely home.

Mary phoned him once, while he was journeying, to say that the kind lady at the local pub in Croydon, "the one who handed out the hot tea and the bacon sandwiches to the police officers", had welcomed her in to re-charge her phone. What a relief that was: at least they were in touch. Gabriel had worried he might have to contact the police station in Croydon and ask them to find Mary if the boy phoned.

He'd never actually been into Mary's home – he had no reason to do so: friends and neighbours, yes, but not so close as to wander into each other's houses. Had he imagined what her home might look like, Gabriel would not have been disappointed in what he found. Poor, yes: there was no top-of-the-range furniture to be seen. He would have expected that was the case: after all, she'd coped alone with two children to raise ever since she turned her no-good husband out onto the street. But clean as a whistle, neat and tidy, comfortable.

A soft rug on the floor in front of the gas fire, fruit in the bowl (being the proprietor of a local grocery store, Gabriel was pleased with the sight), the smell of polish on the air, no dirty dishes in the sink.

Gabriel sat for a moment on the settee, leaning back into the scatter cushions, and looked around. It was a good-sized room with space at the far end for the dining table that looked out over the small back garden through a pair of french windows. The settee on which he sat was accompanied by a couple of matching chairs so that the family could gather in front of the fire around the television set. Gabriel was wondering where Mary kept the phone when he heard it ringing. By the time he reached it in the hallway, the ring had stopped, and so Gabriel checked the messages: there were several – all from the police station at Croydon. He rang back and explained who he was and why he was in Mary Rudge's house.

"We have the boy here," explained whoever it was on the other end of the line.

Gabriel didn't suppose it was an actual policeman: they seemed to employ civilians these days.

"We have him here," repeated whoever it was, "We've been calling you all night."

"As I explained, Mrs Rudge and I have been in Croydon, and she's still there."

"Are you able you contact her?"

"Yes, I think so but if not you'll find her at Reeve's Corner."

"Or what's left of it," replied whoever it was on the other end of the line.

"Are you a police officer?" asked Gabriel.

"Of course! Why do you ask?"

"I just wondered. I ..."

"Would you get in touch with Mrs Rudge as sharp as you like, Mr Pilgrim? We really do need her to come to the station."

"Yes, right away. I'm sorry. I didn't mean to vacillate."

Gabriel heard the sigh on the other end of the line and realised how tired he felt; he wasn't concentrating but waffling irrelevancies. A call to Mary would put her mind at rest, at least temporarily but in what kind of state would she find her son?

*

Neil Stagg (Spike to his friends) – who hadn't intended to steal anything but just join in the fun stoning the police and then had almost wet himself with excitement raiding Currys for over an hour and nicking TVs, Canon lenses, PlayStations, anything – could hardly believe his ears as he stood up facing the magistrates.

"Jurisdiction is declined."

What the fuck did that mean?

"The bench considers that the maximum sentences they can impose are insufficient," explained his solicitor.

"Insufficient?" responded Neil, adopting outrage as his tone, something he'd always found effective when dealing with the likes of teachers and coppers on the beat.

"The maximum sentences this court can impose would be six months in prison ..."

"Six months in prison!"

"... or a fine of £5,000 ..."

"A fine of £5,000. Where the fuck do they think I'm going to find that kind of money?"

His solicitor wanted to say "Exactly" but restrained himself.

"... and so, they are referring your case to the crown court. You will not be granted bail."

"You mean I'll go to prison?"

"You'll be remanded in custody, yes."

In truth, Neil Stagg's solicitor was not happy with the decision and when questioned by reporters said so:

"Defendants who would normally be released on bail are being remanded in custody. The decisions seem to be being taken in a routine manner without enough consideration for the distinct factors of each case. It certainly seems to me that it is being motivated by political pressure."

*

Edward Andrews, who'd fought against the rioters in Edmonton, Lewisham and Blackheath was on his way home at last. He wondered whether he'd remember what his wife, Joan, looked like: the last time he'd really taken a good look at her was on the dance floor at a friend's wedding anniversary in Stoke-on-Trent. It seems decades ago.

He remembered standing hungover at Lewisham police station waiting for orders to head for Edmonton, where they'd been told to guard burnt out shops and ignore the fact that the rioters were setting light to residents' cars; he remembered knowing it went against the grain, went against his instincts as a policeman.

He recalled that later he was jogging the streets of Lewisham with Doreen Manners. Talk about unreal: rioting all over the city and they were jogging the streets! And then it did get nasty – really nasty, when they were called to Bromley Retail park where six police officers faced a mob of fifty rioters – rioters bent on a killing. They'd broken them up and driven them back but it had been a terrible time, a time for reassessment. Why was he a copper? Was it worth being a copper?

When he arrived home, his wife was waiting for him and she had no doubts.

"You were left to fend for yourselves with no food and no water. What does that tell you about how much your superiors care for their people, Ed? If you and the others hadn't arrived at that retail park when you did, what would have happened to those six officers?

"You don't have to ask, do you? You and Doreen would be better off resigning and running a personal training and life coaching company.

"At least you'd be safe, then, and helping others to keep themselves fit and safe, as well. You have the skills, both of you. Use them!"

Ed wasn't sure, but what his wife said made sense; it usually did.

*

Alex Willet, sweeping up the glass and clearing the rest of the destruction at his dad's pub in Tottenham, with the help of his mother, Mabel, his partner, Katy, and several locals had no doubts about his future.

All right, he had felt gutted when he arrived home and saw his parents' lives work in ruins. He wouldn't easily forget seeing his father – a don't-show-your-feelings-man – in tears, but he was back home now. The clear-up had begun and the criminals were on the run. He was back home caring for the people who mattered most in the world to him: his parents, Katy and her daughter, Louise, his neighbours, his community. He was an on-the beat copper and proud of his choice of career.

He'd pass his sergeant's exam easily – he was sure of the fact – and, who knows, he might even make inspector one day.

*

Mary Rudge received Gabriel Pilgrim's call with relief. At last, she could stop standing around and go to her son. She dreaded to think what state he might be in if he'd been held in a police station all night, and the response of the duty officer did nothing to allay her fears.

"He's in one of the cells," she said in response to Mary's first question.

"In a cell? How long has he been in a cell."

"Benjamin did not respond well to questioning," replied the officer, "He became violent."

"Benjamin isn't violent by nature. He probably had one of his turns."

"We had to restrain him."

"You mean he's handcuffed – strapped down?"

"Not now. He's quiet now. In fact, we're less worried about him than we were. He's curled himself up into a ball and is rocking backwards and forwards on the floor. We are keeping him under observation."

"Has he had anything to eat and drink? He shouldn't go hungry for long periods of time."

"He asked for some sandwiches," said the officer, adding with a smile on her face, "He insisted on brown bread and bottled water. He said he didn't drink tea or fizzy drinks."

She drew back the smile when she saw the look on Mary's face. Standing in a public place, Mary wasn't prepared to go into details.

"I'd like to see my son, now, please – somewhere private."

"I'll see what can be arranged."

"Just do it – and fast," Mary replied without raising her voice.

She found herself in a small office, quite cluttered with files and papers but a place that, at least, looked orderly. A policeman – a sergeant she saw by his stripes – entered, smiled and shook her hand.

"We're pleased you received one of our messages at last, Mrs Rudge. I hope you'll be able to help. Benjamin was involved in a serious incident and did not respond well to questioning ..."

"He wouldn't look you in the eye, I suppose?"

"No and when we pressed him ..."

"He became overwhelmed and had one of his turns?"

"He thumped the table and when one of the officers tried to calm him, Benjamin kicked over a chair and became violent."

"It never occurred to you that my son might be different to other people?" asked Mary, adding when she saw the sergeant frown, "Benjamin is autistic. I imagine most people are intimidated when being questioned by police officers in a small room. An autistic person cherishes order, uniformity; they need time to prepare themselves to face any change in their circumstances. Even going to a supermarket different to the one they'd expected can throw them out considerably. Does that help you understand why Benjamin might have thumped the table when pressured by your questions?"

"Yes, of course. He didn't say ..."

"Did you give him the chance? How many times did you thrust the same questions at him – over and over and over again?"

"We had to establish the truth."

"You won't establish any truth by throwing an autistic person into a fit. Now, please, will you bring my son to me?"

As if such a response to Mary's demand had been prearranged, the door opened and Benjamin entered, restrained by a young policeman.

"Mum," he said, "Can I sit down?"

The sergeant, who'd obviously been expecting a more emotionally charged meeting, nodded to the young officer who released what was a relaxed hold on Benjamin's arm and pulled forward a chair for him. Mary walked over slowly and rested her left arm across the boy's shoulder.

"I don't like people grabbing me," he said, "but he was all right."

"Thank you," said Mary, smiling at the young officer.

"I haven't had any breakfast," said Benjamin.

"If you would be so kind, constable," urged the sergeant, "I think the young man prefers brown bread."

"They brought me a cup of tea," said Benjamin, "but I couldn't drink it."

Mary Rudge could see that her son was doing all he could to hold himself together. Breakfast started his day always and he wanted this day to be like all the others so that he knew where he was in the world. She felt wretched that she'd not been with her son during his time of trial and had no idea what charges might be brought against him.

"I need to be quiet," said Benjamin as he tucked into the sandwiches.

How true that was, thought Mary. What she needed was to get her son home, where he could go to his room and begin the long process of going over and over what had happened to him.

"Benjamin, I'm really sorry this has happened to you but we need to put the police officer's mind at rest. You don't need to panic, but I want him to explain why you are here. Do you understand?"

"Yes."

"And you will be all right if he tells me why you are here?"

"Yes."

Mary Rudge listened quietly to the sergeant's explanation, watching her son all the time, but he munched quietly away, never taking his eyes from the sandwiches, the muffin or the chocolate cookie, and occasionally refreshing himself with a drink from the bottle of water.

When the sergeant finished, and he gave a resume of Benjamin's answers, Benjamin spoke.

"They wouldn't let me make notes. I needed to make notes so that I could go over them when I get home."

Mary steeled herself to the thought of what that would mean: days, weeks, possibly months of tracking through the questions and answers, the whys and the wherefores. It had been a long night, now leaning into a long day.

Mary realised how tired she felt and there was still the question of whether Benjamin was believed, whether he would be charged and, if so, whether he would be granted bail. She'd heard that custody was the order of the day, and Benjamin wouldn't survive locked away among strangers, many of them no doubt hostile and ready to make fun of an autistic boy. Her son had suffered fools at work: women laughing when they made suggestive remarks to him, men kidding him he was hearing voices when they whispered messages over the intercom system.

"Sergeant," she said, "My son knows right from wrong. I think what he told you about walking away from his friend, Angus, when he suggested stealing things from the mall, shows you that is true. He was lost and asked for help. He was forced into the car because he remembered the number plate. That's not uncommon with some types of autism. If he says he did not know these men, he is telling you the truth – far easier for him than lying. Autistic people take things literally. Benjamin, in particular, has no time for literary fiction. The use writers make of words confuse him. He did not make any of his answers up: they were the truth. Do you understand?"

"I understand one thing, Mrs Rudge – you'd make an excellent defence barrister."

Chapter 35

PUNISHED WITH THE REST

Andy Warner was looking forward to the next hour or so; it wasn't so much a desire for revenge as a need to settle the score.

Nevertheless, he was concerned: he didn't know much about this gang, in particular, but he didn't underestimate their nastiness and their threat to the safety of his colleagues. He knew there were at least nine of them and he'd rounded up five constables to support him; six against nine weren't bad odds. Certainly, better than those he'd heard that six officers at Bromley Road Retail Park had faced: fifty to six – how the hell did they survive?

His colleagues knew what they were doing; they'd been trained, but Andy Warner had not forgotten his own terror when faced with the three thugs wielding machetes in Tottenham when the riots first broke out. He'd been saved that night by a fellow officer who'd rushed between him and the men who intended to kill him, and who had then discharged his personal issue fire extinguisher into the faces of the men. Needless to say, as well as their batons the men in his command each had their own extinguisher.

The plan was simple. There were only two exits from the abandoned warehouse used by The Blades: two of his men would cover the back, the other four would enter from the front. Two of those entering from the front would move very quickly to prevent any of the gang making a dash for a set of stairs that led to the upper floors of the building; Andy didn't want a situation where one of the gang fell from the roof because there would then be a distracting public enquiry along the lines of whether the police had over-reacted and were, therefore, responsible for the young man's death. He could see the newspaper headlines now.

Once his men were in position and ready to enter the building, he'd signal for the patrol van to be ready to escort their prisoners to the station. Andy's intention was for the whole business to go off as quietly as possible. Once the gang were separated, they could be questioned; that was where the information for their prosecution would be gathered.

It was all in hand. If he could just talk them down, take them in quietly, all would be well, but he was under no illusions: however careful the planning, the situation could get out of hand.

He recalled an incident five years previously. A young man – not himself a gangster – had been shot from a passing car after receiving an educational award at the Broadwater Farm Community Centre. He'd been shot for no other reason than the fact that he was from that area and those in the car, some of the Wood Green Mob, had simply wanted to make a statement by shooting someone on what they saw as 'rival turf'.

These gangs had a kill or be killed mentality. This grew from a fear of what lay beyond their very small worlds – often as small as the housing estate where they grew up. The word was that the gangs had suspended hostilities between themselves to concentrate on attacking the police. It seemed that the gangs themselves were not responsible for engineering the riots but their willingness to resort to violence, their contempt for the lives of others and the property of others played a key role in what happened. In the world of the gang, violence was glamorised, the brotherhood of the gang was everything.

Andy knew these boys would be armed; he hoped they did not possess guns. Guns had been used during the riots but not here, he hoped, not today. Let's get this done and dusted quickly.

The abandoned warehouse was in a rundown area of Tottenham. Officers patrolled it regularly when the need arose, when information led them in that direction, but it wasn't a place where any copper would want to find themselves alone. Grubby walls inviting graffiti, dirt and grime. The whole place needed taking down and affordable housing built to replace it; it needed to become somewhere people could feel proud to call home. Neglect, years of it, surrounded them as the six police officers assumed their positions.

They'd acted quickly, once Alex Willet had gained the information – and he'd been wise to stay out of the way: there was no point in giving the usual carpers a chance to find fault with the operation – and, by a watch kept, Andy knew The Blades were inside, most likely with a variety of stolen property.

Andy looked up. The old building towered over them: windows broken, small upper doors swinging back and forth where they'd become detached from their locks, gantries and pulleys (no doubt used to haul up sacks or boxes of goods or grain at one time) stuck uselessly out from the main framework.

The door didn't give to his touch and he wanted to avoid entering noisily, dramatically: this wasn't television. He tried again, pressing his weight against the latch, trying to force the slanting door upwards to disengage the latch bolt from the latch. He was fortunate both were old and worn; the wooden door had shrunk ages ago and barely met the jamb. They were inside, quietly and unseen.

It was Simon Tippet who saw the coppers first, standing on his palette at the top of the horseshoe, as they emerged from behind a panel that once provided a corridor. His gang sat round, torches in hand. Stored against one of the walls, Andy and his colleagues saw a wide range of stolen goods.

Simon was clearly taken aback. It never occurred to him that coppers would ever enter this hallowed place – not if they knew what was good for them. His gang saw the shock registered on his face and turned without, at first, rising. Two of Andy's colleagues moved swiftly to the stairs. So far, so good.

"Good evening, lads," said Andy, calmly, "I see you're offering storage here for a wide range of companies, judging by the goods next to the wall: Foot Locker, H & M, JD Sports, PC World, Currys. Quite the entrepreneurs, it seems. Don't get hasty!"

Andy added his exhortation quickly, seeing the gang members rising to their feet.

"We have the warehouse surrounded and there's no point in you making this situation worse than it is already. Simon's parents are at the station and those of you other lads will soon be visited. From the law's point of view there's a world of difference between theft and causing actual bodily harm. Now, what we'd like you to do is to place any weapons you have on the boxes you've used as seats, and then to step forward slowly in front of your horseshoe."

But the gang's masculinity was at stake. Simon saw himself cruising around Tottenham in a flashy car, while the little kids admiring him aped him shooting a gun. He wanted the youngsters to copy him. When he'd been at school, especially when he was little, he'd always had the piss taken out of him because he was small and his legs were thin. His legs – he hated his legs! But now he was leader of his own gang he could get his own back. It was him who led the gang, it was him who worked them up, it was him who despised all authority: coppers, teachers, politicians, bosses. He had a great list of grievances and this copper wasn't going to take them away from him now – not now he was on the way up.

"You're not taking us in," he yelled, "It's not us. You're the gang out there."

It was a cry he'd heard before – the police being the gang. It was a chant. It was certain to work up his gang.

"Yeah, you're too fond of stitching us up – beating us up when we don't say what you want to hear," yelled one of the others, a fair-haired youth with a snub nose, stepping forward, his blade thrust in front of his abdomen.

Simon didn't like this; he wanted to lead. It was essential he led if he was leader. He jumped from his palette and pushed his way through the gang members who stood watching, waiting.

"Nip ain't the first to be beaten up in a police van," he shouted, gripping his blade tightly and holding it across his chest, "We've all been stopped and searched for no reason."

Andy cast his eyes over the rest of the gang. If they took up their leader's shout, the situation was going to deteriorate rapidly. He saw one of his two officers who had been guarding the stairway, move to the rear door, ready to let those waiting outside in – if the door wasn't fast locked. If it was, then they'd have to smash their way through – the four inside would have difficulty against the nine youths in such a tight space. Thank god for the protective vests.

"Yeah, like it wouldn't hurt you to be civil, would it?"

Another youth joined Simon and Nip, a boy with long, wavy hair who Andy thought in different circumstances might have been a model or a film star. Why was such a good-looking boy wasting his time defying authority for the love of doing so?

A snigger rose from the gang as a whole: they seemed to find the 'civil' amusing.

"Yeah, you needn't think these riots are about you lot shooting Mark Duggan," called Simon, "It's you we're after – the police gang."

A cheer went up from the remaining youths, the ones who had not as yet moved from the horseshoe. But they would; Andy knew they would.

The officer at the rear door, still unnoticed by the gang, was obviously unable to open it. Andy didn't want to give the signal to smash their way in – not yet: the sound would be the final thing to set these youths off.

"None of you lads want a criminal record of violence against anyone," he said, "even police officers. It'll do you no good. You know that's true. One day, you'll want to start a home, need to get a job ..."

"What job? There ain't no jobs. My old man can't get a job. My mum's always going on at him," shouted a fourth youth, another good-looking lad, dark-haired but with an ugly twist, an affectation, on his lips.

"Get out of Tottenham," replied Andy, "There are opportunities out there. Find out what hard work can deliver. Use your talents."

He was trying. He was sure there were firms who could help these kids – mentor them, showing them what they could achieve.

"You treat us like criminals, whether we've done anything wrong or not!"

It was Simon again, eager to get things on the move, to keep control. He'd heard this kind of talk from do-gooders before. He didn't want doing good to. It was all lies, anyway. His dad hadn't had a job for years. He waved his blade in the air. A shout rose from his gang. Blades out.

"We're together now, ain't we?" asked Simon, "None of this, 'you can't go round in a group, you've got to split up' shit. We're together now and there's nothing you can do about it COPPER."

"No, you're not treating us like shit – not this time. You get poked, you poke back. It's you what's getting poked today, COPPER!"

Simon didn't look back: he knew the voice. Eamon could always be worked up. You could always rely on Eamon. And the word 'copper' – always a hate word.

Andy nodded to the officer who was still standing calmly guarding the stair: only a slight nod – one pre-arranged. As soon as the first youth made a move, it would be time to break in. He'd always liked the word 'copper' when he first joined the force; it was friendly word when used by friendly people – an almost affectionate word like referring to your dad as 'the old man'. Here, among these youths, it had turned into a curse.

"PIGS!"

That had never been nice – always hateful, always used by the contemptuous who had no reason to feel contempt. He'd heard it often: the level of tension that existed in certain parts of their community had obviously gone unnoticed in the force's community engagement programme.

"You ain't taking us in to be abused – PIGS!" cried Simon. Nine against two were good odds; he'd forgotten the two behind his gang, so excited was he at teaching the two in front a lesson. As soon as one of his gang had shouted PIGS, he knew he had them with him.

Simon ran forward and struck out at Andy Warner. It was a foolish jab: once his blow had reached its furthest point, the youth had nowhere to go. Andy struck down at Simon's wrist with his baton. The wrist snapped, Simon screamed with the pain and fell back.

At that same moment, Andy heard crashing at the rear door; the thud, thud followed by a rending of timber. He heard his colleagues at the stairway yell.

"Behind you, lads! Drop your weapons. It's all over!"

Andy saw six of the gang turn as the doorway gave in and the two who had waited outside run in across the broken woodwork. At the same time, the officer who stood beside him called.

"Andy – now with you!"

He'd sprayed a blast of Halon gas into the face of Nip, who'd' rushed at him, and the fair-haired youth with the snub nose was now staggering around, temporarily blinded, rubbing his eyes.

Andy saw the youth's blade on the ground as the wavy-haired gang member rushed at him and struck forward, missing Andy by inches as the policeman stepped aside. The youth turned, raising his blade as he did so. It was a classic mistake: never strike down, always up. Someone had told him that at some time but the youth panicked, exhilarated at the idea he might catch the policeman with speed. Andy closed, applied the armlock, which caused sufficient pain for the youth to drop his weapon. Andy brought him down to the ground, holding him over Simon Tippet. Cuffs, and we have them.

He looked across the warehouse floor. His other four officers seemed to have had no great trouble quelling the remaining six gang members: each had two either by the scruff of the neck or on the floor and were in the processing of cuffing them. Three of the youths were rubbing their eyes – clearly blinded with the officers' personal extinguishers – two had been forced down and were sitting back-to-back, and the sixth was kneeling – as though in prayer, thought Andy. Their six blades were lined up on one of the boxes.

After all the talk and abuse, the matter had been settled more rapidly than Andy thought possible.

"The meat wagon's waiting," he said, "Let's get them aboard."

He regretted afterwards using the slang term but it was a relief at the time; until the moment all nine were in the patrol van on the way to the station, Andy Warner didn't realise just how tense he'd felt throughout the whole business.

It was just a matter, now, of letting Alex know the operation had been successful and, yes, just giving Mrs Marks a call. She might appreciate having her mind put at rest, worried as she was about what might be in store for her daughter, Meghan, who'd not wanted to be an informer, a grass.

*

"You needn't concern yourself, constable" was the mother's reply, "One of them louts will mention her sooner or later. Her name will come up and she'll be punished with the rest. None of them will know it was her who gave you Simon Tippet's address. When thieves fall out, they blame each other. Us parents can't afford to keep our mouths shut. If parents keep their mouths shut, we're no better than the kids."

It was a cry from the heart that Andy Warner was to hear again several times; but he couldn't help feeling sorry for Meghan Marks. She was such an unattractive, wretched girl and he could see how someone like her would be dragged into any kind of trouble in search for what passed as love.

THURSDAY, AUGUST 11TH

Chapter 36

PAIN SUFFERED

David Cameron had not been looking forward to this day since he'd felt obliged to return home from his holiday three days before: it was Prime Minister's Question Time. Nevertheless, it gave him the chance to show that the government, his government, was still in charge and that the responsibility for the chaos of the last few days should be placed quite firmly at somebody else's door.

He would hit a hard note from the very beginning of his speech: thank the House for returning from their holidays, stress the need for a united front, thank David Lammy for his contribution over the past few days and condemn the rioting, looting and arson as "criminality pure and simple" and stress that "there was no need for it". He would also reassure the public that the government would not allow "a culture of fear on our streets". He would make it absolutely clear that it was preposterous to suppose that there was any link between the death of Mark Duggan and the looting, arson, thuggery and rioting that followed.

He would expect a loud cheer from the House when he said that "no phoney human rights considerations would prevent these criminals being brought to justice". Already CCTV images had enabled the apprehension of many of the criminals. He would emphasise that anyone who had committed these offences would be arrested and that anyone convicted would go to jail. Custodial sentences would be the order of the day. Courts had been sitting throughout the night and would "continue to do so as long as necessary".

The issue of face coverings had been raised since criminals were using them to escape detection. At this time the police could only ask for these to be removed in certain places and for a certain time; from now on the police would be able to request the removal of face coverings if they had any reason to suspect criminal activity.

It would also be important, very important, to assure the public that individuals and businesses that suffered through the actions of a thuggish minority would be fully compensated and supported to "get back on their feet". The Prime Minister considered that a good phrase: it suggested that society would be up and running as soon as possible with the government's full support.

And then he would return to what he must describe as "the deeper problems", beginning by pointing out (what he was sure the public at large would agree with) that "responsibility for crime always lies with the criminal". He looked at his speech. One sentence caught his eye: it was a good point:

"These people were all volunteers: they didn't have to do what they did and must suffer the consequences".

But there was more to it than just the criminals themselves. David could see that was true. He read on, wanting to make the assertion that these crimes were not a political issue. He could hear his voice ringing around the chamber.

"This is not about poverty; this is about culture. In too many cases, the parents of these children – if they are still around – don't care where their children are or who they are with, let alone what they are doing. The potential consequences of neglect and immorality on this scale have been clear for too long, without action being taken."

This must be true and David could hear more cheers reverberating throughout the House of Commons.

"We need a benefits system that is on the side of families; we need more discipline in our schools."

Surely those ideas for improving our "broken society" would produce approval?

He felt that at the heart of all the violence stood the issue of street gangs: "territorial, hierarchical and incredibly violent. mainly composed of young boys from dysfunctional homes." He had been told there was evidence that they had been behind the co-ordinated attacks on the police.

"Part of the problem is that fathers have left too many of these communities, and that is why young people look towards gangs."

It was time to revive some old ideas.

"Every single tax and benefit is pro-family, pro-commitment and pro-fathers who stick around."

Yes, that felt right. Gang injunctions! They were working in some places such as Strathclyde. Use them against children and adults. Councils and landlords already had tough powers to evict perpetrators from social housing.

This was the time for our country to pull together. We have already seen it in those people who have gathered to clean up the damage left by the rioters, in people who patrolled the streets to protect their homes, businesses and places of worship.

"The fightback has truly begun."

That would be a phrase to capture the support of the House and stir the imagination of the public. It was important to reassure the law-abiding people, the great majority, to let them know that they will be protected, that their livelihood will be restored and that they would be compensated for the pain suffered; and to make it clear to the small minority that their crimes would be punished.

"We will track you down, we will find you, we will charge you, we will punish you, you will pay for what you have done."

And the world – we need to show them the true face of Britain! What the world has seen is not representative of our country or our young people. We are a year away from the Olympics! We need to show other countries that we are a country that doesn't give up but stands up!

It was going to be a tough afternoon in the House!

*

The house was packed, 'buttock to buttock', as one journalist expressed it, and his speech was supported by the Labour leader, Ed Miliband. He'd expected that to be the case: they had already spoken. Mr Miliband also scored a point or two of approval for thanking, profusely, the police and other public servants such as fire officers for "putting themselves in harm's way".

David was less than happy, however, when Mr Miliband questioned the government's decision to continue cutting police numbers, pointing out that the public felt safer with the presence of officers on the street; and when he asked why there were people who had nothing to lose but everything to gain from wanton vandalism; or the reference to knowing about "the problems posed by gangs *before these riots*." There was a direct suggestion here that the riots might have been avoided if certain actions had been taken by government.

＊

Peter Tapsell, Conservative MP for Louth and Horncastle wondered why the police had been "dispersing these hoods" rather than "rounding them up". The House found this immensely funny, especially when he further suggested that Wembley stadium might be used to accommodate the criminals.

David was reassured by the laughter and pointed out that he would prefer the stadium to be reserved for sporting events.

＊

Watching the proceedings at home, John Chase wondered how close to the streets Peter Tapsell had been when the riots were at their height and how he might have managed to round the hoods up. He remembered having the gun aimed at him when he and Emma came across Machete Man. It wasn't a pleasant experience and it would be nice to have what they did acknowledged – a commendation would be appreciated – but if not, John didn't think he'd leave the force earlier than he must. He was due to retire in four years' time, anyway, and that would be reluctantly.

*

Next to be called by the Speaker was David Lammy. The Prime Minister had already called him on the morning he arrived back in the country, assuring him that order would be restored in the days ahead. The Labour MP for Tottenham had remarked:

"I suspect we are going to hear a lot more about the broken society in the next few days,"

He had replied, "I suspect you may be right.," knowing the Labour MP had been referring to the Conservative Party's pre-election narrative.

As it happened, the first question the Labour MP raised was his constituents asking: 'Where were the police?' He then asked for a public enquiry and invited David to visit Tottenham and explain why forty-five people were homeless and shopkeepers found their premises "in cinders". David leapt to his feet accepting the invitation. It was an opportunity to stress that "the police presence needed to be greater and more robust".

*

One of his own party's MPs, Tobias Elwood (Bournemouth East) asked why social media networks such as Facebook, Twitter and Blackberry were not silenced because these means of communication enabled the rioters to stay one step ahead of the police.

It was a difficult one to answer: safer to say that these private companies should be asked if they felt they had the need for these capabilities. He was aware that a spokesman for Twitter had already made it clear that their 'goal was to instantly connect people everywhere to what is most meaningful to them. For this to happen, freedom of expression is essential ... we keep the information flowing irrespective of any view we may have about the content'.

A view that sounded dogmatic enough; one, perhaps, to involve some consultation between the companies concerned and the Home Office. David took a quick look at the face of Theresa May, the Home Office Minister, and her glum expression supported his cautious reply.

*

Several members of the House harped on about his intention to continue to cut police numbers but he was adamant that this was the right policy, despite the events of the last few days. The solution was not to stop cutting police numbers and certainly not to employ more officers; the solution was to *get police officers out from behind desks and on to the streets*. He hit that one hard to a satisfying round of 'Hear! Hear! from his own benches.

*

It was a long afternoon; by the end, the benches in the Commons were emptying rapidly, members were chatting among themselves, others were engaged on their mobile phones, several of those who'd stayed the course were stifling yawns. His own front bench, obliged to see out the session, were visibly wilting.

One of the last speakers, Eric Ollenshaw (Conservative, Lancaster and Fleetwood) raised the issue of policing by consent, a model enshrined at the very heart of policing in Britain. Would the Prime Minister accept that the public now gives *its consent for the police to balance the question of individual freedoms against its own freedom to act.*

It was an easier question to answer than might have been expected. In Britain, "the police are the public and the public are the police". Police officers come from our own communities.

"It is a very special thing we have but the model has to be updated with new tactics, new resources, new technologies, as appropriate, so that it meets new threats."

David felt it was a good answer, one that covered eventual possibilities, and the support from the House suggested he'd hit the right note. There were smiles all round, smiles that broadened even further when John Bercow, the Speaker, closed the PMQT after one hundred and sixty-five minutes.

*

Sitting at home, Emma Hare wasn't so sure about Mr Cameron's answer to what was almost the final question of the session. Policing by consent, whatever the circumstances and despite her experiences of the past five days, was essential to the British way of life. It was why she and her father and both her grandfathers had joined the force.

Mr Cameron spoke of giving police chiefs more say in methodology and that was fine if you promoted the right people to the top jobs – but only then. It had never occurred to Emma that she might consider moving further in her profession, but she'd never thought beyond policing her own community. Perhaps it was time to do so: Commander, Assistant Commissioner, even Commissioner? Who could say?

Chapter 37
CARRIED BEFORE JUSTICE

Tom Drane had been dreading this day ever since his son, Lewis, insisted upon turning himself in to the authorities. It was the right thing to do, and Tom guided him in that direction but the outcome of Lewis being carried before justice was to be a shredding experience both for the boy and his father.

As it turned out, the boy's mother, Jenny, soon 'winkled the truth' (a favourite phrase of hers) out of the boy and insisted on coming to court with them.

"Did you seriously think you could keep this under wraps, Tom?" she yelled

Tom didn't answer; he supposed not. It had just been an idea, an idea that gave the promise of a bit of peace and quiet, the promise of avoiding a row. He so disliked rows; perhaps the current boyfriend had a way of coping with them, a way that had always eluded Tom.

"I didn't want to worry you unnecessarily," he replied, lamely.

"Worry me! Unnecessarily! Do you think I'm not going to be worried about my son – our son! – going to prison?"

"I suppose not."

"Suppose not! You suppose not! How do you think you were going to keep that one quiet?"

Tom didn't think; he was never one step ahead.

"You didn't, did you? You were never good at thinking, were you Tom? The thinking was always left to me. That was one of our problems. Things would always turn out better tomorrow! There was never any need to think about what might happen *if*, was there? All you ever thought about was your health. All you ever think about is yourself. You're your own favourite person."

"That's not fair, Jen ..."

"Don't call me Jen!" she snapped, keen to maintain her momentum.

"It's not fair," insisted Tom, "I had a good job with the parks department. I brought home a good wage. We were comfortable. I always played with Lewis, took an interest in what he was doing. It was you threw me out and then along came what's-his-name. The new boyfriend! You never liked being without a boyfriend, did you Jen ..."

"Trust you to blame me. You'd gone before ... before Mick and I met."

"I hadn't gone, as you put it. I was thrown out by you!"

Jenny was silent. Tom hadn't expected silence. He paused for a moment and then pursued his grudge.

"With him there – *in our house* – it's impossible for Lewis and me to meet properly."

"You were always full of excuses."

"Lewis doesn't even like the bloke ..."

"He told you that?"

Tom hadn't meant to say what he did. He didn't want to get his son involved. He knew his ex-girlfriend would worry the boy to death talking him round to her way of thinking.

"I just know," he said, realising the argument had gone too far, exhausted its course, "Anyway, there's no point yelling at each other like this. We need to think about Lewis."

"I'm always thinking about Lewis," she snapped, "I'm the one who's there with him all the time."

She couldn't resist it, could she, thought Tom, always has to have the last word, however daft it is. He'd lain awake for nights after that row, getting nowhere with his thoughts and his worries; and now they stood in the magistrate's court facing the District Judge.

*

The two boys, Lewis and Hugo, were to be tried together. Tom didn't understand what had happened with regard to Hugo's parents who he'd read had taken the blame for their son's thieving. He'd read in one of the papers that a mother who'd done a similar thing had been jailed. Perhaps Hugo had come forward? Perhaps the police had intervened. Whatever the case, Martin and Letitia Battersby were with their son today.

The mother was tearful, the father stony-faced; quite the reverse of him and Jenny, but Jenny always hid behind her anger: it was him who tended to be tearful. Both the boys were white-faced; they knew CCTV footage existed of them looting at PC World, "if the presence of the looted goods in Hugo's parents' flat was not sufficient evidence to convict them". Jenny had made that comment, spitefully, on their way to court; Tom felt she enjoyed being spiteful: it helped to build up her anger.

The boys pleaded guilty; the lawyer who'd taken their case in a hurry – along with a dozen other cases – had advised there was no point doing anything else. She had pleaded with the court for clemency:

"I was taken by surprise," she said, "Talking to them and recently talking to their families, they come across as perfectly ordinary, reasonable and – dare I say it? – civilised young men. Their parents have found it really very hard to fathom what's going on. Indeed, the parents of Hugo Battersby – ill-advisedly, no doubt – attempted to take the blame upon themselves. Fortunately for them, their son had the decency to come forward and confess his guilt, an action that indicates his remorse, in my view.

"Both boys have accepted their guilt and there is no doubt they are both remorseful. The parents all work, as do the boys with small jobs at the weekends. If it all kicked off again tonight I don't for one second think you would find these young men anywhere near."

Both sets of parents exchanged looks as the lawyer spoke; they were grateful to her for the plea: it gave them hope because what she said was undoubtably true. In a moment of fear, they felt a togetherness and clutched each other's hands as they waited for the judge to speak.

"I take on board what has been said in your defence," he said, passing an even look towards the lawyer, "The tragedy is that you are both of good character, each of you well-educated. You have jobs, as do your parents. You have plans for your future education. You have shown remorse and you have both pleaded guilty.

"However, I can't ignore the context in which these offences were committed. You have played your part in a wider act where devastation was caused to businesses and local residents.

"In my view, although I'm retaining jurisdiction, the matter is so serious that only a custodial sentence will suffice. That, I hope, will serve as a deterrent to others. You will go to jail for six months."

As the boys were led down to the cells, Tom looked at his ex-girlfriend as tears rolled down his cheeks; Jenny kept her eyes from him, not wanting to share his grief or display hers. This would be the end for what was left of their relationship. Both recalled the day they posted on Facebook 'Tom and Jenny are in a relationship', a relationship that culminated in the birth of Lewis. What had gone wrong?

Martin and Letitia Battersby hugged each other, his stony face immersed in his wife's grief. None of what was happening was possible: all these years they had cared for their son, guided him in the right direction, supported him throughout school, planned to finance him through university, looked forward to the day when he graduated and would enter society as a professional man. All in vain – now this, this disgrace for him and them.

*

Dolly Pilgrim had begged her mother to change her mind and not hand her over to the authorities but Martha was adamant against her daughter and her husband. Gabriel had been on his daughter's side, even though he knew it was no use arguing against his wife's determination, but he now – however reluctantly – shared her views. What he'd seen in Croydon on the night he accompanied Mary Rudge in pursuit of her son had changed his mind; when all was said and done, it was of no use for Dolly to say she'd been led on; at the end of the day, she was responsible for her actions.

The honest shopkeeper, a man who had always shown kindliness towards his customers in their time of need, was wretched with himself. Somehow, all he thought he stood for – decency, politeness, honesty, kindness – left him the day he agreed with his wife.

Martha, tight-lipped but crying inwardly, stood beside him, holding his left hand, knowing – after all their years of marriage – exactly how he felt, appreciating his support on this dreadful day.

In court, Dolly, standing with her friend, Cathy, admitted stealing clothes from H&M and creams from Body Shop in Wood Green on the first night of the riots. Both girls also admitted stealing a wheelie bin to take away their stolen goods. They both denied any criminal damage, saying that they had not joined in the smashing of the shops' windows but had been "caught up in the madness".

They explained that they had gone out to see the riots in Tottenham and had then gone on to Wood Green with someone they met who had a car. "Everyone was going to Wood Green", Dolly explained as the District Judge listened.

"Do you realise how serious this is?" he asked.

"Yes," replied Cathy, "we realise it was more than just messing about."

Gabriel and Cathy's father, a schoolteacher, both told the court that their daughters "were easily led" and that they had urged them to apologise to the court. Their solicitor, too, had urged them to plead guilty.

The judge looked at the girls, both pathetic specimens of the modern generation, he thought, and at their parents. He was aware of the devastating results of the nights of violence across the city and of the government's desire for custodial sentences. At the same time, both sets of parents had not hesitated to turn their girls in; both sets of parents would be keeping a close watch on where they went and what they did. In the end, he said:

"I have decided that in both your cases a referral order is the best solution. You will, therefore, receive a twelve-month referral, during which time you will make restoration to your victims and the wider community."

It was with a huge sense of relief that the parents faced each other outside the magistrate's court. Here were smiles and handshakes all round and promises to meet up more often "in the interests of their girls", as Gabriel put it.

"What does it mean exactly?" asked Dolly as she walked home with her parents.

"It means, my girl, that you're going to find yourself very busy every weekend for the next twelve months. You can put any idea of going around with your friends and enjoying yourself out of your head until you've made full restoration to H&M, Body Shop, your local community and us," replied her mother.

Chapter 38
ON ONE SIDE OF THE COURT

Alex Willet was content: he and his family had come to several key decisions following their experiences during the riots and the arrest of The Blades. He sat in his dad's pub enjoying one of the beers that were, once again, on tap.

Together with the help of Keith's regulars the mess had been cleared and The Blacksmith's Arms looked presentable enough to welcome customers. The famous window bearing Tottenham Football Club's famous emblem was now boarded up, of course, but matters were in hand to have a new one made. The scarves from the away games, the trophies, the notices and the photographs would take some time to replace but word was already out and Mabel had taken many calls and promises over the last twenty-four hours; the locals were as keen as the landlord and his lady to see the old pub resplendent in its former glory.

"Wouldn't be the same, Mrs Willet, to come in here and not feel at home, now, would it?" said one.

Mabel was relieved. Her husband was a stubborn man and so deep was his misery after the ransacking of his pub that she feared he might be determined to call it a day. It had been a close call but their son Alex's decision helped; about that she was over the moon.

Alex had kept in close touch with the station's questioning of Simon Tippet and his gang. He was pleased he'd called in his friend, Andy Warner, to complete the job. It was better that way and there was no one better than Andy, an officer senior to him, due for retirement in four years' time after thirty-seven years as a policeman. Alex always felt that if he could be as good a copper as Andy he wouldn't go far wrong. He wasn't ambitious: making sergeant would be good enough for him. Feet on the ground, close to home. Alex had come to a life-changing decision: he felt – at last, as far as his mum was concerned – that he might be good at being married.

It was a sudden thought brought about by the riots. He'd noticed that nearly all the kids involved had been boys or young men and his mother's comments, as they cleared the mess and cleaned the pub, came home to roost.

"Most of these lads, you'll find, had no fathers worth talking about, no one to show them how a man behaves. I've no sympathy for what they did, the louts, but I do feel sorry for them. You think, Alex, what your dad meant to you when you were a boy. These louts had no one like your dad."

As he swept and polished, alongside his partner Katy and her daughter, Louise, his mother's remarks got Alex thinking. He knew from experience that schools had trouble with boys and that ninety-five percent of those in prison were men. He'd seen the sort on the streets many times: the tough guy, the alpha male, demanding what they liked to call 'respect' but not actually deserving it: always violent, always ready to have a go at someone.

Alex remembered the first time he'd realized he had stubble on his chin, the first time someone at school called him a 'queer' because he wasn't always chasing a bit of skirt. Who'd taught him how to shave; who'd taught him how to stand up for himself in the playground? His dad! All right, his mum could have done it, but it wouldn't have been the same.

He'd known kids at school – some were mates of his – who had no fathers. They'd just cleared off, and their mothers were left to fend for themselves. They didn't all become criminals, of course, but they'd found growing up more difficult than Alex, simply because his dad was always there – working. The kids with no fathers had never seen a working man, someone who went off to work each day, dressed for the job. They had no idea of what it meant to be a man and some of them grew up with a twisted notion of manhood; that was where the gangs came in, and the country had seen the results of that over the last five days.

He'd been lucky enough to have an emotional bond with his dad; the bond came from simple things like being there to help with his homework, reading the last story of the day to him in bed, cooking breakfast – something his mum often seemed to get ratty about doing. They'd been the other activities, of course: the manly things like football and model-making and learning to use the toilet properly and sandcastles on the beach and how to pour a pint and ...

Alex was almost in tears when he realized the list of these small things was endless. He could commit himself to that kind of life if he had a son and Louise was always wondering why she didn't have a younger brother. He and Katy had talked about it, as you do, but he'd always back off, unsure whether he'd be any good at it; and then, there was his role model, the old man crying at the loss of his pub and with his wife's help fighting back, determined again.

He'd talked with Katy when they'd taken a break from the clearing and cleaning, and she'd just smiled.

"I knew you'd come round eventually. Louise will be pleased just to have a proper dad, never mind anything else that might come along."

Alex realized when she smiled and spoke how much he'd always loved her; he didn't know why the realization came at that moment; he must have known before, but the realization was different, breath-taking. It boded well, he thought, and his mother was delighted.

They sat now, together with a bunch of customers that included Phil Meadows alone at the table he usually shared with his cronies, Daniel Solomon and Tom Drane. Word had got around that Charlie Solomon's case was referred to the Crown Court later in the month and the gossip supposed with a good deal of certainty that the boy would spend several years behind bars.

"What do you know about your friend Tom's boy, Phil?" asked Keith.

"I don't. I haven't heard anything as yet. Tom's been quiet about his lad."

"And your boy, Carl?" asked Mabel.

"Kept his nose clean didn't he? No fool, my lad. He knows what's what."

"You're sure about that, are you?" persisted Mabel, annoyed at the man's boastful manner.

"I've heard nothing to the contrary, Mrs Willet."

It was true: since he and his ex-girlfriend, Lynn, hadn't communicated except in one moment of panic when the riots started and Mabel goaded him into taking an interest in his son's doings, Phil had no idea that Carl was safe at home but with his fingers crossed.

Mabel knew why the man annoyed her so much. He was one of those men the papers called an 'absent father'. Phil Meadows wasn't just absent, in her opinion: he was completely disengaged from the boy he'd brought into the world. It was time, she thought, that the government did something about fathers like him, brought them to account. Phil Meadows had an easy ride after his night of pleasure, allowed to walk away from his responsibilities. What should happen with men like him was that maintenance should be taken directly from their salaries. It would be easy enough if the government got its act together: all a mother needed was the man's National Insurance number. If he could afford to drink regularly in their pub, he could afford to keep his son!

Mabel gave Phil Meadows an angry glance and he smiled back; Phil was never ruffled but everybody's friend.

"I'm just popping along to see Martha and Gabriel," she said, "their Dolly was in court today. It's only right to take an interest in what happened. Martha will appreciate it."

"Tell Gabriel to pop along for a swift half," replied her husband, "it'll do him good."

Alex had watched his mother giving Phil Meadows the eye and guessed what was going through her mind. Coppers were always on one side of the court dishing out the law, he thought: they needed to be on the other, active in the neighbourhood.

"Katy, Louise and I will walk with you, mum," he said, "We're about to be on our way home."

Neighbourliness was about keeping in touch with the people in your community, staying engaged and a copper, a local copper, was in the right place to be a good neighbour.

AFTERWARDS

Chapter 39
BENJAMIN'S NOTEBOOKS

Mary Rudge was another whose experiences during the riots brought her closer to her neighbours. She'd never been a reserved person and when Benjamin was at school had shared a drink or two with some female friends of hers at one of the local public houses – not, it is true, The Blacksmith's Arms, which she thought of as essentially a football supporter's place – but at a quieter venue, The Beagle, situated just a twenty-minute drive out of Tottenham.

But now grateful as she was to both Keith Willet and Gabriel Pilgrim, who she knew enjoyed what his wife called a 'swift half', Mary felt obliged to frequent her local, if not often then occasionally; apart from being neighbourly, it gave her the opportunity to engage her son more fully with the local community and he seemed to have no objection to being seen with her in the pub, especially at lunch times. Benjamin didn't drink alcohol, of course – this would not have gone well with his medication – but he enjoyed the food and the company.

*

It had been a real relief for Mary when the police officers accepted Benjamin's story beside her explanation; it also imbued her with great pride that her autistic son had known right from wrong, father or no father.

Benjamin seemed not to have suffered from the dreadful experience of watching the driver shot dead but Mary knew from the past that her son was probably storing the memory, one that might emerge later in nightmares, endless questioning or both. She tried to speak with him when they arrived home but Benjamin went immediately to his room and shut the door. Not a good sign but the following morning he asked if W H Smith sold notebooks indexed alphabetically so that he could record his notes according to the person's name. The stationers did and together they found such a book in a black false-leather binding; true, it possessed red beading along the spine but Benjamin raised no objection, despite his loathing of the colour. He seemed delighted at the book itself and turned it over in this hands that evening while they watched television.

Mary remained puzzled as to why Benjamin wanted the book but refrained from asking: sometimes, it was better to wait. He often showed the same intensity when an obsession – not that she liked the word – took root. Once, at school when the teacher arranged a topic on the Thames, planning to take the children down to the river and then follow it to its source through film and video, Benjamin decided he must study Dinosaurs. It could have been a tense moment on his educational journey had not Mary already liaised with the teacher and gained his understanding.

"I am going to keep a record of the convictions," he said on the following morning.

Mary knew what he meant but, nevertheless, asked.

"The convictions of the rioters and what happens to them and ... I shall need a newspaper every day."

"I'll see Gabriel," Mary replied, "he sells newspapers and he will have one delivered."

"I shall need more than one because they all give different information."

"Which ones will you want, Benjamin?"

"The *Daily Mail*, the *Evening Standard* and *The Guardian*."

"Why those three?"

"The *Daily Mail* is always exciting and has pictures, the *Evening Standard* is a local paper and will keep going longer about the riots and *The Guardian* is more serious and gives more information."

"How do you know all this? We don't have a daily paper."

"There were always papers in the school library and I looked at them some playtimes."

It wasn't the first time a snippet of conversation exposed the loneliness of an autistic child and Mary was used to such moments but her eyes filled up, nevertheless.

"I'll get the papers, Benjamin," she said, "just as long as you need them."

"Thank you."

And so it was that Benjamin's notebook began. He was meticulous and methodical, collecting not only information about convictions but also about commendations and outcomes. He homed in, particularly, on names that he knew, collecting details of local people.

At times, Mary felt his endeavour was intrusive because he asked her for information, not supplied in the newspapers, about people she knew in the neighbourhood. His first entry unsettled her immediately.

Angus Wilson, caught on camera in a Croydon shopping mall, appeared before Tottenham magistrates today, August12th, accused of looting shoes and other items. Images, alleged to be of the accused, had been shown on TV and in the Press. Wilson is accused of stealing shoes from JD Sports and a £429 Notebook from Argos. The youth was arrested yesterday at his home in Tottenham. He is to be remanded in custody for trial at Croydon Crown Court. (Evening Standard: August 12th)

Mary's shock at the youth, Benjamin's age or close, being sent to Crown Court, which implied a custodial sentence in excess of six months, sent her to the telephone and Angus's mother, who had shown such kindness to her son when he was lost in Tottenham. For an hour they spoke and Mary agreed to meet her "for a coffee". They were two women who had never spoken before the riots but were now drawn together by the grief of one and the relief of the other.

Another entry was closer to home.

The mother of one convicted looter told the paper her daughter – who got sixteen weeks for 'threatening or abusive language or behaviour' – had got a much harsher sentence because of the political climate. "If this wasn't the riots she wouldn't even have got a caution," she said, "it's all because of the riots."

Her daughter, Megan Marks, had gone with her boyfriend to see what was going on with no intention of getting involved in trouble. She pleaded guilty, however, to telling officers during the riot: "I'd smash you if I weren't a woman" before being arrested later at her home in Tottenham. She became the first rioter to be jailed at a Tottenham magistrates court session that began on Wednesday morning and ran late into the night.

At her home in Tottenham there was remorse at Meghan's behaviour. But her family's main emotion was dismay at her wasted opportunity, mixed with indignation that, in their view, she had been made an example of. Marks had applied to become an Olympics ambassador. (The Guardian: August 12th)

Another entry was even closer; Mary didn't know whether to laugh or cry but chose the former since it clearly gave her some satisfaction and her son some relief.

Mike Rudge, 53, was arrested for burglary after his van was caught on CCTV outside a Currys warehouse in the early hours of Tuesday during the riots.

Westminster magistrates court was told Rudge was seen running from the van and back to it with a number of electrical goods

Rudge, who has a sixteen-year-old son, denied he was a looter and claimed he was van-jacked by a gang at a petrol station who ordered him to drive them to the warehouse.

He said: "They threatened to kill my wife and my son. I had no choice. I had to drive them to the warehouse while they carried out the burglary. I did not commit a crime. I am innocent. I just want to get back to my family.

He was bailed to appear before magistrates next month.

(Evening Standard: August 12th)

If he was to appear before magistrates, it seemed to Mary that her ex-husband was believed, at least in part, and faced no more than a six-month sentence at the most. She didn't begrudge him that much.

Benjamin did some of his research at The Blacksmith's Arms during their lunchtime visits. It excited him to have his notebook at the ready and his newspapers spread across the table. His right leg would jerk relentlessly up and down as he read, and it was there he came across the following news, which he shared with Keith and Mabel Willet at once, reading from the newspaper.

"Back at Westminster magistrates CPS prosecutors, some of whom had already worked two-night shifts in a row, were admitting they had never experienced work patterns such as these in their careers. Magistrates took it in turn to hear cases overnight as the suspected rioters continue to file through the courts.

"'Chaos reigns downstairs,' a solicitor offered apologetically to the district judge, Dolores Walters, as court number six waited for the first of 9 defendants to be brought in on a charge of violent disorder in Tottenham, late on Tuesday evening. "It certainly does," she replied drily. One by one, the youths, aged between 16 and 18, were brought into the dock, accused of having smashed the windows of a local public house, The Blacksmith's Arms, while the landlord was locking up for the night, of tying the landlord to a chair, carrying weapons and threatening his wife and daughter. The defendants also ransacked the premises, inflicting thousands of pounds worth of damage in the process.

"One of the accused had just secured a place at university to study law, the judge was told. The accused vehemently denied knowing any of the others or of having been involved but police officers, headed by Sergeant Andy Warner, who made the arrests said he was among those apprehended at the time. All were denied bail and remanded in custody to appear at Westminster Crown Court next month'."

As he read, Benjamin's excitement grew; Mary's face showed consternation and Keith's, a resigned tolerance; it was Mabel who spoke.

"I don't think that's anything to be cheerful about, Benjamin," she said quietly.

Benjamin frowned.

"Why not? They smashed up your home. This must be The Blades."

"Yes," replied Mabel, giving Mary a glance, wondering whether she should explain, adding, "It's sad about Meghan Marks, too."

Mary smiled.

*

"What did she mean?" asked Benjamin, after they arrived home and he'd spent an hour in his room.

"She was sad about what happened," replied Mary.

"Why?"

"Because Mabel realises that those boys will one day be dads and she wonders what their sons will grow up like."

Benjamin frowned again: entering into another person's train of thought was difficult.

"What did she mean about Meghan?"

Mary plunged in with the only explanation she could summon.

"Mabel knows Meghan's mum. She knows how upset she'll be."

What else could she say? Her son wasn't going to be able to comprehend how a girl like Meghan was attracted – if 'attracted' was the word – to a thug like Simon Tippet and how, one day, she might have children destined to behave like him. The day was done, there was some recompense, emotionally, for the pillaging of the Willet's pub and their home but the world that made The Blades was still alive and kicking. Who would they kick next and when?

"I was only making conversation."

"Yes, I know, Ben."

"I wasn't asking for advice."

"No, and Mrs Willet wasn't giving any. She was just expressing an opinion."

Benjamin decided he wouldn't go to the pub again; he would read and write in his room; he was relentless and so his notebook grew as the rioters were apprehended and brought to justice, as the police were commended and criticised.

*

By December, Mary's newspaper bill was growing in line with Benjamin's notebooks that now numbered seven; he was at the college working for qualifications that would secure him a place in the hospitality industry and he had started work at weekends as a kitchen porter with the local branch of MacDonalds, but his obsession with the outcomes of the riots still dominated his life. On Sundays he walked along to Gabriel Pilgrim's general store and bought The Observer because one of his lecturers advised that this was one of the best papers for the serious reader. Benjamin's 'political conversations', as he liked to express them did not go down well at work, since nobody was particularly interested but he found Gabriel to be a ready listener, which was a relief to Mary, and on December 3rd, 2011, he came across the following article.

The riots began in Tottenham following the police shooting of Mark Duggan, 29. Confusion over the circumstances of his death led to rumours on social media networks that he had been "assassinated" by police. The report says that it is "essential" in future that an early press statement is available and agreed by senior investigators and all relevant parties.

The findings have been submitted to the ongoing review into public order policing, which was announced in the aftermath of the riots.

The report also reveals that fear of criticism over heavy-handed tactics led to the initially cautious policing approach in Tottenham, which was subsequently blamed for encouraging rioters elsewhere in the country.

Officers were hamstrung, it says, through fear of being condemned by politicians and the media and were mired in a "damned if they do and damned if they don't" mindset as the disorder began.

(The Observer: December 3rd)

"Who was Mark Duggan, Mr Pilgrim?"

"He was a gangster, Benjamin," replied Gabriel, "They say his uncle boasted that he had more guns than the police. At least that's what I read in the Evening Standard."

"And the police shot him?"

"Yes."

"Have they got the right to shoot people?"

"It was an accident, they say."

"It says that he was 'assassinated'."

"That remains to be seen, Benjamin. A lot of people were on his side. There were loads of tributes to him when he was shot. You know – flowers and so on against the railings."

Benjamin was silent for a long time, trying to take in what was and what was not the truth: black and white was easy, shades of grey were not. He read through the article again.

"What does 'hamstrung' mean, Mr Pilgrim?"

"It means to restrict what someone can do. I don't know where it comes from. It's a funny word. Perhaps your mum will know. Give me the paper ... Yes, right, well here it means the police didn't feel they could take decisive action against the rioters because there'd be a public outcry."

"What's an 'outcry'?"

"It means people wouldn't approve of what they were doing."

"So, they did nothing?"

Benjamin remembered the night he and Angus had gone to Croydon and the way the police stood quietly by while the rioters looted the mall and how the rioters taunted the police by running up to their line and dancing in their faces.

"They were careful, son, careful. They could have done more," replied Gabriel, "and probably wanted to. Now, I must get on!"

*

Two photographs, ones he discussed endlessly with his mother, had haunted Benjamin's nights: the photograph of Monika Konczyk leaping from her burning home and the face of the man who died, Richard Mannington Bowes, as he lay unconscious on the pavement in Ealing.

His mother told him that Monika was still living and working in Croydon: she read that in one of his newspapers and wondered, teasingly, how he'd missed the article.

Benjamin's other nightmare was resolved by an article in the Daily Mail of March 12th, 2012.

Just ten minutes after delivering a fatal punch to Richard Mannington Bowes, 16-year-old Darrell Desuze smashed several shop windows and strolled away with a bottle of wine in each hand.

Such was the force of the blow that the 68-year-old retired accountant, who was trying to quell a fire started by a rampaging mob near his home, never awoke and died three days later.

Instead of calling for an ambulance, Desuze dragged the bloodied body of 'wholly innocent' Mr Bowes away from the flames and on to a pavement – before resuming his looting of four nearby shops.

Desuze, now 17, has pleaded guilty to manslaughter and was yesterday warned that he faces a 'substantial' prison sentence for the killing.

The engineering student, who three years earlier had expressed an interest in becoming a police officer, callously attacked Mr Bowes as he rampaged through the affluent West London suburb of Ealing with a large gang in August last year.

He was said by his school to have become interested in a potential career in the Metropolitan Police after a day out at the police training centre in Gravesend, Kent.

However, a year later he was responsible for one of the most shocking events of the riots.

The burly six-foot teenager, whose gang name was Smokey, revelled in violence and boasted of his love of 'beatings' on Facebook, describing his motto for life as: 'If you don't like someone, just beat them up.'

He punched Richard Mannington Bowes, knocking him to the ground and leaving him with brain damage after he banged his head on the pavement in Haven Green, Ealing, west London.

The pensioner was attacked at about 10.30pm on August 8 after being surrounded by a group of youths. He never regained consciousness and died in hospital three days later.

The photograph of Mr Bowes' unconscious body lying unconscious on the pavement became one of the most shocking images of last summer's riots.

Desuze, who admitted manslaughter and violent disorder but denied murder, can now be named after an order banning his identification was lifted at Inner London Crown Court.

(Daily Mail: March 14th, 2012)

It was a Wednesday and Benjamin collected the papers from Pilgrim's General Store on his way home from college. He didn't like reading in the street, preferring to lay the newspapers out in an orderly manner on the desk in his room and turn the pages carefully through them, while his mother cooked the evening meal.

When Mary called him down to the dining table, Benjamin said suddenly, making it clear he didn't want an answer by looking back at his plate immediately:

"They've got him. It's all right now."

Mary knew what her son was talking about but had not been fully aware of how much the thug remaining unpunished had meant to the boy, despite knowing Desuze had been remanded in custody since he was arrested. In her son's mind justice had been done it seemed. All was right with the world. As they finished the meal and Benjamin returned to his studies and his notebooks, Mary washed the dishes and put them carefully away in the cupboard. Benjamin had never spoken of another killing to which he was a witness and his mother wondered just how deeply the shooting of the driver troubled him.

*

Good news followed three months later, not regarding the driver of the car but about one man who had captured the public's imagination during the riots.

Bus driver, Mehmet Avci, from Lewisham has been awarded a commendation by the Lewisham Borough Commander for his bravery and actions during last year's riots in London.

Mr Avci was honoured for going above and beyond the call of duty, a Transport for London spokesman said. He transported police officers into the thick of the troubles using a London bus with no concern for his own life or the views of his superiors

His assistance was 'written up' by the officers he helped..

(Daily Mail: June 16th, 2012)

*

It was a summer of acknowledgements, recorded by Benjamin in his notebooks and talked about at The Blacksmith's Arms by Keith, Mabel and their now regular locals and Tottenham's football fans.

"I see, in Ealing, the Borough Commander has ... here we are 'awarded 173 individual commendations for bravery to police officers, police staff and a member of the public'. Is that right Alex?"

"That's right, Dad, yes, so I hear. John Chase and Emma Hare will be among those officers – and well-deserved."

"You've heard nothing yet, then?"

"No, Dad – not yet."

"Expecting to?"

"I can't' say as I am," replied his son.

"Not for bravery above and beyond the call of duty"

"Not for bravery above and beyond the call of duty – no, Dad."

To be honest, Alex wasn't expecting any recognition and in conversations with fellow officers in other boroughs he'd heard that neither was anyone else. Some were annoyed; others took it as part of the job. In Alex's case, his mind was on the forthcoming wedding, which his mother and father had insisted on paying for and insisted on the reception being held in their now completely re-furbished pub.

"And there's no need for you not to have a honeymoon," persisted Mabel, "Your dad and me can look after Louise here."

It sounded a good idea to Alex and Katy.

Talk of the wedding and the awards gained ground throughout the summer, particularly the awarding of Animal OBEs to dogs and horses.by the PDSA. Among these was Obi, the police dog who suffered a fractured skull after being hit by a brick in Tottenham and ten police horses also received an Order of Merit.

"And rightly so," said Alex, "the dogs and horses stayed on the frontline because their loyalty to their handlers mattered more than the danger they faced. They had all the missiles thrown at them that we did and they stuck with us. Don't tell me that isn't courage!"

*

It was over two years after the riots, on January 7th, 2014, that the inquest into the shooting of Mark Duggan delivered a verdict.

Katy had now presented Alex with a son and Louise with a baby brother. Whereas the public at large had long forgotten the London Riots of 2011, they were still a hot topic in Tottenham and in The Blacksmith's Arms in particular. Quiet though he was about the riots, their causes and outcomes, Alex Willet awaited the long-delayed verdict with avid interest, as any copper might.

"It's here," he said, "waving a copy of the *Evening Standard* at those in the pub, "The jury were asked to deliver a verdict of either 'unlawful killing', 'lawful killing' or an 'open verdict'. The last would be no good to anyone – Duggan supporters or us ..."

"Go on," said his father.

"The jury returned a verdict – and I quote – 'that Mark Duggan's death at the hands of the police was a lawful killing'. Right – now we can all rest from the speculation. The policeman who shot the gangster thought his and his colleagues' lives were threatened and he fired. What else was he supposed to do."

It wasn't a question and no one in The Blacksmith's Arms treated it as such.

*

In his bedroom, Benjamin Rudge also read the article and planned to talk about it with his mother and the people at work. His hospitality course having been completed in 2013, Benjamin was now a full-time employee at Wagamama's. He'd tried elsewhere but found life difficult: the sexual taunts he'd received from female employees upset him and many of the men thought him 'a bit of a weirdo' because he didn't date women; and Benjamin, at nineteen, didn't feel he was ready for such a relationship yet, didn't feel he could cope with being so close in that way to someone else. He knew it was going to be a problem that would haunt him for years but he was content to wait; at Wagamama's restaurant he was treated well, he was happy.

Benjamin was still keeping his notebooks, now numbering twenty-three, keen to find resolution for the one outstanding crime that still haunted him.

"They've still not found the man who shot the driver, Mum," he said as they shared their evening meal.

"I know, Ben, and you must accept they might never find him."

"They found the gun two years ago in 2012 and the police have offered a reward and the police have made some arrests."

"But no one has been charged, have they?"

"No."

"No," said Mary, softly.

"Why, Mum?"

"People who know who it was might be frightened to come forward, Benjamin."

Benjamin didn't ask why: he knew.

"You mustn't keep fretting about it, Ben. You're in no danger yourself – not now, not so long after. It's the man's mum we should feel sorry for: for her it's a continuing nightmare."

"I know," replied Benjamin, and looked at his mother.

Suddenly, he could understand; he could feel for the driver's mother. Mary looked at her son and smiled: for him and for her it was a huge step forward.